"Laura,

Laura felt tempt____ ____ ____ ____ out to this man who was practically a stranger. But before the urge grew too strong, she abruptly stood up.

It was important that he leave; she knew that much.

"Everything's fine," she lied. "Except dinner. It will burn if I don't get into the kitchen."

Nick remained seated. "It smells good."

Good grief, he was angling for a dinner invitation! She was trying to get rid of him and he wanted to stay. Logic told her to ignore her conscience. But good manners—and something else she refused to acknowledge—told her to listen.

She sighed. "Would you like to stay for dinner?"

"As a matter of fact, yes."

His smile warmed her to her toes. But something told her she'd made a big mistake. Something told her that after tonight, her life might never be the same....

Books by Irene Hannon

Love Inspired

IRENE HANNON

is an award-winning author of more than twenty novels, including thirteen for Steeple Hill. Her books have been honored with a coveted RITA® Award from Romance Writers of America and the Reviewer's Choice Award from *Romantic Times BOOKreviews*. Irene, who spent many years in an executive corporate communications position with a Fortune 500 company, now devotes herself full-time to her writing career.

In her spare time, she enjoys performing in community musical theater productions, singing in the church choir, gardening, cooking and spending time with family and friends. She and her husband—an ordained cleric who juggles ecclesiastical duties with a career in international sales—make their home in Missouri.

Irene invites you to visit her Web site at www.irenehannon.com.

Home for the Holidays

Irene Hannon

Steeple
Hill®

Published by Steeple Hill Books™

STEEPLE HILL BOOKS

Steeple
Hill®

ISBN-13: 978-0-373-36095-6
ISBN-10:   0-373-36095-9

HOME FOR THE HOLIDAYS

www.SteepleHill.com

Printed in U.S.A.

Come to me, all you who labor and
are overburdened, and I will give you rest.
Shoulder my yoke and learn from me,
for I am gentle and humble in heart,
and you will find rest for your souls.

—*Matthew* 11:28–29

To Tom
My Friend, My Hero, My Love

Chapter One

Nick Sinclair felt his blood pressure begin to rise and his spirits crash. A few moments ago he'd been on a high, elated by the news that he'd won the commission to design a new headquarters building for the Midwest Regional Arts Center. It was a coup destined to move his architectural career into the limelight.

Then George Thompson dropped his bombshell. On behalf of the building committee, he had strongly suggested—more like mandated, Nick thought grimly—that the firm of Sinclair and Stevens use some unknown landscaping company to design the grounds.

"Taylor Landscaping?" Nick cleared his throat. "I don't believe I've heard of them," he said in a pleasant, conversational tone that betrayed none of his turmoil.

"You will," George replied with a decisive nod. "Great company. Small. Relatively new. But dynamic. Creative, yet practical. I like that." George always spoke in clipped sentences, a habit that Nick suddenly found irritating.

"How do you know about them?"

"Several of the board members have used them. Did the landscaping at my new house, in fact. Wonderful job! My wife said they were great to work with. Very professional. And stayed right on budget, too."

Nick struggled to keep his face impassive as a wave of panic washed over him. On his own, he knew he could assemble a team of contractors that would do the firm of Sinclair and Stevens proud. But one weak link was all it took to ruin an otherwise great job. Or, at the very least, to make his life miserable.

Nick carefully smoothed down his tie. Not that there was anything out of order in his appearance. His navy blue pin-striped suit, starched white cotton shirt and maroon-and-gray paisley tie sat well on his just-over-six-foot frame. Broad shouldered, with dark hair and even darker eyes, he didn't particularly care about clothes one way or the other, but he'd invested a good number of his thirty-six years to reach this point in his career, and he was smart enough to know that appearances *did* count. Today he looked every bit the part of a rising young architect, and nothing was amiss—including his tie. But that little maneuver bought him a few seconds of time—all he needed to recover from his surprise at George's suggestion and to rapidly formulate his response.

"Well, I'm sure they're very competent, but commercial landscaping is on an entirely different scale than residential," Nick said smoothly. "Now, I've worked with an established firm for several years that I think you'll find very—"

"Nick." George held up his hand, cutting the younger man off. "Providing opportunities for young talent is in keeping with the philosophy of the Arts Center. And it's one of the reasons we chose *your* firm to design it. I think it's only fair that we at least give this company a chance, don't you?''

Nick looked at the man across from him in silence. Checkmate, he thought grudgingly. George Thompson's years as a respected trial attorney served him well in the business world. You couldn't raise an objection that he hadn't already considered.

And, Nick had to admit, he was right. The Arts Center board could have chosen a well-established architectural firm for this project. Instead, the board members—all of whom were influential business people in St. Louis—were giving him a shot at it. He couldn't argue the point that this Taylor Landscaping deserved a chance, too. It was just that he didn't relish the idea of some wet-behind-the-ears firm getting its chance at his expense. However, it looked as if he didn't have a choice.

"I see what you mean," he said, his even tone revealing nothing of his frustration.

"Good, good. Give them a look, get a bid…I think you'll be impressed."

"I'll get in touch with them immediately," Nick promised. "Now, about the schedule…"

By the time Nick left George's office, all of the details had been finalized. He should have been on top of the world. Instead, the sudden gust of cold March wind and the overcast, threatening sky that greeted him when he stepped through the glass doors better matched his mood, and he scowled at the dark clouds overhead.

There had to be a way around this, he reasoned as he climbed into a sleek red sports car parked in the visitors' lot. Obviously, the board wanted a first-class job. The Arts Center would be a St. Louis showpiece, and anything less than the best would reflect poorly on the city. Just as obviously, the board members were convinced this landscaping firm could handle the job. And maybe they were right. But *Nick* wasn't convinced. Not yet, anyway. And before he agreed to work with this company, he had to feel confident in its abilities. George *had* given him an out. A slim one, true, but it was there. And he intended to use it unless Taylor Landscaping did one terrific sell job on him.

Suddenly Nick found himself walking through the door of his office, with no recollection of the drive from downtown. For a man who prided himself on his alertness and attention to detail, it was an unsettling experience. Frowning, he nodded distractedly to the receptionist, glanced at the two part-time draftsmen at work in a large, airy room and stuck his head into his partner's office.

Jack Stevens glanced up from his drafting table and grinned hopefully, his short-cropped sandy hair giving him a fresh-faced, all-American-boy look. "Well?"

"Well what?"

"How'd it go?"

"Fine."

"You mean you got the job?"

"Yeah."

Jack tilted his head quizzically. "Well, try to contain your enthusiasm," he said dryly.

Nick shook his head impatiently and raked his fingers through his hair, jamming his other hand into the pocket of his slacks. "There's a complication."

"What?"

"Have you ever heard of Taylor Landscaping?"

Jack frowned thoughtfully. "Taylor Landscaping... No, I don't think so. Why?"

"Because the board of the Arts Center *strongly* recommended them to do the landscape design."

Jack leaned against the drafting table, propping his head

on a fist. "Is that bad? What do *you* know about Taylor Landscaping?"

"Nothing. That's the point. It's some new outfit that's probably fairly inexperienced."

"Sort of like Sinclair and Stevens?" Jack said with a mild grin.

Nick glared at him. "Don't you start, too. That's exactly what George implied."

Jack shrugged. "Well, it's the truth. Why don't you keep cool until you check them out? Might be the proverbial diamond in the rough."

"It also might be a lump of coal."

"Maybe. Then again, maybe not."

Nick gave him a disgusted look. He was in no mood for humoring, not with the commission of his career facing potential disaster at the hands of an inept landscape designer. "Aren't you just a little worried about how this might affect the future of Sinclair and Stevens?" he said tersely. "Most people will only see the outside of the Arts Center, and a bad landscaping job could ruin the lines."

"You're really worried about this, aren't you?"

"You better believe it." Nick walked restlessly over to the large window on one wall and stared out unseeingly for a long moment before he turned back to his colleague. "You of all people know how hard we've worked to get this far. Fourteen-hour days for three long years, working in a cramped office with barely room for two drafting tables. It's beyond me where you ever found the time or energy to have two kids along the way! We've done okay, but you know as well as I do that we've been waiting for our real break, the one job that will move us into the big leagues. This is it, Jack. It may sound dramatic, but our future could depend on this commission. This is what will make or break our reputation with the people who count in this town. We blow it—we might as well close up shop because we'll never get another chance."

Jack stared at his partner thoughtfully for a few minutes, his demeanor now just as serious as his friend's. "I'm sorry, Nick. I didn't mean to make light of it. I realize how important this is. But if this landscaper doesn't cut it, we don't have to use them, do we? You said the board *recommended* them. So at least the door's open to other possibilities if they don't work out, isn't it?"

"Yeah. About half an inch."

"Look, before we jump to any conclusions or panic unnecessarily, why don't you check out this Taylor Landscaping? I trust your judgment. If you're not satisfied with them, we just have to tell George. I'll back you up, but this project is really your baby, Nick. You went after it and you did the preliminary design that the committee selected. I know it's coming out of the Sinclair and Stevens shop and I'll help peripherally, but you're the one who needs to feel comfortable with this company because you're the one who'll have to work with them."

"Yeah, I know. And you're right. I need to check them out. I'm condemning without a trial, and that's really not fair." He glanced at his watch and gave an exasperated sigh. "Six o'clock! Where did the day go?" He shook his head. "It's too late to do anything today, but I'll follow up on this first thing in the morning."

At nine o'clock the next morning Nick punched in the number for Taylor Landscaping. He waited with an impatient frown as the phone rang once, twice, three times. By the sixth ring he was drumming his fingers on the desk. What kind of an outfit was this, anyway? Every business office he knew of was open by this hour. Hadn't anyone ever told this company that an unanswered phone meant lost business? Nick was just about to hang up when a slightly breathless voice answered.

"Taylor Landscaping."

"This is Nick Sinclair from Sinclair and Stevens. I'd like to speak with Mr. Taylor."

There was a long pause at the other end of the line. "Do you mean the owner?" There was a hint of amusement in the voice.

Nick bit back the sarcastic retort that sprang to his lips, confining his response to a single, curt syllable. "Yes."

"Well, everyone's out at the job site right now."

Nick debated. He could just leave a message. But it might not be a bad idea to see this outfit at work. "All right. Just give me the address," he said in a clipped, authoritative tone.

"Well, I guess that would be okay." The voice sounded uncertain. "Hang on a minute." A sound of papers being shuffled came over the line, and after several interminable minutes the information was relayed. Nick jotted it down. A residential job, in a nice area of large homes and expansive grounds. But not a commercial commission.

"Thanks," he said.

"My pleasure." The amused tone was back.

Nick frowned at the receiver, perplexed by the woman's attitude. But he wasn't about to waste time trying to figure it out. Instead, he glanced at his watch. If he hurried, there was time to pay a quick visit to Taylor Landscaping before his eleven o'clock meeting.

A half hour later Nick pulled up at the address provided by the woman on the phone. Four people, dressed in jeans and work shirts, were visible. Two wrestled with a large boulder. Next to them, a guy with a mustache fiddled with a jackhammer. Another slightly built worker, who appeared to be only a teenager, stood apart with a hose, watering some freshly planted azalea bushes.

Nick had no idea who the owner was, but the kid with the hose was closest to the street. Besides, he had no desire to approach the group with the jackhammer. It was now in use, and the bone-jarring noise was already giving him a headache.

Nick stepped onto the lawn and took a moment to look over the grounds. It was a new house, built on a vacant lot in an already established neighborhood. The ground had been cleared during construction, and it was obvious that a complete landscaping job was under way. The work appeared to be just beginning, and it was difficult to tell whether a cohesive plan had been developed. But a well-maintained pickup truck bearing the name Taylor Landscaping stood parked in the circular driveway, and the crew seemed energetic.

The jackhammer stopped momentarily, and Nick opened his mouth to speak. But before he could make a sound the annoying noise started again. Shaking his head in irritation, he moved forward and tapped on the shoulder of the teenage boy who held the hose.

It happened so quickly Nick had no chance to step aside. The boy swung around in instinctive alarm, maintaining a death grip on the hose and drenching him in the most embarrassing possible place. Nick was stunned, but not too stunned to lunge for the hose and yank it in a different direction. He glanced down at his soggy gray wool slacks, and for the second time in less than twenty-four hours he felt his blood pressure edge up.

"Just what exactly were you trying to do?" he demanded hotly. "Of all the stupid antics..."

"I'm...I'm really sorry," the teenager stammered.

Nick removed his pocket handkerchief and tried to sop up the moisture, a task he quickly realized was futile. "Yeah, well, that really solves everything, doesn't it?" he said sarcastically. "I have an important meeting in less than forty-five minutes. How do you suggest I explain this?"

The teenager stared at him blankly.

"You could say you had an accident," replied a mildly amused voice.

Nick glanced up. The worker who had offered the suggestion wore a baseball cap and dark sunglasses.

"Very funny," he said icily. "Which one of you is Mr. Taylor?"

His question was met with silence, and he frowned in irritation. "I'm looking for the owner," he said through gritted teeth.

"Well, why didn't you say so," the worker in sunglasses spoke again, the husky voice now even more amused. The baseball cap was flipped off, releasing a cascade of strawberry blond hair caught back in a ponytail. She removed the glasses to reveal two startlingly green eyes. "You're looking at her."

Nick stared at the woman across from him. Several moments passed while he tried to absorb this information. And in those few moments Laura Taylor quickly summed up the man across from her. Rude. Arrogant. Overbearing. No sense of humor. Probably a male chauvinist, judging by his reaction to her gender.

"Laura, I—I'm really sorry."

Laura turned her attention to the young man holding the hose. He looked stricken, and she reached out and gripped his shoulder comfortingly. "It's okay, Jimmy. No permanent damage was done. But those azaleas could use some more water. Why don't you finish up over there."

She turned to the other two men. "I'll be with you guys in a few minutes. Just do what you can in the meantime."

They nodded and headed back to work, leaving Laura alone with the stranger. She tilted her head and looked up at him, realizing just how tall he was. At five-eight, she wasn't exactly petite, but this man made her feel... vulnerable. It was odd...and unsettling. And it was also ridiculous, she told herself sharply.

"What can I do for you?" she asked, more curtly than she intended.

Nick stared down into the emerald green eyes that now held a hint of defiance. How had he failed to notice, even from a distance, that one of the workers was a woman? Sure, the glasses and the cap had effectively hidden two of her best features, but the lithe, willowy figure definitely did not belong to a man!

Laura saw the quick, discreet pass his eyes made over her body, and she resented it. She put her hands on her hips and glared at him. "Look, mister, I don't have all day. I've got a lot of work to do."

It suddenly occurred to Nick just what kind of work she was doing, and he frowned. "You shouldn't be trying to move that boulder," he said. "Why isn't he doing the heavy work?" He gestured toward Jimmy, the young man with the hose.

The question took Laura by surprise, and she answered without even considering the appropriateness of the query. "He's only sixteen. It's too much for him."

"And it's not for you?"

"I'm used to this kind of work. He isn't."

"How can you run this company if you're out in the field actually doing the manual labor?"

Her eyes narrowed. "Not that it's any of your business, but we happen to be one person short today."

"As a matter of fact, it does happen to be my business."

Laura frowned. "I'm not following you."

"I'm Nick Sinclair, of Sinclair and Stevens. We're designing the new Regional Arts Center, and you happen to own the firm of choice for the landscape portion, or so George Thompson tells me."

Now it was Laura's turn to be shocked into stunned silence. She stared at the man across from her, her initial elation at the news suddenly evaporating as her stomach dropped to her toes. What had she done? The Lord at last had answered her prayers, sending a dream commission her way, and she'd blown it by insulting the man who held the key to that dream. Why couldn't she have overlooked his bad manners long enough to find out his business?

Nick saw the conflicting emotions cross her face, debated the merits of trying to put her at ease and decided against it. Let her sweat it out. He certainly was. From what he'd seen so far, he wasn't impressed with Taylor Landscaping. Not by a long shot. He'd started the day off with the disorganized receptionist and then arrived on the scene to find that half of the crew consisted of a high school kid and a woman. Not a promising first impression.

Nick remained silent, his arms crossed. He noted the flush of color on her face, the look of despair in her eyes, the nervous way she bit her lower lip. His resolve began to waver. After all, he was the one who had appeared on the scene uninvited and disrupted what otherwise seemed to be a relatively smooth operation. And then he'd behaved arrogantly over a simple mistake. Not to mention his reaction to the discovery that a woman owned Taylor Landscaping. What had come over him? He wasn't a chauvinist. At least, he didn't think he was. But this woman sure must think so, and he couldn't blame her.

Nick had just decided that maybe an apology was in order when the woman across from him took a sudden deep breath, distractedly brushed a few stray wisps of hair back from her face and fixed those green eyes unflinchingly on his darker ones.

"Do you think it might be a good idea if we start over?"

"It couldn't hurt."

A quick look of relief crossed her face. She wiped her hand on her jeans and held it out. "Mr. Sinclair, I'm Laura Taylor. And as you've already discovered, I own Taylor Landscaping."

Nick took the hand that was offered, surprised by the firmness of the grip.

"Look, I'm sorry about that," she said, gesturing vaguely in the direction of the embarrassing water spot. "I guess Jimmy didn't hear you coming up behind him because of the jackhammer."

"Maybe not, but isn't sixteen a little young to be working in a crew like this?" he asked pointedly.

As if to say, can't you afford more experienced help, Laura thought.

She bit back her first reaction, then shrugged. "I hired Jimmy through Christian Youth Outreach. Have you heard of it?"

"No, I don't think so."

She sighed. "Unfortunately, not enough people have. It's an organization that provides support for young people from troubled homes," she explained. "A lot of the kids have been abused. Anyway, Jimmy is part of a work-study program sponsored by Outreach. He just works for me part-time, to earn money for college." She looked over at him, a frown marring her brow. "He'll need all the help he can get. I'm just doing my bit."

Nick felt embarrassed now by his question. He took a closer look at the woman across from him. She was older than he'd first thought. Early thirties, probably. A fan of barely perceptible lines radiated out from her eyes, and there were faint shadows under her lower lashes. Although she'd stopped frowning, slight creases remained. She seemed tense and serious, and he had a strong suspicion that she'd worked very hard to get where she was. Yet she still found time to help others. All of which was admirable. But it didn't alleviate his concerns about Taylor Landscaping's role in the Regional Arts Center. Hard work was important, but talent and creativity were the critical components. He still had no idea how her company would fare on that score, and he had to find out before he made any commitments.

"Ms. Taylor, I suggest that we defer our discussion about the Regional Arts Center to another time. You're obviously busy, and—" he glanced at his watch with a frown "—I'm late for a meeting. How about tomorrow at one?"

"That would be fine."

He withdrew a business card from his pocket and handed it to her. "Sorry for the interruption today."

"And I'm sorry about that." Again she gestured vaguely toward his slacks.

"Well, as someone suggested, I'll just say I had an accident."

Laura caught the faint teasing tone in his voice and looked at him in confusion. Was this the same arrogant man who had been ranting at them less than ten minutes ago? It didn't seem possible.

Unsure how to respond, she chose not to. Instead, she

reached back and twisted her hair up, securing it firmly under the baseball cap before once more settling the dark glasses on the bridge of her nose.

"I'll see you tomorrow, then."

Nick was taken aback by her abrupt goodbye, and watched for a moment as she strode back toward her crew. Despite the fact that she'd been unfailingly polite once the purpose of his visit had been revealed, she obviously didn't like him. His attempt to lighten the mood at their parting had been clearly rebuffed. As he turned toward his car, the jarring reverberations of the jackhammer started up again, and the headache he'd had earlier returned with a vengeance.

The partnership of Taylor Landscaping and Sinclair and Stevens was definitely off to a rocky start.

Chapter Two

Nick turned sharply, swinging neatly into his reserved parking space. As he set the brake, he glanced at his watch with a frown. He was twenty minutes late for his meeting with Laura Taylor, and judging by the unfamiliar, older-model hatchback in the small parking lot, she was waiting for him.

For some odd reason, he still felt off balance from their meeting the previous day. From the moment he'd arrived at the job site, things had gone wrong. And being twenty minutes late for their meeting today wasn't going to help.

Nick strode into the reception area and stopped at the desk to pick up his messages.

"Laura Taylor is here," the woman behind the desk told him, confirming his assumption about the Toyota's owner. "I was going to have her wait here, but when you weren't back at one Jack came out and got her. I think they're in his office."

"Thanks, Connie. Did any of these sound urgent?" he asked, waving the stack of pink message slips in his hand.

"No. I told everyone it would probably be late afternoon before you got back to them."

"Thanks. Would you handle my calls until Ms. Taylor leaves?"

"Sure."

Nick heard the sound of voices from Jack's office as he paused at his desk to deposit his briefcase. He couldn't make out the conversation, but Jack's sudden shout of laughter told him that his partner and Laura Taylor had hit it off. Good. Maybe if Jack had kept her entertained, she'd be less judgmental about his tardiness. He shrugged out of his jacket, rolled up the sleeves of his crisp white cotton shirt and loosened his tie, flexing the muscles in his shoulders. He wasn't in the mood for another encounter with Laura Taylor, not after the marathon lunch meeting he'd just attended with a difficult client, but he didn't have a choice.

As Nick approached Jack's office, the sounds of an animated conversation grew louder. Through the open door he could see half of Jack, who was leaning against his desk, ankles crossed and arms folded over his chest. But he gave his partner only a passing glance, directing his attention to Laura Taylor instead. She was sitting in one of the chairs by the desk, angled slightly away from him, legs crossed, her attention focused on Jack. Nick stopped walking, taking a moment to watch her unobserved. She was dressed the same as yesterday, in worn jeans and a blue cotton work shirt, her feet encased in heavy tan work boots. The baseball cap was missing, and her hair was once again caught back in a ponytail, the severe hairstyle emphasizing the fine bone structure of her face. Her full cotton shirt was neatly tucked in, a hemp belt encircling a waist that seemed no more than a hand span in circumference. The worn jeans molded themselves to her long, shapely legs like a second skin, he thought as his eyes leisurely traced their contours. It suddenly occurred to him that even in this workmanlike attire, Laura Taylor radiated more femininity than most of the women he knew, freshly manicured and dressed in designer clothes.

Manicures were obviously not part of Laura Taylor's life, he thought as his gaze moved to the hands that rested quietly on the arms of her chair. He remembered the strength of her handshake, and noted with surprise the long, slender fingers. Her nails were cut short and left unpolished, and her hands looked somewhat work worn. He thought again about her struggle with the boulder yesterday, and frowned. She was too fragile looking for that kind of work. He eyed her more critically, noting that despite her fabulous shape, she bordered on being too thin. The dark shadows under her eyes that he'd noticed yesterday were still there, speaking eloquently of tension and hard work and lack of rest. A powerful, unexpected twinge deep inside brought a frown to his face. Now what was that all about? he wondered, jamming a hand into the pocket of his slacks.

The sudden movement caught Laura's attention, and her gaze swung to the doorway. The image she saw was not comforting. Nick Sinclair stood frowning at her, and her stomach began to churn. She was painfully aware of the poor impression she'd made on him yesterday, but at least he'd agreed to meet with her today. She couldn't blow it. She couldn't! *Please, God, let him give me a chance with this project,* she prayed silently.

Nick's eyes locked on hers, and she returned the gaze unflinchingly, although it took all of her willpower. Based on his expression, it appeared that he might already have had second thoughts about using her company, she thought dispiritedly. He was an intimidating figure, even in shirtsleeves. The angular planes of his face and prominent cheekbones held a no-nonsense look, and his dark eyes seemed fathomless—and unreadable. At the same time, there was an almost tangible magnetism about him that seemed somehow...unsettling.

Jack, sensing the change in mood, leaned forward to look out the door.

"Nick! Come on in. Laura and I were just getting acquainted."

Nick tore his eyes away from the deep green ones locked on his. "Sorry about the delay. My lunch meeting took a lot longer than I expected. I hope the wait doesn't inconvenience you," he said, turning his attention back to Laura.

Laura struggled to present an outward facade of calm as questions and doubts raced through her mind. Had he changed his mind about giving her a chance? Was her behavior yesterday going to cause her to lose this job? Were his chauvinistic attitudes going to work against her? She struggled to control her inner turmoil, and when at last she spoke her voice sounded cool and composed.

"No. I've enjoyed chatting with Jack. I'm just going back to the job site when I finish here."

"Still one person short?"

"Yes."

He nodded curtly. "Then let's try to make this as brief as possible." He turned back to his partner. "Do you want to sit in, Jack?"

"I'd like to, but I have a two o'clock that I need to prepare for."

"Okay. Ms. Taylor, why don't we go into the conference room? There's more space to spread out the plans," Nick smoothly suggested.

"It's Mrs.," she corrected him, noting that his eyes

automatically dropped to her left hand, which displayed no ring. "I'm ready whenever you are," she said, ignoring the question implicit in his look. She reached for the portfolio beside her chair and stood. "Jack, it was nice meeting you," she said, holding out her hand. Her voice was tinged with a husky warmth Nick had never heard before, and he noted that they were on a first-name basis.

"My pleasure."

Nick stepped aside for her to pass, catching Jack's eye as he did so. Jack grinned and gave a thumbs-up signal, but Nick just gave a slight shrug. Jack might have been impressed with Laura Taylor personally, but Nick was more interested in her abilities as a landscaper.

He followed her down the hall, conscious of a faint, pleasing fragrance that emanated from her hair. Again he felt a disturbing stirring deep within, which irritated him. "Right here," he said, more sharply than he intended. She shot him a startled look. "Go on in and I'll grab the plans from my office," he added, purposely gentling his tone.

She nodded and disappeared inside. He returned to his office, pausing to lean on his desk, palms down, and take a deep, steadying breath. For some reason, Laura Taylor had the oddest effect on him. She seemed so cool and composed, so strong and independent, yet she'd shown moments of touching vulnerability—yesterday when she'd found out who he was, and just now when he'd spoken to her in an unexpectedly harsh tone.

He couldn't quite get a handle on her. She was a small-business owner, apparently with enough smarts to weather the many pitfalls inherent in that situation. You had to be tough to survive, and he had seen the results of that struggle in many of the women he dated. He was inherently drawn to women who displayed independence, toughness, intelligence and drive. Women who were savvy and sophisticated in the business world, but who knew exactly what buttons to push to turn him on after hours. The only problem now was that these very qualities seemed to make his relationships mechanical, gratifying on a physical level but lacking some essential ingredient.

Lately his thoughts had been turning to a more serious involvement, to marriage and the kind of family Jack had. The only problem was that the women he'd been involved with put their careers first and relationships second. Like Clair. He was beginning to feel as if he was just one more appointment on her calendar. Their dates were always penciled in, and it was understood that if a business conflict arose, the personal commitment would be sacrificed. Nick understood that—he'd lived that way himself for the past ten years—but now he wanted—needed—something more. Once or twice he'd thought about suggesting marriage to Clair, but he'd never been able to bring himself to do it. Because, while he admired her and was physically attracted to her, he knew deep in his heart that she would never put her first priority on their relationship—as he intended to do with the woman he married. As a result, he saw her less and less. She was so busy with her own independent life that he sometimes wondered if she even noticed that he rarely called anymore.

Nick walked over to the window and ran his fingers through his hair, uncertain why his emotional dilemma had surfaced just now, in the midst of a business meeting. He supposed Laura Taylor had triggered it in some way, but he wasn't sure why. Maybe it was those intriguing glimpses of vulnerability, a surprising contrast to her usual businesslike demeanor. That vulnerability wasn't something he usually saw in the professional women of his acquaintance. Yet she obviously didn't let it get in the way of her business.

Impatiently Nick walked over to his desk and picked up the rolls of plans. An analysis of Laura Taylor's psyche was not on his agenda today, he told himself firmly.

Laura was grateful to have a few moments alone. It gave her a chance to compose herself and prepare for her next encounter with the unpredictable Nick Sinclair. She had no idea why he'd spoken to her so sharply just now. But she did know that this job was a once-in-a-lifetime opportunity, and she *had* to get it. *She* knew she could handle it—the question was, how could she convince the man in the next room?

As she often did when faced with a question or situation or decision that baffled her, Laura closed her eyes and opened her mind and heart to the One who had guided her so well in the past. Her faith had always been important to her, but only in the difficult years, when it had been put to the test, had she realized how powerful an anchor it could be. It had provided calm in the midst of turbulence, hope in the face of despair. She had learned to accept God's will without always understanding it, and she knew that whatever happened today was part of His plan for her. All she could do was her best and leave the rest in His hands.

Laura took a deep breath and opened her eyes. The panic was gone, and she felt ready to once more face the intimidating Nick Sinclair.

By the time Nick returned, Laura was bent over studying the model of the Regional Arts Center. She straightened up when she heard him enter, impressed despite herself by the clever integration of contemporary and classical features. "Very nice," she remarked.

"Thanks."

With an unconscious grace, she moved around the conference table and unzipped the portfolio that lay there, taking another deep, steadying breath before she spoke.

"I think it makes sense for us to be honest with each other about the possibility of working together. I realize that you probably have no idea of the capabilities of Taylor Landscaping, and based on our encounter yesterday I have the distinct impression that our services are being— to put it bluntly—shoved down your throat. So I thought it might be helpful for you to see some examples of our work. I've brought some drawings and photographs of some of our jobs over the past two years. While there's nothing in here on the scale of the Regional Arts Center, I have every confidence that we can do an exceptional job for you. I've also brought a list of all of our jobs since the business began six years ago, as well as a review of my academic and professional credentials."

As she talked, Laura arranged the contents of her portfolio on the table, keeping her eyes averted from the man across from her. Last night, as she'd prepared for bed, she'd had a chance to think about their encounter yesterday. It had become clear to her that Nick Sinclair was probably extremely uncomfortable with the whole arrangement. If he was like most architects, he had established relationships with a group of proven, reliable contractors. Naturally, for a prestigious job like the Regional Arts Center he would have preferred to use one of those firms. Laura understood that. She also understood that he might still do so, providing he could justify it to George Thompson and the Arts Center board. So she had come prepared. This commission was vitally important to her business, and she wasn't about to let it slip away without a fight. She carefully finished arranging the contents of her portfolio on the table before she spoke again.

"Now, what would you like to see first?" she asked, looking up at last.

Nick Sinclair's attention was entirely focused upon her now. His grim expression made her feel uncomfortable, as if he was sure she'd never measure up. She dropped her eyes, a faint flush staining her cheeks.

Nick saw the look on her face and slowly settled himself on the edge of the conference table across from her. He opened his mouth to speak, then closed it. This project obviously meant as much to her as it did to him—maybe more, he thought, his jaw tightening as he once again pictured her struggling with the boulder.

"Let's look at some of the photos first," he suggested quietly.

Laura glanced up, their eyes locked and she saw nothing but sincerity. Maybe he'd give her a fair chance after all, she thought, pulling the photos toward her.

They worked their way through the photos and the designs, and then Nick quickly scanned the list of projects, spending more time on the sheet with her credentials. He was impressed by her background and by the quality of the jobs Taylor Landscaping had done, but he still wasn't honestly convinced that her firm could handle a job the magnitude of the Arts Center.

"What I've seen here looks very good," he said carefully, his eyes meeting hers as he handed back her list of credentials. "But most of what you've done is residential work, with the exception of a few small commercial jobs. Do you really think you're equipped to handle the Arts Center?"

"Yes," she said steadily. "I realize we'll have to expand. I've been wanting to do that anyway, but I was waiting for the right commission to come along. And as for our ability to do the design itself, all I'm really asking for is a chance to give you some ideas. I won't even charge for spec time.''

"No one is asking you to work for free."

"I'll do anything it takes to convince you that we can handle this job," she said steadily, her gaze locked on his.

She wants this assignment so much, Nick realized with a sharp pang of sympathy. He knew what it felt like to be in that position. But earnestness didn't guarantee talent or results, he reminded himself.

"Suppose we take a look at the plans," he suggested. "You've already seen the model, and I'll fill you in on the terrain."

"I've already been to the site," she informed him.

He looked at her in surprise. "You have?"

She nodded. "This morning. I knew where it was from all the articles in the paper, so I went over there early and walked around a bit. But I had no idea what you have in mind architecturally, or even what direction you want the building to face, so I need to see the plans before I can talk intelligently about the landscaping."

Nick nodded, impressed by her initiative. "Of course." He unrolled one of the elevations, and for the next two hours they worked their way through the plans. Laura's questions were astute, and the preliminary ideas she voiced were intelligent, appropriate and interesting. She took extensive notes as they talked, and Nick couldn't help notice the enthusiastic sparkle in her lovely green eyes.

When the last of the elevations had been rerolled, Laura leaned back in her chair. "I'm impressed," she said honestly. "It's a spectacular building, and I like the use of natural materials. This will lend itself beautifully to landscaping that features native plants and trees. I can just imagine the entrance in the spring if we do a design with dogwoods and azaleas and redbuds. And the reflecting pool in front could be flanked with gardens that feature seasonal flowers.'' She paused thoughtfully, and then looked over at Nick. "Those are just preliminary thoughts, of course. I'd like to get some rough designs on paper and then meet with you again before you make a decision on your landscaper.''

Despite her calm, professional tone, Nick saw the strain around her mouth and eyes, and could sense the tenseness in her body as she waited for his answer. He had a totally illogical urge to reach over and smooth away the smudges under her lower lashes with his thumb, which he firmly stifled.

She's married, for heaven's sake, he chastised himself. Get a grip, pal. That's really not your style.

He cleared his throat and forced himself to glance away from those mesmerizing eyes. "That would be fine,'' he said, gathering up the plans. "I'll have a set of prints run for you. When would you like to get together again?''

"How about a week from today?''

He looked up in surprise. "Will that give you enough time?''

She shrugged. "Enough to do some preliminary work. It won't be detailed, but it should be sufficient for you to decide whether you want my firm for this job.''

"All right. Should we try one o'clock again?''

"That will be fine.''

"And next time I promise to be punctual,'' he said, his eyes twinkling.

She gave him a fleeting smile and then shrugged. "I enjoyed chatting with Jack. He's a nice guy.''

"Give me a minute and I'll have those copies made for you.''

By the time he returned, Laura had gathered up all of

her material. He handed her the copies and she slipped them inside the portfolio, zipping it before extending her hand.

"Thank you, Mr. Sinclair. I appreciate the chance you're giving me."

"It's my pleasure. I do have one favor to ask, though."

"Yes?" she asked quizzically.

"Could we use first names? This Mr. and Mrs. business is too formal for me."

She shrugged. "Sure."

He smiled. "Good. Then I'll see you next week, Laura."

Three nights later, the phone's persistent ringing finally penetrated Laura's awareness. She sat bent over the drawing board in a corner of her living room, working on the Regional Arts Center designs, and had no time for social calls. And it had to be a social call, she thought when a quick glance at her watch showed that it was after seven. So she ignored it and went back to work.

An hour and a half later, the doorbell rang. Laura looked up and sighed. She'd promised designs in a week with full knowledge that the commitment would appreciably lengthen her already long work days. But they were going to be even longer if she had too many interruptions.

The bell rang again, and this time the caller kept the button depressed. With a frown Laura slid off the stool where she'd been perched and, massaging her neck muscles with one hand, made her way to the door. Her eyes widened when she glanced through the peephole.

"Sam!" she said, swinging the door open. "This is a surprise! Come in."

The slim, fashionably dressed woman on the other side

sauntered over the doorway and glanced around. "Have you had your phone fixed yet?"

"My phone?" Laura asked blankly, shutting and bolting the door.

"Well, it must be out of order. I keep calling, and it just keeps ringing. And you're obviously here."

"Oh." Laura's face flooded with color. "Sorry," she said apologetically. "I just didn't pick up. I'm on a deadline for what could be the commission that will finally put Taylor Landscaping on the map, and I just don't have time for anything else until next week."

"Including food?" Sam asked.

"I've been eating," she hedged.

"What did you have for dinner?"

"Well, I haven't had dinner yet," Laura admitted.

As Sam pointedly glanced at her watch, her shoulder-length red hair swung across her face. "May I ask at just what hour you plan to dine?"

"When I get hungry."

"You're not hungry yet? You must have had a big lunch," Sam persisted.

"Not exactly." Suddenly Laura realized she felt ravenous. She'd eaten only an apple for lunch, and that had been hours ago. As enticing smells emanated from the brown sack that Sam held Laura felt her empty stomach growl.

"You wouldn't want to share some Chinese with me, would you?" Sam asked, waving the bag under Laura's nose.

Laura grinned. "I could probably be persuaded. Why are you eating so late?"

"I was showing a house and my clients had to poke into every nook and cranny."

"Well, I'm glad you decided to share your dinner with

me," Laura admitted as Sam opened cartons and doled out Mongolian beef and cashew chicken, with healthy servings of rice. "Although I never have understood this mothering complex you have," Laura teased. Sam certainly didn't look like the nurturing type, but she watched over Laura like a mother hen. "Not that I'm complaining, you understand. But I really can take care of myself," Laura mumbled around a mouthful of food.

"Right," Sam said with mild sarcasm. "That's why you don't eat right and work such long hours."

"Getting a business off the ground isn't easy, Sam," Laura said, spearing a piece of green onion. "Mmm, this is delicious," she said with a smile, closing her eyes. "Anyway, right now I don't care if I have to stay up every night until two in the morning for the next week. It will be worth it."

"Is that when you've been going to bed?" Sam asked. "How long can you keep up this pace?"

"As long as it takes. Sam, this could be it! You know the new Regional Arts Center that's going to be built?"

"Yeah, I've read about it in the paper."

"Well, I may get a shot at doing the landscaping!"

"No kidding!" Sam said, duly impressed. "How did this come about?"

Laura explained briefly, concluding with the day she'd met Nick Sinclair at the job site. "Although I haven't yet figured out how he knew where I was," she said with a frown.

"I think maybe I can enlighten you on that," Sam said slowly.

Laura looked at her in surprise. "You can?"

She nodded. "Uh-huh. When I stopped by your office the other morning to drop off the book you loaned me, the phone rang and I just answered it automatically. That was the guy's name—Nick Sinclair. He asked for *Mr.* Taylor and didn't seem to take my amusement too kindly. Anyway, your job schedule was right there, and I didn't think it would hurt to give him the address. You know,'' she said thoughtfully, ''he was pretty heavy-handed, but he did have a really intriguing voice. What does he look like?''

Laura frowned. ''I don't know,'' she said with a shrug. ''He's attractive enough, I guess. Mid to late thirties, pretty tall, dark hair, high cheekbones, brown eyes. But to be honest, Sam, I've been so intimidated the two times we've met it's everything I can do to speak coherently let alone take inventory. After all, we didn't exactly get off to a good start,'' she said, a touch of irony in her voice.

''Hmm'' was all Sam said.

''What does that mean?'' Laura asked suspiciously.

Sam shrugged. ''Nothing. But do me a favor, kiddo. Next time, take inventory.''

''Why?''

''Why do you think?'' she asked with an exasperated sigh.

''Sam, for all I know the man is married. Besides, we've been over this before,'' Laura warned.

''Yes, and I still haven't changed my mind. After all, it's been nearly ten years, for Pete's sake! You could do with some male companionship.''

''I can do *without* it,'' she said emphatically.

Sam sighed dramatically. ''I wish you would at least make an effort. Is this guy nice?''

Laura frowned. ''He wasn't the first time we met. He was arrogant and rude, and when he found out I was the owner his shock was almost comical.''

''Well, after all, the man had just been doused with a hose,'' Sam reminded her.

"That's no excuse," Laura said.

"What about the second time you met?" Sam persisted.

Laura shrugged. "He seems to be a good architect. The plans for the Arts Center are very impressive."

Sam rolled her eyes. "Why don't I just give up? Laura, was he nice?"

Laura remembered the way he'd patiently looked at all the material she'd brought, and then spent two hours explaining the plans, finally agreeing to let her have a shot at the job. But she also remembered the way she felt around him—intimidated and uncertain. "He makes me nervous," she said.

"Well, it's a start," Sam said optimistically.

Laura smiled and shook her head, reaching for a fortune cookie. "Don't get your hopes up," she said, breaking it open.

Sam watched her friend's face turn slightly pink as she read the slip of paper. "What does it say?" she asked curiously.

In reply, Laura crumpled the paper between her fingers. "These things are stupid," she said.

"What does it say?" Sam repeated.

Laura sighed. "If I tell you, will you promise not to make any comments?"

"Sure."

Laura looked at her friend skeptically, and then read, "His heart was yours from the moment you met."

Sam didn't say a word. She just smiled.

Chapter Three

❧

The harmonies of the string quartet could barely be heard above the voices of the crowd, driven under the large tent by a sudden June shower. Nick, alone for a moment, grimaced as he adjusted his bow tie. The late-afternoon air felt unusually muggy and warm, even for St. Louis, and his glass was almost empty. Not that he could stomach much more of the bubbly champagne being served, anyway. Maybe he could find something more thirst quenching if he made a search, he thought halfheartedly. But it didn't seem worth the effort of fighting his way through the dense crowd. Besides, he preferred to remain on the sidelines for the moment. The ground-breaking party for the Arts Center had brought out all of the "beautiful" people, the wealthy St. Louisans who could be counted on as patrons for anything arts related. He'd said hello to all the right people and smiled for the photographers, and now all he wanted to do was go home, shed his tux and relax. It had been a long week. Despite the festive surroundings, his spirits felt as flat as the residue of champagne in his glass.

It was odd, really, that he wasn't in a more upbeat mood. His plans had been given enthusiastic praise in the press, and the ground-breaking party today for the project he'd worked so hard to win should have left him filled with excitement and energy. Instead, he was suddenly bone weary.

Nick's gaze swept over the crowd once more and, with a sudden jolt, he realized that, unconsciously, he was doing what he'd been doing ever since he'd arrived—searching for Laura. That realization also revealed the surprising reason for his glum mood—he had needed her presence to make this party a success.

Nick frowned, honest enough to admit the truth but still taken aback by it. He readily acknowledged that he enjoyed Laura's company. Ever since he'd awarded Taylor Landscaping the job two months ago, he'd seen her regularly as she more fully developed her plans and brought them to the office for his approval. He had grown to look forward to their meetings, to respect her intensity and creativity, and to experience a sense of satisfaction every time he elicited one of her rare smiles.

And *rare* was an appropriate word, he thought grimly, shoving his free hand into the pocket of his slacks. She worked too hard. He'd suspected as much at their first encounter, and the suspicion had been confirmed at subsequent meetings. Not that she ever complained. It was more subtle than that. Like the time he'd asked if he could keep the designs and review them after his full day of meetings, and she'd assured him she could just stop by on her way home from the office that evening about eight to pick them up.

But why wasn't she here today? He knew she'd been invited, and she deserved a party after the work she'd put into this project. A chance to get out of her customary jeans and— Suddenly his thoughts were arrested by a startling possibility. Maybe she didn't have anything to wear to a black-tie occasion! He knew she operated on a shoestring, and it was conceivable that her budget was too tight to allow for frivolities like cocktail dresses. He still had no idea what her husband did for a living, although he obviously wasn't involved in the landscaping business. Maybe he was ill, or out of work, leaving Laura to carry the burden of support.

"Nick! Here you are! Just wanted to say congratulations again on an outstanding job. I've heard nothing but compliments from everyone who's looked at the model."

The familiar voice brought Nick back to reality, and he turned to smile at George Thompson. "Thank you. It's been a great party."

"All except for the weather. But it's brightening up now. Well, enjoy yourself. I'll see you soon, Nick."

The fickle weather had, indeed, changed once again. Rays of sun peeped through the clouds, and the guests began to make their way out of the tent. Nick breathed a sigh of relief as the crowd thinned and his eyes began to scan the gathering again, this time hoping to spot a waiter with a fresh tray of something other than champagne.

His eyes had completed only part of their circuit when they were arrested by a tantalizing view. A woman was seated in the far corner of the tent, angled sideways. Her body was blocked from his view by a tuxedoed figure, but her crossed legs were clearly revealed under a fashionably short black skirt. His appreciative gaze wandered leisurely up their shapely length, his thirst forgotten for the moment. This was the most enjoyable part of the event so far, he thought with a wry smile.

Suddenly the legs uncrossed and the woman rose. She now stood totally hidden from his view by the man in the tuxedo, and Nick shook his head ruefully. So much for that pleasant interlude, he thought.

He was just about to go in search of a drink when he saw the woman attempt to move out from behind the man, only to have him take her arm and forcibly restrain her, backing her even farther into the corner.

Nick frowned. He didn't fancy himself a Sir Galahad, and besides, most women today were quite capable of taking care of themselves in situations like this. His intrusion could only cause unpleasantness. The man was probably her husband or, even worse, someone very important who it would not be wise to offend. Yet he was unwilling to leave the woman unassisted if she actually needed help.

Nick hesitated uncertainly. He watched the woman make another attempt to walk away, moving to one side. The glimpse he caught of her face made the swallow of champagne catch in his throat, and he almost choked as he stared in disbelief. It was Laura!

No wonder he hadn't noticed her earlier, he thought. She wore a black crepe cocktail dress, with double spaghetti straps held in place by rhinestone clips on the straight-cut bodice. The dress gently hugged her figure, ending well above her knees. She was gorgeous, Nick thought, stunned. Loose and full, her hair fell in soft, shimmering waves against the creamy expanse of her exposed shoulders. Her subtle makeup enhanced her picture-perfect features and wide eyes. She looked chic and sophisticated and polished, and she seemed as comfortable here as she did on a construction site.

Nick's perusal was abruptly interrupted as Laura made yet another futile attempt to extricate herself from the man's grasp. His indecision evaporated and he surged forward, adeptly maneuvering his way through the crowd, his eyes never leaving her face. She looked pale, and though poised and obviously trying her best to be polite, he also saw that a trace of fear lurked in her eyes. His stomach tightened into a hard knot, and as a waiter passed, he removed two glasses of champagne from the tray, never stopping his advance.

"Laura! I've been looking everywhere for you. I finally found the champagne," he greeted her, forcing a pleasant, conversational tone into his voice.

Laura's eyes flew to his, and he could see the relief flood through them. "Thanks, Nick. I wondered where you went." Her voice sounded a bit unsteady, but she took his lead gamely. His hand brushed hers as he offered her the champagne, and he noted that her fingers felt icy as she took the glass, holding it with both hands.

The fortyish, balding man looked from Nick to Laura, his flushed face indicating that he'd had his share of the freely flowing champagne. "You two are together? Sorry. Why didn't you say so?" he mumbled, his hands dropping to his sides. Nick saw the red mark his grip had left on Laura's arm and his jaw tightened. "I think I'll go find some more champagne," the man said, glancing around fuzzily.

"Maybe you've had enough," Nick suggested curtly, but the man had already turned and disappeared into the crowd.

Laura carefully set her champagne glass down on the table next to her and took a deep breath. "Thank you," she said quietly.

"I didn't do much." He watched her closely, aware that she was deeply upset.

"Well, your timing was perfect," she replied, a forced lightness in her tone. She reached for her purse, unsnapped the clasp and retrieved a mirror. "I think I'm about to lose an earring," she said, buying herself some time while she regained her composure. She reached up and tightened the already secure rhinestone clip.

She was putting on a good show, Nick thought. But he wasn't fooled. He could hear the strain in her voice and he could see the unsteadiness of her hands. "Maybe you should drink this," he suggested quietly, picking up her glass of champagne.

She looked at it distastefully and shook her head. "No, thanks."

He glanced in the direction of her "admirer." "I guess I don't blame you."

She shrugged. "I don't have anything against moderate drinking," she said. "But I have no tolerance for abuse." Her eyes dropped to the silver filigreed mirror in her hands, and she played with it nervously before setting it on the table. She took a deep breath, and when she spoke again there was a husky uncertainty in her voice. "I do appreciate your help, Nick. I—I'm not very good at handling those kinds of situations."

"You shouldn't have to be," he said, with an edge to his voice that made her look up in surprise. "No woman should."

She was taken aback by the vehemence of his tone, given that she'd labeled him a male chauvinist. "Yes, well, it sounds good in theory." She paused and took a deep breath. "Look, Nick, I think I'm going to head home. It's been a long day."

"Did you work all day?"

She nodded. "Up until about three hours ago."

"That hardly looks like your usual work attire," he said, hoping that the warmth of his smile would ease some of the tension he sensed in her body. "If I may say so, you look stunning."

"Well, you didn't expect me to come in my jeans, did

you?'' she asked, unexpectedly pleased by his compliment. When he didn't reply, her eyes widened in disbelief. ''Or did you?''

''No, of course not,'' he said quickly. He didn't tell her that he thought she might have stayed away due to lack of appropriate attire rather than lack of taste. ''It's just that I've never seen you wear anything but work clothes.''

She tilted her chin up slightly, and there was a touch of defensiveness in her voice when she spoke. ''Jeans and overalls suit my job. This outfit would hardly be appropriate at a construction site. I don't have an office job, Nick. And I'm not afraid to get my hands dirty.''

Nick frowned at her misinterpretation of his remark. ''I realize that,'' he said quietly. ''I didn't mean to offend you, Laura. My comment was meant as a compliment, not a criticism.''

Laura looked at him, lost for a moment in the depth of his eyes. What else did he realize? she wondered. Did he realize that for some unaccountable reason her heart was hammering in her chest? Did he realize that her breathing had become slightly erratic? And did he realize that neither of those reactions was a result of her unpleasant encounter? Distractedly she pushed the hair back from her face. ''I've really got to be going,'' she said, retrieving her purse from the chair at her side.

''Are you here alone?'' Nick asked in surprise.

''Yes.''

''Well, can I at least walk you to your car?''

''I'm fine, really. But thanks for the offer. Good night, Nick.''

He hesitated, reluctant to let her leave alone, knowing he couldn't stop her. When Laura looked at him curiously, he found his voice. ''Good night, Laura.''

He watched her thread her way through the thinning

crowd, frustrated by his inability to…to what? he wondered. He'd done all that was necessary by helping her out of an offensive situation. Yet he felt she'd needed something more, something he couldn't give. She'd seemed unaccountably shaken by the encounter, and he doubted whether she'd fully recovered. Certainly it had been unpleasant, but there'd been no real danger. Yet he'd caught the glimmer of fear in her eyes, of vulnerability. He wished she had at least let him walk her to her car. And where was her husband? he wondered, suddenly angry. She did have one. Or at least he assumed she did. Yet she always seemed so alone.

He continued to stare pensively into the crowd long after she'd disappeared from sight. Only when he realized that the majority of guests had departed did he rouse himself to do the same. It was time to call it a day.

Nick turned to set his glass on the table, and his eyes fell on Laura's silver mirror, obviously forgotten in her haste to depart. He picked it up and weighed it thoughtfully in his hand, turning it over to examine it more closely. It looked quite old, perhaps a family heirloom, he mused. He'd have to call Laura immediately and let her know it was safe. Hopefully he could reach her even before she realized it was missing. She'd had enough stress for one day, he thought, a muscle in his jaw tightening.

And then an idea slowly took form in his mind. Why not drop it off on his way home? That way he could assure himself that she had gotten home all right and, perhaps in the process, meet the elusive Mr. Taylor.

Nick slipped the mirror into the pocket of his jacket and turned to go, only to find a board member at his elbow. His patience was stretched to the breaking point by the time he could tactfully disengage himself from a discussion of the importance of art to the St. Louis community. Then it took another ten minutes to find a phone directory so he could look up Laura's address. With a frustrated sigh, he glanced at his watch. Seven o'clock. Laura was probably home by now. He *could* just call and let her know he had the mirror, he told himself. There was no urgency about returning it. But somehow that wasn't good enough. He *wanted* to go. And he wasn't going to waste time analyzing the reasons why.

Laura stirred the spaghetti sauce, raising the spoon to her lips for a taste. Perfect, she thought with a satisfied smile. But then, Grandmother's recipe never failed. It was one of those things you could always count on. And there weren't a lot of them in this world, she mused, her smile fading. There was her faith, of course. It had been her anchor in the difficult years of her marriage and the struggle for survival that followed. Her trust in the Lord was stable, sure and strong, and even in her darkest hours, it had offered her hope and comfort. The Lord had always stretched out his hand to steady her when she felt most shaky and lost. Yes, she could count on her faith.

She could also count on her family. And Sam. But certainly not men. Or at least not her judgment of them. How could she have been so wrong? she asked herself again, as she had countless times before. But the answer always eluded her.

As her mood started to darken, Laura fiercely took herself in hand. She refused to become melancholy over a stupid little incident that she'd blown out of all proportion, she told herself angrily. Okay, so the man's steel grip on her arm and the smell of liquor on his breath had brought back painful memories. So what? She wasn't the only one in the world with painful memories, and it was about time that she laid hers to rest.

At the same time, she had made progress, she consoled herself. She turned the spaghetti sauce down to simmer, removed her large white apron and headed for the bedroom to change clothes. Three or four years ago she probably would have been a basket case after that scene. She'd held up all right. Of course, if Nick hadn't come along...

Nick. Her arm froze as she reached around to unzip the black cocktail dress. Thoughts of him were almost as disturbing as thoughts of the unpleasant encounter. Both caused her breathing to quicken and her pulse rate to accelerate. Both made her stomach churn and her legs grow weak. Both made her nervous and uncertain.

But for very different reasons, she acknowledged honestly. Ever since Sam had planted the seed of romance in her head about Nick, Laura had reacted like a skittish colt whenever she was around him. And the explanation was simple. She felt attracted to him. Heaven help her, but she did. There was simply no way to honestly deny it, and Laura had learned through the years that being honest with herself was essential to her survival.

Slowly she unzipped the dress, stepped out of it and made her way toward the closet. When she passed the full-length mirror behind her door she hesitated, and then glanced at her reflection. It wasn't something she did often; for too many years she had disliked herself and her body so intensely that she avoided mirrors whenever possible. She was still much too thin, but at least her self-image had improved enough in the past few years that she could now look at herself without cringing.

One thing for sure, she thought with a wry smile, her job might be physically demanding, but it helped keep her in shape. Her body was that of a twenty-year-old—muscles toned, stomach flat, thighs firm. Joe had enjoyed her body once, she thought, allowing a moment of wistful recollection. At least he had until the problems started and she'd begun to lose weight. Then he'd started making fun of her thinness. And her looks. And her ambition. And her faith.

His loss of faith and belittlement of hers had been one of the most painful things to endure during those last difficult months. As their relationship had deteriorated, she'd turned more and more to her faith to sustain her, finding great comfort in the Bible. Joe, on the other hand, had found no solace there, had laughed when she suggested they spend some time each evening reading a few verses out loud. It was almost as if he was jealous of her faith, resenting the consolation she found there. She had tried to help, tried to share her faith with him, but he had resisted every attempt she'd made. In the end, his ridicule of all she had been raised to believe in had killed whatever love still survived in their relationship.

A lump formed in her throat, and she forced herself to swallow past it. The power of love—both constructive and destructive—never ceased to amaze her. Her faith had survived, but little else had, including her self-esteem. Even now, more than ten years later, she was still self-conscious about her body. ''Bony,'' Joe had called her. She'd gained a little weight since then, but she was still probably too thin to be desirable. Not that she'd cared about that over the years. But for some reason Nick had activated hormones that she'd thought had died long ago. After Joe, Laura had been convinced that she would never be attracted to another man. With a shudder she recalled how the sweetness of their young love had gradually soured, how in the end lovemaking had become an ordeal, an act devoid of all tenderness, to be endured, not enjoyed. Even now the memories filled her with shame and disgust. It had taken her years to accept emotionally what she'd always known intellectually—that Joe's actions had been the result of his own sickness rather than anything she had done. She had dealt with the guilt—as much as she would ever be able to, knowing that some would always remain. And she had stopped asking the "what if?" questions ten times a day. But she had never recovered enough to risk another relationship.

Until she met Nick, Laura had been content to live the solitary life she'd created for herself, a life where no one made demands of her, no one belittled her, no one hurt her. It was a safe, if insulated, existence. Sam had been after her for years to reconsider her self-imposed physical and emotional celibacy, but, until Nick, Laura had never even been tempted. The idea of opening up again to any man had turned her off completely, and her passionate side was kept firmly under wraps.

So why were her hormones kicking in now? she wondered. Sure, Nick was a handsome man. And he seemed nice enough. After their initial confrontation, he'd proven to be a fair and considerate business associate. But until this afternoon she'd never related to him on anything but a professional level. Not that she should consider today's encounter very significant, she reminded herself. He had simply helped her out of an awkward situation, his action prompted more by good manners than personal interest. Yet the way he'd looked at her, as if he sensed the trauma of the situation for her and cared how she felt, had sent shock waves along her nerve endings and filled her with an almost forgotten warmth.

Laura took a deep breath and closed her eyes. What was wrong with her? Had she suppressed her needs for so long that even the slightest kindness and warmth from a man sent them clamoring for release?

Impatiently Laura pulled on a pair of shorts and a

T-shirt. She had to get a grip on her emotions. Nick was a business associate. Period. Her reaction to him was just the result of long-suppressed physical needs. She would never again give herself to a man, now or in the future. It was simply too dangerous. No matter what Sam thought!

By the time Nick turned down Laura's street, it was nearly seven-thirty. He'd grown more uncertain with every mile he'd driven. Maybe her husband wouldn't appreciate his visit. And the last thing he wanted to do was cause Laura any further distress.

He still felt undecided when he pulled up in front of her apartment. He parked the car but remained behind the wheel, glancing around the neighborhood. Not the best part of town, he thought grimly. She lived in a four-family unit in the south part of the city, on a side street lined with similar brick flats. The buildings in this part of the city were probably at least seventy years old, and judging by the cars lining the street, it was not an affluent area. In fact, the longer he sat there, the more he began to realize that the surroundings were actually a little seedy. He frowned. He'd known money was tight, but she had a nice storefront office, albeit small, in one of the nicer suburbs, so he hadn't expected that she would live in such a run-down area.

He thought of his own West County condo, with its tennis courts and swimming pool and health club, and a surge of guilt washed over him. Nick was certain that Laura worked just as hard—if not harder—than he did, and she obviously had much less to show for it. Even in his leaner years, Nick's life-style had never been this impoverished.

He glanced at Laura's apartment building, still undecided. Why was he agonizing over a simple decision? he asked himself impatiently. After all, the worst that could happen would be that he would be treated as an unwelcome intruder. If so, he could make a hasty departure. It was no big deal.

Determinedly, Nick stepped out of his car, which was attracting interested glances from a few teenagers gathered on a neighboring porch. He felt them staring at the back of his tux as he bent to carefully lock the door, and he paused uncertainly, fiddling unnecessarily with the key. Was it wise to leave the car unattended? But he wouldn't be staying long, he assured himself. He strode inside, found that Laura lived on the top floor and took the steps two at a time.

Laura heard the doorbell and frowned, glancing at the clock. Sam was out of town until tomorrow, so it couldn't be her. Curiously she walked over to the door and peered through the peephole.

Her eyes widened, and with a muffled exclamation she stepped back from the door in alarm, her hand going to her throat. She began to take deep breaths, trying to steady the staccato beat of her heart. This wasn't good. This wasn't good at all. Not after the thoughts she'd just been having. Maybe she could just ignore him, she thought hopefully. Surely he'd go away if she didn't answer the door. But then logic took over. Why was he here? It must be something important for him to track her down at home. Was there a problem with the Arts Center, something he'd discovered after she'd left the party? That must be it, because he hadn't even bothered to change out of his tux. He'd come directly from the party. It had to be urgent.

Laura took another deep breath and stepped forward,

sliding back the bolt and swinging the door open. "Nick! Is something wrong?" she asked without preamble.

Nick stared at the woman across from him. Her hair still swung loose and full, but she'd changed into shorts that snugly hugged her hips and revealed even more of her incredible legs than the cocktail dress had. A T-shirt clung softly to her upper body, the sea blue color complementing her hair and eyes. Suddenly aware that the silence was lengthening noticeably, he cleared his throat. "That's not the most enthusiastic welcome I've ever received," he said, flashing a quick, uncertain grin.

"Sorry," she said, flushing as she stepped aside. "Come in."

He hesitated. "I don't want to intrude…"

"I'm just making dinner."

"Well, only for a minute." He crossed the threshold into a tiny foyer and Laura shut the door behind him, sliding the bolt into place.

"Make yourself comfortable," she said, gesturing toward the living room, and Nick stepped into the softly lit room, which Laura had decorated in an English country style. Floral-patterned chintz covered the couches and chairs, and an old trunk served as a coffee table. Baskets of dried flowers and the soft yellow walls gave the room a warm, homey feel. A drafting table stood in one corner, with a wooden desk nearby, and lace curtains hung at the windows. There was a dining nook to one side, separated from the galley kitchen by a counter, and a glance down the hall revealed a bathroom door slightly ajar and a closed door that must be a bedroom.

"You've done a good job with this place," he said approvingly. "These older buildings are hard to decorate."

He regretted the words the moment he said them, thinking she might interpret his comment as criticism, but he was wrong.

"Thanks. It's amazing what a little paint, a needle and thread and some elbow grease can do."

She seemed skittish, not offended, and Nick wondered if her husband was in the bedroom or expected soon. He'd better do what he came to do and get out, he decided, withdrawing the mirror from his pocket and holding it out to her.

"I think you forgot this."

"Oh!" She gasped softly and reached for it.

"I thought you might be worried. It looks like it might be valuable."

She shrugged. "I have no idea about its monetary worth. But it has a lot of sentimental value." Her voice grew soft. "My grandfather gave this to my grandmother on their wedding day." She shook her head. "I can't believe I forgot it."

"Given the situation, I can. You were pretty upset."

She looked at him and took a deep breath. It seemed foolish to deny what had clearly been quite apparent. "Was it that obvious?" she asked quietly.

"Mmm-hmm."

"Like I said, I'm not very good at handling that sort of thing. Would you like to sit down for a minute?"

"The offer is tempting," he hedged, his eyes traveling around the room. "You've made this a very welcoming place." His eyes fell on the dining table and he noted with surprise that only one place was set. So Laura was here alone. But why? He decided to probe, knowing it was a gamble. "It's too bad your husband couldn't join you today," he said casually, strolling over to one of the overstuffed chairs. "That scene probably would have been avoided."

His back was to her when he spoke, and as he turned he caught the sudden look of pain in her eyes. Then they went flat, and she turned away. "My husband is dead," she said in a curiously unemotional voice. "Will you excuse me for a minute? I need to check something in the kitchen."

Nick felt as if he'd been kicked in the stomach. He had wondered if she was divorced, although divorced women rarely asked to be called Mrs. anymore. Yet the idea that she might be a widow had never entered his mind. He'd satisfied his curiosity all right—at her expense, he thought, gritting his teeth. He jammed his hands into his pockets, his fists tightening in frustration at his lack of tact.

When Laura reappeared a few moments later, he turned to her, feeling that some comment was called for. "Laura, I'm sorry. I didn't know."

She looked at him, startled, as if surprised he'd reopened the subject. Then she shrugged. "No reason you should have. Please, sit down."

Nick hesitated for a moment, and then settled his large frame into a chair, noting that she perched nervously on the edge of the couch. Why was she so tense? Was it his presence that made her uncomfortable? And if so, why? He'd given her no reason to be nervous. In fact, since their first explosive encounter he'd gone out of his way to treat her with consideration.

"Laura, is there something wrong?" he asked quietly, knowing he was taking a chance but willing to accept the consequences.

The deep, mellow tone of his voice had a curiously soothing effect on Laura, and she looked down at the hands clasped tightly in her lap. At last she glanced up, aware that Nick's relaxed posture was at odds with the intensity of his eyes, which seemed to say "I care." And for just the briefest moment she felt tempted to pour her heart out to this man who was practically a stranger. But before the urge grew too strong to resist, she abruptly stood.

Nick seemed taken aback by her sudden movement, but he remained seated, waiting for her to speak.

Now that she was on her feet, Laura was at a loss. It was important that he leave, she knew that much. Never mind that she'd just invited him to sit down. Something intuitively told her that he represented danger. "No, everything's fine," she lied. "Except dinner. I'm afraid it will burn if I don't get into the kitchen." Her voice was pitched above normal, and even to her ears it sounded strained.

Nick remained seated. "It smells good," he said with a smile.

Dear Lord, why couldn't the man take the hint and just leave? Laura thought desperately. But she forced a bright smile to her lips. "Thanks. It's an old family recipe. I really hadn't planned to fix dinner tonight, but I didn't get a chance to eat much at the party," she said, trying to talk away her nervousness.

"Me neither."

Laura stared at him. Good grief, he was angling for a dinner invitation! This was great. Just great. She was trying to get rid of him and he wanted to stay. They were obviously not on the same wavelength. But how could she ignore the blatant hint without sounding ungracious? After all, he had come to her assistance today, and he'd gone out of his way to return the mirror.

Logic told her to ignore the prickling of her conscience. But good manners—and something else she refused to acknowledge—told her to listen. She sighed, capitulating.

"Would you like to stay for dinner?"

Nick smiled, the tense muscles in his abdomen relaxing. "As a matter of fact, yes." Then, suddenly, a shadow of doubt crept into his eyes, which narrowed as they swept over her too-thin form. "On second thought, maybe I won't. I don't want to take part of your dinner."

This was her out! All she had to say was "Maybe another time," and she'd be safe. But other words came out instead. "Oh, there's plenty. I made a whole batch of sauce and I was going to freeze what I didn't use. It's just a matter of cooking a bit more spaghetti."

Relief washed over his features, and he smiled. "In that case, I'll stay."

Laura smiled back. At least, she forced her lips to turn up into the semblance of a smile. But something told her she'd just made a big mistake.

Chapter Four

"What can I do to help?" Nick asked, his engaging smile making her heart misbehave.

"There's really nothing," Laura said vaguely, still off balance by the unexpected turn of events. A visitor for dinner was the last thing she'd expected—especially this particular visitor.

Nick placed his fists on his hips, tilted his head and grinned at her. "Were you going to make a salad? I'm not too great on cooked stuff, but I can handle a head of lettuce."

Laura found herself responding to his lighthearted warmth, and a smile played at the corners of her mouth. "Well, I wasn't planning to. But since you offered…"

Nick gestured toward the kitchen. "Lead the way."

Laura was conscious of him close behind her as she walked toward the tiny kitchen, and she was even more conscious of him as they worked side by side in the cramped space, only a few inches apart. She suddenly felt all thumbs as she stirred the sauce and put the spaghetti into the boiling water. Nick, on the other hand, seemed totally relaxed. He was humming some nondescript tune under his breath as he worked, detouring occasionally to peer in her refrigerator and withdraw some other ingredient. So far she'd watched him chop lettuce, cut up tomatoes, slice red onion, sprinkle cheese and add croutons, all with a dexterity that surprised her. She had never expected him to be so at home in a kitchen.

"Voilà! A masterpiece!" he exclaimed finally, turning to her with a smile. "I just hope your spaghetti lives up to the standards of this creation," he said with an exaggerated French accent and an aristocratic sniff.

Laura found herself unexpectedly giggling at his comic antics, but her face quickly sobered when she saw an odd expression in his eyes. "What's wrong?" she asked uncertainly.

"Nothing. It's just that you should do that more often," he said quietly, suddenly serious.

She frowned in confusion. "What?"

"Laugh. It makes your face come alive."

Laura turned away, embarrassed, and stuck her head in the freezer on the pretense of looking for something. In reality, she hoped the cool air would take the flush from her cheeks. "Thanks, I think," she said over her shoulder, her voice muffled.

"You're welcome."

Her eyes fell on a package of garlic bread, and she reached for it gratefully. "I thought I had some of this left," she said glibly. "Should be perfect with our menu."

"Looks good," he agreed.

Suddenly the kitchen seemed even smaller than before. Nick leaned against the counter, his arms folded across his chest, one ankle crossed over the other. His cool confidence unnerved her, especially at this proximity. He was so close that if he wanted to he could simply reach over and pull her into his arms, she realized, quickly trying to stifle the unbidden thought. But it remained stubbornly in place, and her heart rate took a jump.

"Um, Nick, maybe you could set another place," she suggested. Anything to get him just a few feet farther away! she thought.

"Sure," he said easily, straightening up and walking around to the other side of the counter. "If you hand the stuff through, I'll take care of it."

Laura breathed a sigh of relief, feeling somehow safer now that they were separated by a counter. "Okay." She stood on tiptoe to open the overhead cabinet, unaware that when she reached up for the extra plate and glass, her T-shirt crept up to reveal a bare section of creamy white midriff and a perfectly formed navel.

Nick took a sharp, sudden deep breath and reached up to loosen his tie.

"Oh, you must be warm in that outfit," Laura said innocently as she handed the plate through. "I'm sorry I don't have the air on. I usually only run it during heat waves. Why don't you take off your tie and jacket?"

Nick swallowed with difficulty. "I think I will," he said, turning away, needing a minute to compose himself. Did Laura have any idea just how attractive she was? Even in shorts, her face now almost wiped free of makeup from the steamy kitchen, there was an appeal about her that he found strangely compelling.

He pulled off his tie and undid the top button of his shirt, slipping his arms out of the jacket and automatically rolling his sleeves to the elbows in his customary fashion. His hand hesitated for a fraction of a second on the cummerbund, and then he unsnapped it. He'd be a whole lot more comfortable without it.

Laura watched the cotton fabric of the shirt stretch

across his broad shoulders as he went through these maneuvers, and a profound yearning surged through her. It had been so long, so very long...

With harsh determination she turned away and opened a cupboard to search for some cloth napkins. Her eye fell on an unopened bottle of red wine, a Christmas gift from a client. She'd been saving it for a special occasion. Thoughtfully, she reached for it, then hesitated. Was she asking for trouble? This wasn't a romantic tryst, after all. It was just a thank-you, and Laura didn't want Nick to read any more than that into this invitation. Still, wine would be a nice complement to the meal. With sudden decision, she grasped the bottle firmly and pulled it out. She was already flirting with danger merely by having him here. Why be cautious now?

Laura turned to find Nick in the doorway, and she paused, her eyes drawn to the V of springy, dark hair revealed at the open neck of his shirt. She clutched the bottle to her chest, suddenly at a loss for words, sorry now that she'd taken the wine out.

Nick glanced at the bottle curiously. "I'm surprised," he commented. "After your encounter today, I wouldn't think you'd be inclined to drink."

"I told you, Nick. I have nothing against alcohol. Wine goes great with some food. But I can't tolerate abuse. It freaks me out."

"So I noticed," he said, watching her closely, searching for a clue to the reason why.

Laura's eyes flew to his, then skittered away at their intensity. "Well, shall we eat?" she asked a bit breathlessly.

He took the hint gracefully and dropped the subject, and Laura's heart stopped hammering quite so painfully. Nevertheless, she was sure she wouldn't be able to swallow a bite of food. Her stomach was churning, and even as he held her chair—an unexpected courtesy—she was fighting waves of panic. She was having a pleasant, intimate dinner with a man for the first time in more than a decade—never mind the circumstances. It would have been nerve-racking enough with any man. But it wasn't just any man. It was Nick Sinclair, the man who only this afternoon had awakened her dormant hormones.

Nick sat down across from her and smiled. "Shall I pour?" he asked, picking up the bottle of wine.

"Yes, please."

"Everything smells delicious," he commented, aware of her tension, struggling to put her at ease. "Your grandmother must have been some cook."

"Yes, she was."

"Was she Italian?"

Laura found herself smiling. "Hardly. She just loved to experiment with dishes from foreign lands. And in Jersey, Missouri, Italy is about as foreign as you can get."

"Jersey," he mused. "I don't think I've ever heard of it."

"Not many people have. It's a tiny town in the southern part of the state."

"Is that where you grew up?" he asked.

"Mmm-hmm."

"It must have been nice growing up in a small town. I've spent all of my life in big cities. I grew up in Denver."

"Small-town life has some advantages," Laura said. "But not many opportunities."

"I suppose that's true. So how's the salad?"

Laura looked down in surprise at her half-empty plate. Nick's gentle, nonthreatening conversation had made her relax and she'd begun to eat without even realizing it. "It's very good," she said.

"Well, you don't have to look so surprised," he said in mock chagrin.

She laughed. "Sorry. You just don't look like the type of man who would spend much time in the kitchen," she admitted.

"As a bachelor, it's a matter of survival to learn some of the basics," he said.

As the meal progressed, Laura found that the tension was slowly ebbing from her body. She realized how much Nick's quiet, attentive, undemanding manner had calmed her. With a little prompting, she even found herself telling him about her work with Christian Youth Outreach and sharing her views about the importance of a Christian influence on young people and the difference it could make in troubled lives.

By the time the last crust of garlic bread had been eaten, Laura felt mellow and relaxed, and she smiled at Nick, no longer intimidated or frightened. He was easy to be with, she realized.

"I'm afraid I can't offer you dessert," she apologized. "I don't keep sweets in the house. It's just too much of a temptation."

"Well, I have a suggestion."

She looked at him curiously. "What?"

"How about Ted Drewes?"

Laura hadn't been to the South Side landmark in years, but the famous frozen custard was considered the ultimate summertime treat for many St. Louisans.

Nick watched her surprise turn to delight, and he grinned. "Why do I think this won't be a hard sell?"

She smiled back. "I must admit that I've always had a

weakness for Ted Drewes," she confessed. "But it is getting late."

Nick glanced at his watch and let out a low whistle. "Is it actually ten o'clock?"

"I'm afraid so."

Nick looked up and saw the disappointment in her eyes. "Well, this is the peak time for Ted Drewes on a Friday night," he reminded her. "I'm game if you are."

"Nick…are you sure?" she asked uncertainly. "You've already gone to so much trouble for me today…"

He reached over and covered her hand with his, his touch sending sparks along her nerve endings. "Laura, I'm doing this for *me*," he said softly.

She looked into his eyes, trying to read his thoughts, but all she saw was a warmth and tenderness that made her breath catch in her throat. His hand still rested on hers, and she loved the protective feel of it. She'd almost forgotten that a touch could be so gentle.

"Well…in that case…okay," she said, her voice uneven.

"Good." He squeezed her hand and then released it. "I'm parked out in front."

"Let me just get my purse," she said, feeling as nervous as a teenager on her first date.

When Laura reached the sanctuary of her bedroom she groped in her purse for her lipstick and applied it with shaking hands. Then she ran a comb through her hair. All the while Nick's words kept replaying in her mind. *I'm doing this for me.* They made her feel good…and scared, all at the same time. But maybe that was okay, she thought. Maybe it was the Lord's way of reminding her to be cautious and move slowly.

When Laura returned to the living room Nick stood

waiting, his jacket slung casually over his shoulder. He smiled as she walked toward him, and Laura felt nearly breathless. He really was a very handsome man. Maybe too handsome, she reflected.

"Ready?"

"Yes."

He opened the door for her and stepped aside as she carefully locked it, then followed her down the steps. When they reached the ground floor she found his hand at the small of her back as he guided her toward the red sports car, which was thankfully still in one piece, he noted.

Laura let him lead her to the car, enjoying his touch, impersonal though she knew it was. She sank into the cushions of the two-seater, the unaccustomed luxury making her smile.

"Nice car," she said, reverently running her hand over the leather cushions.

Nick flashed her a grin. "Thanks. It was a splurge, but we all deserve those now and then, don't you think?" He suddenly remembered her older-model hatchback and clenched his jaw, realizing that she probably had little discretionary income. He was afraid he might have offended her, but when she spoke her voice was friendly and conversational.

"Of course! What good is success if you can't enjoy the fruits of your labors?" she replied promptly. Her tone held no resentment, no envy, no self-pity that her own financial situation was not yet secure enough to allow for such luxuries. She was quite a woman, Nick thought— not for the first time that day.

As always, the lines at Ted Drewes stretched nearly into the street, and a good-natured crowd milled about. Families, couples young and old, teenagers in groups, all mingled. A stretch limo was even pulled up to the curb, but that was not an uncommon sight.

"This place never ceases to amaze me," she said with a smile, shaking her head as Nick jockeyed for a parking place.

"It's pretty incredible," he agreed, stopping by a spot that was being vacated. "We're in luck," he said triumphantly, skillfully pulling into the tight slot. By the time he turned off the ignition and started to come around to open Laura's door, he discovered that she'd already alighted, and he stopped in midstride.

Laura looked at him guiltily. It had been so long since she'd dated that she'd forgotten the niceties. Over the years she had grown accustomed to doing everything herself.

"Sorry," they said in unison.

Laura smiled. "Why are you sorry?" she asked.

He shrugged sheepishly. "I thought maybe you were one of those women who felt offended by men opening doors and holding chairs. I've run into a few who let me know in no uncertain terms that they considered such behavior the height of chauvinism. But my mother did a good job training me, and now it's a habit. If I offended you, I'm sorry."

"No, it's not that," Laura assured him quickly. "As a matter of fact, I enjoy it. I just…" Her voice trailed off. How could she tell him that it had been so long since she'd been with a man that she had simply forgotten the rules? "I'm sorry," she finished lamely, seeing no way she could possibly explain her behavior without telling him things that were better left unsaid.

"No problem," Nick assured her with a smile. "I just want to make sure we're on the same wavelength."

After braving the long line at the order window they

returned to Nick's car, leaning against the hood as they ate their chocolate chip concretes, so called because of their thick texture. As they enjoyed the frozen concoction Nick kept her amused with comments and outrageous speculations about various people in the crowd.

"See that guy over there? The one in the Bermuda shorts who looks like he's made too many visits here? He's a spy," he said solemnly.

"How do you figure that?" Laura asked, smiling up at him.

"It's elementary, my dear. Spies are picked to blend in with the crowd. Would *you* think he was a spy?"

"No," she admitted.

"Well, there you have it."

Laura giggled. "Nick Sinclair, you're crazy. Has anyone ever told you that?"

"I've been called a few things in my life," he admitted. "But 'crazy'...no, that's a new one. Should I be insulted?"

"No. You're crazy in the best sense of the word," she said, laughing.

"Well, it must not be so bad if it makes you laugh," he said softly, his voice suddenly serious.

Laura was thrown off balance by the change in mood, preferring the safe, easy banter of moments before. She shifted uncomfortably and focused on scraping the last bite of custard out of the bottom of her cup.

Nick sensed her withdrawal. For some reason, relationships with men made her uncomfortable, he realized. She seemed fine when the give and take was light and friendly, but introduce an element of seriousness or intimacy and she backed off, retreating behind a wall of caution. Why? He felt certain there was an explanation. And probably not a pleasant one. But he was equally sure that at this stage in their relationship she was not about to share it with him. He'd have to earn her trust first. And pushing or coming on too strong were not the right tactics, he warned himself. In fact, he instinctively knew that doing so would be the surest way to lose her.

"Well, I see you've managed to polish off that entire concrete," he said lightly, peering into her now empty container. His head was so close that Laura could smell the distinctive scent of his aftershave, could see the few flecks of silver in his full, incredibly soft-looking hair.

"Uh, yes, I did, didn't I? And on top of all that pasta, too." She groaned. "This was not a heart-healthy meal. And it wasn't so great for the waistline, either."

"You don't have to worry about that," he assured her.

Laura looked at him sharply. "What do you mean?"

Nick was taken aback by her prickly reaction. "It was a compliment, Laura. You don't have an extra ounce of fat on your entire body."

She looked down dejectedly, playing with her spoon. So Nick thought she looked scrawny, too. And scrawny was not attractive.

"Laura?" Nick's voice was uncertain. When she didn't look up, he reached over and gently cupped her chin in his hand, turning her head, forcing her to look at him. He gazed into her eyes, which suddenly looked miserable and lost, and felt an almost overwhelming desire to pull her into his arms. He resisted the urge with difficulty. "Laura?" he repeated questioningly, his voice now husky. "What is it?"

She couldn't lie, not when his eyes were locked on hers with such intensity. "I'm just sort of paranoid about being skinny," she said softly. "It's not very...very—" she searched for the right word "—appealing," she finished.

Nick frowned. Good grief, did Laura think she was unattractive? It wasn't possible. No one could look like her and be unaware of her effect on the opposite sex. Or could they? he wondered incredulously. She didn't seem to hold a very high opinion of her physical attributes. Yes, she was on the thin side. But most models would kill to have her figure. And he personally preferred slender women. Voluptuous beauty had never appealed to him.

"Laura, you can't be serious," he said quietly, deciding that honesty was the only tactic. "You are a gorgeous woman! You knocked me off my feet today at the party in that slinky little black dress you had on." Usually he didn't lay his cards out on the table so early in the game, but her need for reassurance outweighed his need to protect his ego.

Laura's eyes reflected disbelief. "You're being very kind, Nick, but—"

"Laura, stop it," he said fiercely, cutting her off abruptly. Her look of shock made him soften his tone. "Look, I am not giving you empty compliments. I respect you too much for that. I'm telling you the truth. You are an extremely attractive woman, and if I wasn't looking into your eyes right now and reading the uncertainty, I'd think you were just fishing for compliments. It's almost beyond my comprehension that someone who looks like you should have any doubts about her attractiveness."

Laura swallowed past the lump in her throat and felt hot tears forming behind her eyes. She wanted to believe Nick. Wanted to desperately. But life had made her wary. And you didn't lose that wariness overnight, no matter how kind a person was.

"It's a long story, Nick," she said softly.

"I figured it might be." He casually draped an arm around her shoulders. "Sometimes it helps to talk," he offered.

"Sometimes," she agreed, conscious of the warmth of his fingers gently massaging her shoulder. His simple touch made her yearn for too much too soon.

"But not now?" he suggested.

"Not yet," she amended, knowing she was leaving the door open for the future.

"I'll settle for that," he said. "Ready to call it a night?" At her nod he stood and, extending a hand, drew her to her feet. He kept his hand familiarly in the small of her back as they walked around the car, releasing her only after he'd opened the door and she made a move to slip inside.

"Thank you," she said, suddenly shy.

"You're welcome."

The ride home was brief and quiet, but it was a companionable silence. Only when he pulled up in front of her apartment and came around to open her car door did he speak, glancing around as he did so.

"It's not very well lit here, is it?" he said.

"I've never thought about it," she replied truthfully.

"You don't wander around here at night, do you?" he asked worriedly.

"No. Nick, it's a safe neighborhood, if that's what you're asking," she assured him.

"If you say so," he replied, but he sounded unconvinced.

They walked up the dimly lit stairway to her second-floor apartment, and Nick silently took the key from her hand and fitted it into the lock.

Laura looked up at him, her eyes suddenly sad. She'd had a wonderful evening, an evening she'd never expected to have again. Now she felt a little like Cinderella at midnight as the chiming clock broke the magic spell, knowing that today had been a chance encounter that was unlikely to be repeated.

Nick saw the melancholy look steal over her eyes and reached up to brush a few stray strands of hair back from her face. Laura's breath caught in her throat at his intimate touch, and her heart began to pound.

"You look suddenly unhappy, Laura," he said, his voice edged with concern. "Didn't you have a good time tonight?"

"Oh, yes! I did! I'm just sorry it's over," she admitted. "It's the nicest evening I've had in a long time," she told him honestly. "I just hope I didn't disrupt any of your plans. This was so unexpected."

"Yes, it was. And yes, you did. But I'm not complaining," he said with a gentle smile that warmed her right down to her toes.

"Well…" Should she ask him to come in? she wondered. What was the protocol? Did an invitation to come in automatically include an invitation for more? She'd been out of the dating world too long to know. What she *did* know was that casual intimacy wasn't her style. It went against everything she believed as a Christian.

Nick, sensing her dilemma, solved the problem. He would have liked nothing better than to follow her through that door, to hold her in his arms until she melted against him, to leisurely taste her sweet kisses. But now was not the time, and he knew it.

"I'll see you soon, Laura," he said, his voice strangely husky. "Get a good night's sleep."

Nick hesitated. He knew she was scared. He didn't know why, but her fear was real. And he knew he couldn't push her. At the same time, he had to let her know that tonight's chance encounter had turned into a great deal more than that for him.

Carefully, so as not to frighten her, he lifted her hair back from her face, letting its silky strands slip through his fingers. He caressed her cheek with his thumb, his eyes locked on hers. He thought he detected desire, but if so, it was so tangled up with fear that the two were indistinguishable. Suddenly fearful himself, he slowly leaned down and gently pressed his lips to hers in a brief but tender kiss. He had followed his instinct, which told him to do that. But the same instinct told him to do no more. So with one last stroke of his thumb, exercising a degree of self-control that surprised him, he reluctantly stepped back.

"Good night, Laura," he said with a smile. "Pleasant dreams."

And then he disappeared down the dim stairway, leaving her filled with a deep, aching emptiness tempered only by the tender new buds of a frightening, uninvited hope.

Chapter Five

"I haven't heard you mention our friend, Nick Sinclair, lately," Sam said, helping herself to another potato skin.

Laura glanced around the popular eatery, crowded on Saturday night with singles, and shook her head. "Why in the world did you pick this place?" she asked, the incessant din of high-pitched voices and laughter giving her a headache.

"It's a hot spot," Sam informed her.

"It's a meat market," Laura replied flatly.

Sam shrugged. "Same difference. So how's Nick?"

Laura sighed. "Sam, do you ever give up?"

"Nope," she replied without apology, taking a bite out of a potato skin and chewing it thoughtfully. "That's the problem with you, you know. You've given up."

"Given up?"

"Yeah. On men."

"How is it we always end up talking about men?"

"Because good friends should discuss important things. And men certainly fall into that category."

"Sam, you've been married—right?"

"Right."

"And it was a disaster, right?"

"Right."

"So how come you want to find another man and repeat the mistake?"

"Laura," Sam said patiently. "Just because we married two losers doesn't mean all men are bad. So, we got unlucky. There are plenty of good men out there who would love to meet a wholesome, hardworking woman like you and a straightforward, slightly kooky woman like me. And I bet if we found the right ones, they'd treat us like queens."

"Yeah?" Laura said skeptically. "Well, I'm not willing to take the chance. By the way, how did your date turn out last night? Who was it this week? The accountant?"

"Jay. The engineer. It was okay," Sam said with a shrug. "We went to a movie, stopped for a drink, had a few laughs. You know, the usual."

"No. I don't know," Laura replied.

"You could if you wanted to."

"Maybe," she said skeptically. "Anyway, that's not the point. I *don't* want to."

"That's precisely the point. This may not be your scene," Sam said, gesturing to the bar, "but there are other ways to meet men. I'm not saying you need to go out twice a week. But twice a month would be nice. Just for diversion. How about twice a year?" she teased her.

"I don't have time for diversions," Laura replied matter-of-factly. "But I must admit I'm in awe of your technique. How do you do it?"

"Do what?"

"Find all these men you go out with."

"I *look*, Laura. That's your problem, you know. You

don't look. Even when there's a perfectly good specimen right under your nose, do you notice? No. Which reminds me...what about Nick?'' she prodded.

''What about him?''

''Do you see him much?''

''When necessary.'' And sometimes when not, she added silently, recalling the previous night's impromptu dinner and trip to Ted Drewes.

Sam gave a snort of disgust. ''When necessary,'' she mimicked. ''Laura, for Pete's sake, you've got to let a man know you're interested or you'll never get anywhere!''

''I don't want to get anywhere,'' she insisted firmly.

''Of course you do. You just don't know you do. So when did you see him last?''

''Sam.'' There was a warning note in her voice.

''What? Is it a state secret? I only asked a simple question.''

''Okay, okay. Last night.''

''Last *night?* As in after work?''

''Yes,'' Laura admitted. ''The ground breaking for the Arts Center was yesterday, and I forgot my mirror there. You know, the one my grandmother gave me?'' At Sam's impatient nod, Laura continued. ''Well, anyway, he dropped it by the apartment after the party.''

''And?''

''And what?''

''What happened?''

''Nothing.''

''You mean he just handed you the mirror at the door and left?'' Sam asked, disappointed.

''Well, not exactly. Neither of us ate at the party...and he...well, he smelled the spaghetti sauce and...I mean, he did go out of his way. I—I couldn't very well not ask him to stay,'' Laura stammered.

''Are you telling me you invited him to dinner?'' Sam asked incredulously.

''Yes,'' Laura admitted reluctantly. ''But don't jump to any conclusions,'' she warned quickly. ''I felt like I owed him a favor. And besides, he practically invited himself.''

''You don't have to justify it to me,'' Sam assured her. ''I think it's great! So what happened then?''

''What do you mean?''

''Laura, it is like pulling teeth to get any information out of you,'' Sam said in frustration. ''I mean, you ate, you talked…then what?''

''We went to Ted Drewes for dessert,'' Laura offered.

''Good. He extended the evening. Did you have a good time?''

''Yes. Well, sort of. Sam…'' She took a deep breath. ''I was really nervous,'' she admitted, playing with her glass.

''That's okay,'' Sam assured her. ''It's perfectly natural. You haven't dated for a while.''

''Try fourteen years,'' Laura said wryly.

''Well, there you go. You're just out of practice. Do you think he'll ask you out again?''

''What do you mean, 'again'? He didn't ask me out this time.''

''Laura, you know what I mean.''

Laura shrugged. ''I don't know. I think he had a good time,'' she said cautiously.

''Is he attached?''

''I—I don't think so. Sam, he…he kissed me goodnight,'' she said, her cheeks turning pink.

''And you let him?'' Sam asked incredulously. ''Well, hallelujah!''

"But, Sam, I'm not ready for this yet!" Laura protested.

"Laura, you're past ready. You're ripe," Sam said with her usual blunt, earthy honesty.

Laura smiled. Leave it to Sam to home right in on the problem. The woman across from her might be too outspoken for some, but she'd been a true friend and a real lifesaver to Laura during the rough times. Sam could always be counted on to remain steadfastly loyal and supportive.

"I'm not sure I'd go that far," Laura replied with a smile.

"Well, I would. So tell me, what does he look like? I assume you've taken inventory by now."

Laura flushed. "Sam, I'm not good at describing people."

"Well, does he look like anyone here?" Sam persisted.

Laura let her gaze roam over the room, first through the restaurant and then through the adjoining bar. "No. I'm not good at seeing resemblances. I told you that... Oh, no!"

"Laura, what is it?" Sam asked, alarmed by her friend's sudden pallor.

"I don't believe this," Laura muttered incredulously, sinking lower into the booth.

"What's wrong?" Sam asked again.

"It's him!"

"Him?"

"Yes. Him!"

"*Him* him?" Sam's head swiveled. "Where?"

"Sam! Will you please turn around," she hissed. "Maybe he won't see us," she said hopefully.

Nick leaned against the bar, swirling the ice in his drink, trying to figure a way to make his escape without looking rude. He fervently hoped that this was the last bachelor party he ever had to attend. They were so predictable and boring. He was tired of the singles scene, tired of going home alone every night, tired of wondering if he would ever find someone to spend his life with, as Jack had. He envied Jack and Peggy their satisfying existence. Sure, Jack complained good-naturedly about being nothing more than a Mr. Mom and a general handyman, but Nick knew he was deeply content. And that was the kind of life Nick wanted.

He let his eyes idly roam around the room, sipping his gin and tonic. His contacts were already drying out from the cigarette smoke that hung in the air, and he sighed wearily. At least there was a no-smoking area in the restaurant, he thought enviously, his gaze sweeping over the crowd. The faces were just a blur until his eye was caught by a redhead openly staring at him. She was attractive enough in a flamboyant sort of way, and he smiled lazily back. For a moment he thought she was alone, and then he realized there was another woman slumped in the booth beside her. Nick could only see the back of her head, but the unique strawberry blond hue caught his eye. Laura had hair that color, he thought. And then he frowned. Could it be her? he wondered. He tried to dismiss the possibility as too much of a coincidence, but he had a gut feeling that it really was her. Should he check it out? And what if he was wrong? Well, what if he was? he asked himself impatiently. He had nothing to lose. He could just make some innocuous remark to the redhead and beat a hasty retreat. It was worth a try.

"Sam," Laura hissed again, this time more urgently. "Will you please turn around? He's going to notice you if you keep staring.''

"Too late," Sam replied. "He just smiled at me."

Laura moaned. "Well, will you at least stop encouraging him?" she pleaded.

"You didn't tell me he was such a hunk," her friend said accusingly, still looking over her shoulder. Suddenly she straightened up. "Hey! He's coming over!"

Laura gave her a panic-stricken look, and then searched wildly for an escape. But they were wedged in a corner booth, and the only way out would take her directly in Nick's path.

"Laura, chill out," Sam advised, aware that her friend was panicking. "You spent hours with him alone last night. This is no big deal."

"Maybe not to you," Laura replied tersely, her heart banging painfully against her rib cage. What was she going to say to him? she wondered. Would he mention last night? Oh, why hadn't Sam picked some other place!

"Hello, Laura. I thought it was you." Nick's deep, mellow voice intruded on her thoughts and she slowly raised her eyes. He smiled at her, looking utterly relaxed, dressed in a pair of khaki trousers and a striped cotton shirt. He held a drink in one hand and nonchalantly leaned on the corner of their booth. He looked fantastic, as always, and Laura suddenly wished she'd dressed in something more flattering than twill slacks and an oversize cotton sweater.

"Hello, Nick."

There was a moment's awkward pause while Nick waited for her to ask him to join them and Laura prayed he would go away.

Sam looked from one to the other, decided it was time to step in and salvage the situation and smiled brightly.

"I don't believe we've met. I'm Sam Reynolds," she said, extending her hand.

Nick took it, looking at her quizzically. "Are you sure we haven't met? Your voice sounds familiar."

"Not exactly," Sam said with an impudent grin. "But we have spoken before."

"We have?"

"Mmm-hmm. I've had a spare key to Laura's office ever since she locked herself out a couple of years ago, and I answered the phone the day you called looking for her."

Nick had the grace to flush. "Then I think I owe you an apology. As I recall, my manners were somewhat lacking that day."

"Well, I would hardly have described you as Mr. Congeniality," Sam agreed. "But that's okay. I survived."

"Well, maybe we can start over. After all, Laura gave me a second chance, and I was even more rotten to her," he said with an engaging grin.

"I don't know..." Sam said, pretending to think it over. "What do you think, Laura?"

Laura couldn't think, period. "Sure. I guess so," she mumbled.

"All right. If Laura says it's okay, then I guess it is. Would you like to join us?"

Laura gave her a venomous look, which Sam ignored.

"As a matter of fact, yes. Thanks." Nick slid into the booth next to Laura, and she quickly tried to move over, only to find her progress blocked by Sam who had relinquished just a few measly inches of the seat. Nick didn't seem to mind the close proximity, but Laura was all too aware of his body whisper-close to hers.

"Help yourself to some potato skins," Sam offered.

"No, thanks. I've been eating bar food all night."

"I hope we're not taking you away from your friends," Sam said.

"No. It's a bachelor party, and like they say, if you've seen one, you've seen them all. I was about to make my excuses, anyway."

"Good. Then you can stay awhile. Isn't that great, Laura?"

Laura felt Sam's elbow in her ribs and realized that she hadn't taken any part in the conversation. "Oh. Yes, that's nice."

Nick casually draped his arm across the back of the booth, and the tips of his fingers rested on Laura's shoulder. She tried to move slightly away, but Sam had her wedged in.

"Can I buy you ladies a drink?" Nick asked.

"Thanks. I'll have a tonic water," Sam said.

"Laura?"

"Iced tea, please."

Nick signaled to the waitress and relayed the orders before resuming the conversation.

"So what brings you two to this mecca for swinging singles?" he asked.

"What do you think?" Sam said pertly. "We're looking for men. Are you available?"

Laura looked horrified, but after a moment of stunned silence, Nick chuckled. "Your friend here doesn't pull any punches, does she?" he said to Laura with a smile.

"Sam's pretty direct," Laura agreed. "But that's *not* why we're here. At least, *I'm* not. Sam picked this place."

"And I'm glad she did," Nick replied smoothly. "Otherwise there wouldn't have been anyone to rescue me from that bachelor party. And, Sam, to answer your question, yes, I am." He turned to look at the bar for a moment. "Would you excuse me for a minute? I think the group is leaving and I need to give the groom my best wishes.''

"Sure," Sam said. "We'll still be here."

"Will you?" Nick asked quietly, directing his question to Laura. He was aware of her tension and he wouldn't put it past her to bolt the moment he was out of sight.

The thought had crossed her mind, and she flushed guiltily. It was almost as if he'd sensed her impulse to flee, and now he was asking for a promise to stay. But as long as Sam was here, what could be the harm? "Yes."

He smiled at her. "Good. I'll be right back."

The moment he was out of earshot Laura turned on Sam. "Sam, how could you? First you invite him to join us, then you ask personal questions. I'm not only a nervous wreck, I'm embarrassed."

"Why?" Sam asked innocently. "He didn't seem to mind. And you should thank me. Now you know for sure that he's available," she said smugly.

"So what? Available and interested are two different things."

"Oh, he's interested," Sam said confidently.

"How do you know?"

"Because."

"That tells me a lot," Laura retorted.

"Look, he came over here because he thought it was you. The man wasn't exactly trying to avoid an encounter—he arranged it. And when he talks to you there's a soft, gentle look in his eyes that makes me feel mushy inside," she said dreamily. "Yeah, the man's interested."

"Well, maybe the woman isn't."

"Oh, she's interested, too."

"What are you, a mind reader?"

"No. It doesn't take a sixth sense to pick up the vibrations between you two. Laura, you're scared, right?"

"Yes."

"And why do you think you're scared?"

"Because I haven't been around a man for a very long time."

"Nope. Wrong answer, kiddo. Not just any man could make you feel like this. It's Nick. Because you're attracted to him, too, and for the first time in years you sense a threat to that insulated existence you've created for yourself. You're not scared because he's a man. You're scared because he's Nick—a very special man. And by the way, I approve. He's not only a hunk, he's got a great personality and a good sense of humor."

Nick chose that moment to slip back into the booth, giving Laura no time to respond. She had been about to protest Sam's quick assessment, but in retrospect she had to admit that maybe Sam was right.

"Did you miss me?" Nick asked with a grin.

"Oh, were you gone?" Sam asked, feigning surprise.

"Well, that's a surefire way to deflate a man's ego," Nick replied good-naturedly.

Laura listened with envy to the exchange. Sam was so at ease with Nick, while she was a mass of vibrating nerves. She couldn't even think of any witty remarks to add to the repartee. Miserably she stirred her iced tea. The ice was slowly melting and diluting the color, washing it out to a pale image of its former self. Sort of like her, she thought. Sometimes, emotionally, she felt like an empty shell of the woman she used to be.

"...so I'll leave you two to carry on."

Laura's attention snapped back to the conversation and she realized that Sam was sliding out of the booth.

"Sam!" There was panic in her voice. "Where are you going?"

"I knew you were daydreaming," Sam declared. "I've

got to go, kiddo. I have to show a house very early tomorrow morning and I want to be thinking clearly when I meet the client. He's only in town for the weekend, so it's now or never for the sale. Nick, it was nice meeting you.'' Sam extended her hand and Nick stood, taking it in a firm grip.

"Can I walk you to your car?" he offered.

"I'm parked right at the door," she assured him. "Besides, I just spotted someone at the bar that I know and I want to stop and say hi. But do me a favor, will you? Walk Laura to hers when she leaves, no matter what she says. She's at the far end of the lot."

"Done," he said with a smile.

Laura suddenly felt like an idiot child, being talked over instead of to. "Sam, I'm quite capable of taking care of myself," she said stiffly.

"Now don't get all huffy," Sam said. "If you're with a gentleman, let him act like one. Good night, Nick."

Nick watched Sam leave and then slid into the booth again next to Laura. "I like her," he said with a smile. "Her candor is very…charming."

"I can think of another word for it," Laura muttered.

Nick chuckled. "Come on, be nice. She's obviously a good friend. She's graciously bowed out, leaving you alone with me, and she's made sure you get to your car safely. What more could you ask?"

"That she butt out?" Laura suggested. "Look, Nick, you don't have to keep me company. Actually, I was thinking about heading home. This," she said, gesturing around the crowded, noisy room, "isn't my style, anyway."

"Mine, neither. And as for keeping you company, I wouldn't have come over here if I hadn't wanted to see you."

"That's what Sam said," Laura admitted, her eyes searching out her friend, who was now carrying on an animated conversation with an attractive man at the bar.

"Well, Sam is very insightful."

"But why?" Laura turned her attention back to Nick, truly bewildered by his interest.

Nick placed his elbows on the table and steepled his fingers, staring at her pensively. Then he shook his head. "You amaze me, Laura. I told you last night. You're an extremely attractive woman. I admire your determination. You are a great conversationalist and fun to be with when you're not totally stressed out, which you seem to be tonight. Is it me?"

Laura shifted uncomfortably. "I'm not stressed," she lied, avoiding his question.

In response Nick reached over and captured her fingers. "Your hands are trembling." His thumb moved to her wrist. "Your pulse is rapid. With any other woman, Laura, I might attribute those symptoms to something else," he said bluntly. Then his voice gentled. "But you're just plain scared, aren't you?"

Laura snatched her hand away and groped for her purse, making Nick realize he had pushed too hard.

"Laura, I'm sorry. Forget I asked, okay, and don't run off. Besides, there's something I want to ask you."

Laura looked at him uncertainly. "What is it?"

"Jack and his wife, Peggy, are giving a little party next weekend. Sort of a pre-Fourth-of-July barbecue. I wondered if you'd like to go."

It took a moment for the invitation to register, and then Laura realized that Nick was actually asking her for a date. A real date, not an unexpected, spur-of-the-moment get-together.

"When is it?" she asked.

"Saturday. About four."

"I work on Saturdays, Nick."

"All day?" he asked with a frown.

"Sometimes."

"Maybe that's one of the reasons you always look so tired," he said gently, reaching over with one finger to trace the shadow under one of her eyes. "Everyone needs some fun in their life."

Laura swallowed. "I don't have time. I'm a one-person operation, Nick. Saturdays are a good time to get caught up on the books. Besides, I'm going home for a long weekend over Fourth of July, so I need to make up the time."

"We could go to the party late," he offered.

"I don't want you to miss any of it because of me," she protested.

"Laura, to be perfectly honest, I'd rather be at *some* of the party with you than *all* of it alone," he replied with a smile.

"Well…" Nick was being completely accommodating, and there was no reason to refuse. Besides, she liked Jack. They would be in a crowd, so what could happen? Sam was always telling her to make an effort to improve her social life, and this was a good opportunity.

She looked toward the bar again, just in time to see her friend heading for the door on the arm of the man she'd been talking to. Sam never seemed at a loss for male companionship. Maybe there was a lesson to be learned here, Laura thought. Her best friend had more dates than she could handle and was always telling Laura to spice up her social life. Perhaps, Laura reasoned, the Lord had put her in this uncharacteristic setting tonight so that she and Nick would cross paths. It seemed like an awfully strange coincidence to have happened purely by chance.

There must be a message here. And maybe it was simply that if Sam could go out with dozens of men, she could at least go out with one. Taking a deep breath, she turned back to Nick. "Okay," she agreed.

Laura was rewarded with an ecstatic grin. "Great! I'll call you this week to firm up the plans."

"All right." She withdrew her keys from her purse. "I really have to go, Nick. It's been a long day, and frankly the smoke in here is killing my eyes."

"Yeah, I know what you mean," he concurred. He thought of suggesting a quieter lounge nearby, but decided against it. He'd already gotten more than he expected out of the evening when she'd agreed to go to Jack's party with him. He wasn't about to push his luck. "I'll walk you to your car."

"It's really not necessary. Sam's just overprotective."

"A promise is a promise," Nick said firmly.

"Well, have it your way," she capitulated.

Nick signaled the waitress again and quickly settled the bill before sliding from the booth. He reached for her hand, and, short of rudely ignoring it, Laura was left with no option but to take it. Once on her feet, she assumed he'd release it, but Nick had other ideas, tucking it into the crook of his arm. Laura's heart went into fast-forward at the protective gesture. Calm down, she told herself sharply. Nick probably treats every woman he's with the same way. You're nothing special.

As they threaded their way through the crowd, Laura wasn't even aware of the glances directed her way from the bar. But Nick was. He looked down at her, noted that her eyes were focused straight ahead and realized that she was oblivious to the admiring glances. She was a woman with absolutely no conceit, he thought. Actually, she went the other direction in terms of self-image, which wasn't good, either. Why? he wondered for the hundredth time.

As they stepped into the warm night air, Laura drew a deep breath. "I hate those kinds of places," she said vehemently.

"Then why come?"

"Sam likes them. She drags me along occasionally because she thinks it will enhance my social life," Laura joked, sorry immediately that she'd made such a revealing comment. She knew Nick was too attentive to let it pass unnoticed.

"If your social life is lacking, I can only believe it's by choice," he said.

Laura shrugged. "The business keeps me busy," she said noncommittally.

They had arrived at the corner of the parking lot, and Nick finally released her hand, making no comment. He leaned against the side of her car and folded his arms across his chest, apparently in no hurry to leave. Self-consciously, Laura fumbled for the right key and unlocked the door.

"Well…thank you for walking me to my car," she said breathily.

"No problem. I would have, even if Sam hadn't asked."

"I know." And she did. Nick's impeccable manners seemed inbred.

Nick gazed at her shadowed face and his throat tightened painfully. She always seemed so alone, so in need of loving. Without even stopping to think, tired of weighing the consequences of every action, he reached out and drew her toward him, looping his arms around her waist. Laura seemed stunned by this unexpected action and stared at him wide-eyed. Because he was leaning against the car, their eyes were on the same level, and his held hers compellingly, searchingly. At last he sighed. "Laura, what are you doing to me?" he muttered under his breath, shaking his head. He moved a hand up to cradle the back of her neck, rubbing his thumb gently over her skin as he spoke.

"Nick…I don't… You can't…" She drew in a sharp breath, tears of frustration hot behind her eyes. "Look, I'm scared, okay?" she choked, wanting to find a hole and crawl in.

Nick tightened his hold in a manner that was comforting, not threatening. "I know," he whispered hoarsely. "I just don't know why. I would never do anything to hurt you." He pulled her close, and she found herself pressed against the hard planes of his body as his hand guided her head to rest on his shoulder. He could feel her trembling, and gently he stroked her back, hoping she would relax in his arms. He felt as shaky as she did, and he forced himself to take deep, even breaths.

With her cheek pressed against the soft cotton of his shirt, her ear to his chest, Laura could hear the thudding of his heart, could feel his breath on her forehead. She knew she should pull away. Warning bells were clanging inside her head. But it felt so good to be held like this. So good. She would take this moment, take what was being offered, with no questions. A moment to enjoy being held in strong but gentle arms, that was all she asked.

Nick felt her relax slightly. Not much, but it was a start, he told himself. Whatever demons were in her past were powerful, and he'd have to be patient. If he wanted Laura, it would have to be on her own terms and in her own time.

As her trembling subsided, he eased her back, smiling at her with an achingly tender look in his eyes. "Laura,

I'm going to kiss you good-night," he said softly. "I want you to know that this warning isn't part of my standard goodnight spiel," he admitted with a quirky smile, "but I don't want you to be scared. Okay?"

Laura hesitated, and then realized she was nodding. It had not been a conscious choice.

His eyes held hers for a moment longer, and then his lips gently closed over hers. Slowly, coaxingly, they began to explore, seeking a response. Her lips were stiff and uncertain at first, but when at last he felt them begin to yield, he intensified the kiss, pacing himself, allowing the embrace to progress only in small increments. Without intending to, without wanting to, she found herself responding to his touch as he fanned into life an ember of passion that had long lain dormant.

Laura didn't know how long they kissed. She just knew that the flame of passion Nick had ignited in her was more intense than any she had ever experienced. His caresses were knowing and sensitive, designed to draw the deepest possible response from her. Laura was not accustomed to such a tender touch. Joe had been her only lover, and she his. Together, through trial and error, they had learned about making love. But long before they had discovered all the things that made it so special, their marriage had started to turn sour.

Nick knew he might be pushing her too fast, and realized he had to stop, but her sweetly tender lips made the blood race through his veins. At the same time, he knew that if he kissed her any longer, tomorrow she might regret her ardent response and cut him off. It was a risk he wasn't willing to take.

With one last, lingering caress, Nick's lips broke contact with hers. Both of them were breathing raggedly, and Laura's hands were pressed flat against the front of his shirt. She stared at him, fear and wonder and uncertainty mingling in her eyes. Nick almost pulled her back into his arms, but forced himself to straighten up.

He opened her car door, and she silently slipped inside. When she rolled down the window, he leaned in and once more brushed his lips over hers.

"Until next week," he said quietly.

"Until next week," she agreed.

Chapter Six

Laura was a little surprised to find a message from Sam on her answering machine when she arrived home, considering her friend had left the bar with an attractive man. But she might as well return the call tonight, she thought with a sigh. Sam would keep bugging her until she had a full report on the evening.

"I've been sitting by the phone waiting for you to call," Sam said eagerly before even one ring had been completed. "So, did my timely departure do the trick?"

"It was a little obvious," Laura said dryly.

"I'm sure Nick appreciated it," Sam replied smugly.

"Yeah, he did," Laura admitted. "He likes you."

"Great. I like him, too. But I'm more interested in how he feels about you. What happened after I left?"

"We didn't stay much longer," Laura said. "By the way, who was your friend?" she asked, more to buy time than out of any real curiosity. She'd long ago given up trying to keep track of Sam's male admirers. There seemed to be an ever-changing cast of thousands.

"Rick? Just a guy in my office. We've gone out a few

times, had a few laughs. Nothing serious. He just walked me to my car. I have an early appointment tomorrow, remember? But why are *you* home so early?'' Sam said worriedly. ''Did you clam up or do something to dis-, courage him?''

''I said I was tired and needed to get home.''

''Oh, great,'' Sam said with disgust. ''I should have hung around, after all. There would have been more action if I *had* stayed.''

''No, I don't think so,'' Laura said slowly, playing with the phone cord.

''What does that mean?''

''Well, he asked me out next weekend.''

''And you're going, I hope.''

''Yes.''

''All right! Now we're getting somewhere.''

''He kissed me again, too.''

''Well! This is definitely progress,'' Sam said enthusiastically.

''Sam…'' Laura climbed onto a bar stool and propped her elbow on the counter, resting her chin in her hand. She frowned, unsure why she was having so much difficulty discussing this with the uninhibited Sam, who was never shocked by anything.

''Yes,'' Sam prompted.

''Um, Nick…he kisses…differently…than I've ever been kissed,'' she said awkwardly. ''More…intimately, you know? And what's worse, I—I wanted him to…well, to kiss me even more. Oh, what's wrong with me?'' she moaned in despair.

''Absolutely nothing,'' Sam said flatly. ''You're a young, vibrant woman who's been living in an emotional cave for a decade. Frankly, I'm surprised those penned up hormones haven't revolted before now. Look, Laura, enjoy it. There's nothing wrong with physical affection. I understand your need to move forward slowly, and, believe it or not, I actually think it's wise. But at least move forward.''

As usual, Sam's straightforward advice sounded logical enough. But move forward…how far? Laura wondered. She had never made love to a man outside of marriage. Her morals and her faith just wouldn't allow it. A few kisses didn't seem that serious. But with Nick, she feared she'd be playing with fire.

''But, Sam, I—I just don't want to get hurt again,'' she admitted finally.

Sam knew how much that admission had cost Laura. Since the two had become friends nearly eleven years ago, Laura had never talked about the emotional scars of her first marriage. Sam knew they were breaking new ground, thanks to Nick. He'd gotten under her skin, opened some old wounds. She realized that it was painful for Laura, but at least now the wounds would have a chance to heal.

''Laura, not every relationship is built on hurt,'' Sam said, treading cautiously on what she knew was shaky turf. ''You've never said much about your marriage to Joe, but I could read between the lines. When I used to run into you at night school you always seemed so sad. And I saw what he did to you the night you left him,'' she said, her voice tightening. ''You did the right thing by walking away. Randy might have been a bum, but he never beat me.''

For a moment there was silence on the line, Sam wondering if Laura would deny the abuse, Laura lost in remembrance.

''Joe wasn't always like that, Sam,'' she said softly.

''I'm sure he wasn't,'' Sam said gently. ''But sometimes people change.''

"He just couldn't take the pressure," Laura said with a sigh. "Something inside of him broke, and I didn't know how to help him fix it. He…he made me feel like his problems were my fault, and for a long time I bought into that," she said, a catch in her voice. "But I finally realized that he was sick. I knew he needed help, but it infuriated him when I suggested it. And when he started expressing his anger with violence, I was too scared to push him. Maybe I should have."

"You did the right thing," Sam said firmly. "From what I saw, you might not be around if you'd pushed."

"But what you said before, Sam, about people changing…that's what I'm afraid of. How do I know Nick won't do the same thing? I survived the last time, thanks to you and my family and my faith, but I'm not sure I would again."

"Honey, I don't have the answers for you," Sam said with a sigh. "Commitment means risk, that's for sure. Relationships don't come with a money-back guarantee or a lifetime warranty. All you can do is use your judgment and then take your best shot."

"You know, despite my faith, I wouldn't have made it through the last time if you hadn't stuck with me," Laura said quietly.

"Of course you would," Sam said briskly. "You are one strong lady, Laura Taylor."

"Lately I haven't been feeling all that strong."

"You'll be fine. Like I said, don't rush things. Take it slowly, if that makes you more comfortable. But give it a chance, for your own sake."

Laura lay awake a long time that night. She tried to push thoughts of Nick from her mind, but it was no use. She supposed she'd been attracted to him almost from the beginning, but her well-tuned defense mechanisms simply had not allowed her to admit it. Now that he had made his interest clear, she found that her defenses were not nearly as impenetrable as she'd assumed.

Laura thought back to her early years with Joe. She couldn't remember exactly when the disintegration of their marriage had begun. Joe's growing despondency had been the first sign, she supposed. Eventually he sought solace in liquor, which made him belligerent and abusive, both emotionally and physically. The deterioration had been a gradual thing that had slowly worsened until one day Laura realized that her life had become a living hell. In trying to appease him, to meet his unreasonable demands, she'd cut herself off from family and friends and lived in isolation, growing more desperate every day, trying to make it work, eventually realizing that she couldn't. It had taken a crisis to convince her that she couldn't go on that way anymore. She'd spent days in prayer and soul-searching, but in the end Joe's untimely death had taken the decision out of her hands. Somehow she'd pulled herself together and found the courage to start over alone, but the scars were deep.

With a strangled sob of frustration, Laura punched her pillow, letting the tears slide down her cheeks unchecked. Her stomach was curled into a tight knot, and the taste of salt was bitter on her lips. She had to let go of the past, like Sam said, and move forward—in her personal life as well as with her business. But she simply didn't know if she had the courage to take another chance on love.

By Friday, when she hadn't heard from Nick, Laura's nerves were stretched to the snapping point. He'd said he'd be in touch about Jack's party, but there'd been no call. What was he going to do, wait until nine o'clock tonight, leaving her dangling until the last minute? Or maybe he wasn't going to call at all, she thought in sudden panic.

Laura glanced at the sheet of paper in front of her. She'd been sitting at the drafting table in her office for the past hour, doodling instead of working, and she was disgusted with herself. See what caring about a man does to you? she chided herself angrily. Your emotional state becomes dependent on his whims. No way was she going to let that happen again, she told herself fiercely.

The sudden ring of the telephone at her elbow made her jump, and she snatched it up in irritation.

"Taylor Landscaping," she said shortly.

"Laura?" It was Nick's voice, hesitant and uncertain, and her heart jumped to her throat.

"Yes."

"Is everything all right?"

"Yes. Everything's fine," she said tersely.

"No, it's not. I can tell."

"Look, Nick, I said everything's fine. Let's drop it, okay?"

She heard him sigh. "I don't have the time or the energy to argue with you now, Laura. We'll talk when I see you," he said, and she realized that his voice sounded weary. "Unfortunately, that won't be until next week. That's why I'm calling."

He was canceling their date! Laura felt her heart dive to her shoes.

"Laura, are you still there?"

"Yes," she said in a small voice.

"I'm really sorry about tomorrow night. I talked to Jack, and you're still welcome to attend if you like."

"I'll probably pass," she said, her voice strained. "I have plenty of work to do."

"Laura, there isn't much in this world that would have

made me break this date. But my dad had a heart attack Wednesday and I flew out to Denver on the red-eye Thursday morning. To be honest, I haven't really been thinking straight since then. I'm sorry for the last-minute notice.''

Laura closed her eyes as a wave of guilt washed over her, and she gripped the phone tightly. "Nick, I'm so sorry," she said contritely. "How is he doing?"

"Okay. It turned out to be a fairly mild attack, but he had us all worried for a while."

"You sound tired," Laura ventured.

"Yeah. I am. I don't think I've had but five or six hours of sleep since Tuesday night."

"Well, don't worry about tomorrow," she said. "Obviously you need to be with your family. That takes priority."

"I hoped you'd understand. Can I call you when I get back?"

"Sure. I hope everything turns out well with your father," she said sincerely. "And get some sleep, Nick. You sound beat."

"I'll try. Talk to you soon, okay?"

"Okay."

The line went dead and Laura slowly hung up the receiver. She felt sorry for Nick and his family, but she had learned one thing. She was letting Nick become too important to her, so important that he could control her emotional state. And that was dangerous.

By the time Nick called Monday afternoon, Laura had convinced herself that, Sam's advice notwithstanding, it would be better if she didn't see him anymore except professionally. She just wasn't ready to trust a man again, it was as simple as that. Now all she had to do was tell Nick—which wasn't quite as simple.

"How's your dad doing?" she asked as soon as he said hello.

"Much better. They're pretty sure he'll make a full recovery."

"I'm really glad, Nick."

"Thanks."

"You sound more rested."

"I got in at a decent time last night and slept ten hours straight," he admitted.

"I have a feeling you needed it."

"Yeah, I did. Jack tells me you didn't make the party."

"No." She played with the phone cord, twisting and untwisting it.

"You would have enjoyed it, Laura. I'm sorry I couldn't take you."

"It's okay."

"Well, I feel like I should make it up to you. How about dinner Wednesday?"

Now was the time. She took a deep breath. "Nick, I can't. I'm going home next weekend for Fourth of July and if I want to take off an extra day I really need to put in some longer hours this week."

"But you have to eat," Nick stated practically. "Can't you spare time for a quick dinner?" he coaxed.

"Nick, I really can't."

There was silence on the other end of the line for a moment, and Laura knew Nick was frowning.

"Maybe I'll stop by one night and we can make a late run to Ted Drewes." There was a note of caution in his voice now.

"I don't think I'll have time. But thank you."

Nick stared at the wall in his office, thinking quickly. Laura was obviously giving him the brush-off. And he shouldn't be surprised, considering she'd admitted before

that she was scared. It didn't take a genius to figure out
what was going on here. She'd gotten cold feet, decided
not to risk any sort of involvement. But he wasn't going
to let her go this easily. She obviously wasn't in a recep-
tive mood, so now was not the time to discuss it. Besides,
he was sure he could be much more convincing in person.
So he'd play dumb, ignore the message being sent, let her
off the hook for this date, but renew the attack next week
when she returned.

"I understand, Laura. I know how it is when you're
trying to take a little vacation," he said sympathetically.
"We'll try again next week. I'll call you soon."

"Nick, I—"

"Laura, it's okay," he cut her off. "You don't have to
apologize for begging off. Duty calls. Believe me, I've
been there. I'll talk to you soon. Take care, okay?"

"Yeah, I will."

Laura heard the click as the line went dead and stared
at the receiver in her hand. Well, she'd certainly handled
that well, she thought in disgust. Why hadn't she just
come right out and said "Listen, Nick, this isn't going to
work out. You're a nice guy, but I don't want any complications in my life." Period. That's all it would have
taken. Instead, she'd tried the more subtle backdoor route.
Unfortunately, he hadn't gotten the message. He was
probably so used to women falling all over him that it
had been beyond his comprehension that someone would
actually not want to date him. Well, the next time he
called she'd be more straightforward.

By Friday, when Nick still hadn't contacted her, Laura
began to think that maybe he'd gotten the message, after
all. But instead of feeling relieved, she was filled with
despair. Which made no sense at all.

As Laura left her office Friday night, she was determined to put Nick out of her mind. She'd been looking forward to this rare long weekend at home for months, and she wasn't going to let anything ruin it. Once she got there, she wouldn't have time to think about him, anyway. The Anderson Fourth of July gathering was legendary, drawing family from far and wide for what had become an annual family reunion. Laura had missed several during her marriage to Joe, but none since.

She climbed into her car, depositing a portfolio on the seat beside her. Lately she'd been swamped, but she wasn't going to complain. The lean years were still too vivid in her memory. If she had to work a little more tonight at home before calling it a day, so be it. She'd have four glorious days of freedom after that.

Suddenly her stomach rumbled, and Laura grinned at the message. She'd worked through lunch, and now she was ravenous. With any luck she could have a simple meal on the table within an hour, she thought, placing her key in the ignition.

But luck was against her. When she turned the key, the engine sputtered but didn't catch. She tried again, with the same result. A third attempt was equally futile.

Laura stared at the dashboard in disbelief. Her little compact car might be old, but it had always been reliable. How could it pick tonight to act up? Without much hope, Laura climbed out of the car and lifted the hood. She had some rudimentary knowledge of mechanics, but nothing appeared to be out of order. Which meant that the car would have to be towed to the shop, she thought resignedly.

Two hours later, the mechanic emerged from the garage, wiping his hands on a greasy rag. Larry had been working on her car for several years, mostly doing routine maintenance, and Laura trusted him implicitly. He'd gone out of his way for her more than once, including tonight, staying well beyond quitting time to help her out.

"Well?" she asked hopefully.

"Sorry, Laura," he said, shaking his head regretfully. "There's nothing I can do tonight. She's got a problem, all right, but it'll take me a while to figure it out. I'd come in tomorrow, but I'm taking the family down to Silver Dollar City for the holiday. We've had the reservations for months," he said apologetically.

Laura's spirits sank. "I understand, Larry."

"I'll work on it first thing Tuesday, though," he offered.

"I guess that's the best we can do," she said, suddenly weary.

"Can I give you a lift somewhere?" Larry asked.

"Well..." Laura hesitated, loath to put him to any more trouble. But she only lived a couple of miles from the garage. "If you're sure it's not a problem..."

"Not at all. Just let me turn off the lights."

By the time Larry dropped her off at her apartment, it was nearly eight o'clock. She let herself in, too tired now to even consider making dinner. Besides, she'd lost her appetite.

Dejectedly, Laura sank into one of her overstuffed chairs and weighed her options. Sam would have been the logical one to turn to for help. But Sam had left today for a week's vacation in Chicago. Besides, asking for a ride to the office was one thing. Asking for a ride halfway across the state was another. Even if Sam was here she doubted whether she could bring herself to impose to that extent.

On a holiday weekend like this one she'd never find a rental car—at least not one she could afford. She could take a bus, but with all the stops and time spent waiting for connections it hardly seemed worth the effort. Besides, long bus rides inevitably made her feel carsick.

The apartment gradually grew dark, but Laura made no move to turn on any lights. The gloom suited her mood. She'd been looking forward to this family weekend for so long. This just wasn't fair. But then, life wasn't, as she well knew.

Laura thought ahead to the weekend stretching emptily before her. She ought to call and let her mom know she wouldn't be coming. But she knew how disappointed her mother would be, and she couldn't bring herself to do it quite yet. Maybe her fairy godmother would appear with a coach, she fantasized. There were plenty of mice in this building to turn into footmen, she thought ruefully.

Laura rested her head against the back of the chair and closed her eyes. She desperately needed some R and R. There had to be a solution to this dilemma, but at the moment she was too tired to figure it out. So she put it in the hands of the Lord. *Please help me find a way to get home,* she prayed silently. *I need to be with my family this weekend. Please.*

She must have dozed slightly, because the sudden ringing of the phone jolted her upright. Sleepily she fumbled for the light, squinting against its sudden brightness, and made her way to the phone.

"Hello."

"Laura?"

"Nick!" She was suddenly awake. "Hi."

"Hi. You didn't sound like yourself for a minute there."

"I was half-asleep," she admitted.

"At nine-thirty? That doesn't fit your normal pattern. Are you sick?"

"No. Just tired."

"It's a good thing you're taking a few days off," he said. "You need a break."

"Yeah, well, it doesn't look like I'm going to get one, after all," she said tiredly.

"What do you mean?"

"My car gave out. It's in the shop, and they won't be able to get to it until Tuesday."

"Laura, I'm sorry." The deep, mellow tones of his voice stroked her soothingly. "I know how much you've been looking forward to this. Is there any other way for you to get there?"

"Actually, I was sitting around waiting for my fairy godmother to come and conjure up a coach," she said, trying to keep her voice light.

"What?" He sounded puzzled, and she had to laugh.

"Nothing. You obviously didn't read fairy tales when you were growing up."

"Oh." She heard the glimmer of understanding dawn in his voice. "Cinderella."

"Very good. The only problem is, my fairy godmother seems to have taken off for the weekend, too." There was silence on the other end of the line, and Laura frowned. "Nick? Are you still there?"

"Yeah, I was just thinking. Listen, Laura, I may not be a fairy godmother, and my car may not be a coach, but why don't you let me give you a ride?"

There was a moment of silence while she absorbed this offer. "Are you serious?" she said at last, her voice incredulous.

"Absolutely."

"But…that's really generous of you… My family lives three hours from here," she stumbled over her words, too taken aback by the offer to be coherent. "And besides, I don't want to disrupt your plans for the holiday," she added more lucidly.

"You won't be. As a matter of fact, I was just going to go over to Jack's on the Fourth for a barbecue. I didn't have anything else scheduled. And, to be honest, I'd much rather spend the time with you."

Laura bit her lip. The temptation to accept was strong, given her desperate desire to go south and the lack of any other options. But how could she accept his offer, knowing she was planning to end their relationship? It wouldn't be honest, or fair.

"Look, Laura, I'm not inviting myself to your party. There must be a motel in town, and I'll settle for whatever time you can spare during the holiday," he said quietly.

"Nick, it's too much to ask."

"You didn't ask. I offered."

"No," she said firmly. "If you come, you come as my guest. There's always plenty of room at the house, even with all the relatives there. Mom loves company. It's no problem, and she'd never forgive me if I let you stay at the motel."

"I don't want to impose," he said firmly.

"I think you've got it backward. I'm the one who's imposing. Giving you a place to sleep is small compensation in return for the favor."

"Oh, there may be other compensations," he said lightly.

Laura stiffened. "Look, Nick. Your offer is generous. But I can't accept it if there are strings attached."

"You mean you won't even feed me?" he said disappointedly. "Man, I was hoping to at least get a good, home-cooked meal out of this."

"Oh." Laura was confused. Had she read too much into that last comment? Besides, what made her think he was that interested in her? Sure, they'd kissed a time or two. But that was probably the way he said good-night to every woman he dated. She took a deep breath. "Well, of course we'll feed you. Mom puts on quite a spread on the Fourth. In fact, it's sort of like a Norman Rockwell scene—long tables covered with checkered cloths and loaded down with every kind of all-American food you can imagine."

"Now you're talking," he said enthusiastically. "What time do we leave?"

"Well, I have a Christian Youth Outreach board meeting at eight-thirty. It should be over by eleven. I could be ready by noon," she replied. Somehow the conversation had gotten out of hand. She didn't remember ever saying she'd go with him, and now they were making departure plans.

"Do you need a ride to the meeting?"

"No, but thank you," she said, touched by the offer. "There's another board member I can call."

"Okay. Then your coach will be there at twelve o'clock sharp, Cinderella. We'll grab some lunch on the way. Now go to bed and stop worrying. We're going to have a great weekend," he said confidently.

Laura replaced the receiver slowly, wishing she felt half as confident as Nick sounded. Being in his presence for four days was more apt to be nerve-racking and unsettling than relaxing, she thought. But as long as they stayed around the family she should be safe, she told herself. Besides, instead of focusing on the pitfalls, she should be grateful for his offer. Without Nick, she'd spend the holiday weekend sitting alone in her apartment. She'd asked the Lord for help, and He had come through for her. Okay, so it was a two-edged sword. She was going home, but she also had to deal with Nick. She'd just have to make sure they were never alone, she thought resolutely. Considering the size of the group, that wouldn't be too hard to arrange. Or would it? she wondered, suddenly sure that if Nick wanted to get her alone, he would find a way. And worse, she would let him.

Chapter Seven

Laura was waiting when Nick arrived the next morning, still unsure how this had all come about, still uncertain about the wisdom of it. But Nick seemed to be on top of the world, reaching over to smooth away her frown lines with gentle fingers when he greeted her.

"What's this? Worried? Did you think your coach wouldn't materialize?" he teased.

"No, I knew you'd come. You're a pretty reliable guy."

"Thank you. Then why the frown?"

Laura crossed her arms over her chest in a self-protective hug. She'd wrestled with this problem all night. She knew she should have told him earlier in the week that she didn't want to see him socially anymore, and she should never have agreed to this arrangement. But she wanted to go home so badly, and the offer of a ride had been too tempting to refuse last night. Now she had second thoughts.

Taking a deep breath, she faced him. "Nick, I'm just

not sure this is right. I feel like I'm misleading you at best and using you at worst.''

''Why?''

''Because…because I…I really don't think that getting involved with each other is a good idea.''

Nick felt a knot forming in his stomach. He wasn't surprised. He'd sensed earlier in the week that she was backing off. But he hadn't expected to confront it now.

''No? Why not? Don't you like me?'' He grinned at her engagingly, his easy manner giving away nothing of his inner turmoil. He'd been planning to put off this discussion until after the holiday, but as long as he was going with her—and he *was* going with her, no matter what she said—they might as well get it out in the open now.

Laura found herself smiling at his teasing tone. ''Of course I like you.''

''Well, that's a start.''

''Nick,'' she said reprovingly. ''Will you be serious?''

''On a beautiful day like this? Mmm…that's asking a lot.''

''Well, could you try for just a minute?''

''Sure. I'll give it my best effort.'' He settled himself on the arm of her sofa. ''Shoot.''

Laura moved restlessly over to the window, double-checking the lock she knew was in place. Now that she had his attention, how could she explain her reluctance? ''Nick, you remember two weekends ago, in the parking lot?'' she asked tentatively.

''You better believe it. It's been on my mind all week.''

Laura gave him a startled look, then glanced away, nervously tucking a stray strand of hair behind her ear.

''Well, do you remember what I said about being scared?''

''Yes.'' Now his tone was more serious.

"I still am. Maybe more than ever. I'm just not ready for any kind of..." She stopped, fumbling for the right word, reluctant to make him think she was jumping to conclusions about his interest in her.

"Intimacy?"

She flushed. "Yes. And I have the feeling that's what you may be after."

"Guilty," he admitted readily.

She stared at him, taken aback at his unexpected honesty. The words she'd been about to say evaporated.

Nick stood and moved in front of her, placing his hands on her shoulders as his eyes locked on hers compellingly. "So now you know," he said quietly. "I like you a lot, Laura Taylor. I think something could develop here. I think you feel the same, and that's why you're scared. I've been completely honest about my feelings and my intentions, because some instinct tells me that you respect total honesty. No games. And I'm also being honest when I say that I realize you have some problems that prevent you from moving as quickly as I might want to. I also respect that. You can set the pace in this relationship."

Laura hadn't expected such a direct approach, and she was momentarily confused. Nick cared about her. He'd made that clear. Cared enough not to rush her. All he was asking her to do was give it a chance. "Nick, I—I'm not sure what to say. You may be wasting your time. I can't make any promises."

"I'm not asking you to. I'm willing to take my chances. Who knows? Maybe my charms will win you over," he said with a grin, his tone suddenly lighter. "Now, is the serious discussion over for the day?" he asked, casually draping an arm around her shoulders.

"Yes, I guess so."

"Good. Then your coach awaits."

Laura still wasn't comfortable. She respected Nick's honesty, and she'd made her position clear, so the guilt was gone. But in its place was a knot of tension so real it made breathing difficult. Because now there was no question about Nick's interest. He wanted to date her; he wanted to see where their relationship might lead. Only God knew why, considering how messed up she was emotionally, but he did. And what was worse, she was beginning to want the same thing. Nick was a handsome, intelligent man with an engaging manner and an easy charm. But beyond that, he was also considerate and caring and gentle. Or at least he seemed to be. And there lay the problem. Laura no longer trusted her judgment when it came to men. She'd made one mistake, and the price had been high. More than she was willing to pay a second time. So where did that leave her with Nick?

Maybe, she thought, she should just take this one day at a time. And perhaps this weekend she should try to forget about heavy issues and just enjoy herself. After all, she'd been looking forward to this trip for weeks. Why ruin it by worrying about her relationship with Nick for the next few days? She needed to unwind, and that wasn't the way to do it.

Nick also seemed eager to relax, she thought as they headed south, through rolling wooded hills and farmland. He kept the conversation light, chatting about inconsequential things, and even made her laugh now and then. Without even realizing it, she began to relax, her pressures and worries slowly easing as they drove through the restful, green countryside.

"So...are you getting hungry?" he said, turning to her with a smile.

"As a matter of fact, I am," she admitted.

"Well, considering that I haven't spent a lot of time

down in this area, Bennie's Burgers is about the extent of my suggestions," he said, nodding to a drive-though hamburger spot off the interstate.

She laughed. "Not exactly gourmet fare, I bet. Actually, there is one place I've been wanting to try. But it's a little out of our way," she said hesitantly.

"Are we on a schedule?"

"No."

"Then let's give it a shot. Where is it?"

"St. Genevieve. It's just a few miles off the interstate."

"Ah, St. Genevieve. The old French settlement," he said. "I was there a couple of times on class assignments when I was getting my degree."

"Isn't it charming?" she said enthusiastically. "My minister's sister opened a tea room there a year ago, and it's gotten some good press in St. Louis. I've been wanting to try it, but I just never seem to find the time to drive down there. Plus, I haven't seen her in a long time, and it would be nice to say hello. We all grew up together in Jersey," she explained.

"Sounds great to me," he said agreeably.

They found the restaurant with little trouble, right in the heart of the historic district. Laura's eyes roamed appreciatively over the charming country French decor as they were led to their table, and after they were seated she turned to the hostess, a slightly plump, white-haired woman with a pleasant round face. "Is Rebecca here today?" she asked.

The woman chuckled. "Rebecca is *always* here," she said, her eyes twinkling. "Would you like me to ask her to come out?"

"If you would. Tell her it's Laura Taylor."

"Mmm, this all sounds great!" Nick said, perusing the menu appreciatively. "And very imaginative."

"Rebecca studied at the Culinary Institute of America and did internships with a couple of the best restaurants in St. Louis," Laura told him, debating her own selection before finally settling on an unusual quiche.

Just as they finished placing their order, a slender, attractive woman appeared at the kitchen door. Her delicate facial structure and high cheekbones were accented by the simple but elegant French-twist style of her russet-colored hair. But her large, eloquent hazel eyes were her most striking feature. She scanned the room, and when her glance came to rest on Laura she smiled broadly and moved quickly in their direction.

Nick rose as she approached, and Laura stood up as well.

"Laura! It's so good to see you!" Rebecca said, giving the other woman a hug.

"Thanks, Becka," Laura said, reverting to her friend's childhood nickname. "I've been meaning to come down, but what with trying to get the business established…" Her voice trailed off apologetically.

The other woman smiled ruefully. "Tell me about it."

"Becka, this is Nick Sinclair. Nick, Rebecca Matthews."

Nick smiled and held out his hand. "It's a pleasure to meet you, Rebecca."

"Thanks. It's mutual," she said, returning his firm handshake. Then she turned to Laura. "I'm so glad you stopped in. May I join you for a minute?"

"Please," Nick said, retrieving a chair from an empty table nearby.

"What brings you to St. Genevieve?" Rebecca asked as she sat down.

"We're on our way to the Anderson Fourth of July reunion," Laura replied.

"Oh, yes. I should have remembered," Rebecca said with a smile. "Those gatherings are legendary in Jersey."

"See," Laura said, glancing at Nick with a smile. Then she turned her attention back to Rebecca. "So how is it going here? I've read about this place in the papers."

"The publicity has definitely helped," she admitted. "And it's going well. Just a lot of hard work and long hours. It doesn't leave much time for anything else. But it's very gratifying to see the business grow."

"I know what you mean," Laura concurred.

"Brad tells me you're doing well, too."

"Brad's her brother—my minister," Laura informed Nick before responding to Rebecca. "Yes. I can't complain. The Lord has been good to me. Hard work really does pay."

"But too much work isn't a good thing, either," Nick interjected smoothly. "Remember that old saying about all work and no play." He turned to Rebecca. "Laura is a hard sell, but I'm trying."

Rebecca smiled at Nick. "Well, keep trying. I've known Laura all my life, and she's always pushed herself too hard."

"Look who's talking," Laura chided teasingly.

Rebecca grinned and gave a rueful shrug. "What can I say?"

"I'm sorry to interrupt, Rebecca." The white-haired woman paused at their table, her voice apologetic. "But the repairman is here."

"Thanks, Rose. I'll be right there." She turned back to Nick and Laura. "Sorry to run. Although I suspect that three's a crowd anyway," she said, smiling as a flush rose to Laura's cheeks. She reached across and took her friend's hand. "It was so good to see you," she said warmly. "Stop by again, okay? And let me know in advance the next time. We do very romantic dinners here on Friday and Saturday nights,'' she said, directing her remark to Nick.

"I'll keep that in mind,'' he promised, rising to pull out her chair.

"It was nice meeting you,'' she said. "And take care, Laura. Don't work too hard.''

"I'll try not to. But remember your own advice,'' she replied with a grin.

As Rebecca disappeared, Nick sat back down and turned to Laura with a smile. "She seems very nice.''

"She's wonderful. Brad says she's making quite a go of it here. But he worries about her being alone. And about how hard she works.''

"I feel that way about somebody myself,'' Nick said quietly.

Laura flushed and glanced down, playing with the edge of her napkin. The conversation was getting too serious—and too personal. Fortunately the timely arrival of their food kept Nick from pursuing the topic, and when the waitress left Laura deliberately turned the conversation to lighter subject matter. He followed her lead, and by the time a delicious and decadently rich chocolate torte arrived, compliments of the house, she was starting to relax again. Maybe this weekend would turn out all right after all, she thought hopefully, as they left the restaurant and resumed their drive.

Conversation flowed easily during the remainder of the trip, and as they approached her hometown, Nick turned to her with a smile. "How about a rundown on the agenda and the cast of characters?'' he said.

"Okay,'' she agreed. "Let's start with the agenda. Today and tomorrow will be pretty low-key. We'll have dinner at Aunt Gladys's tomorrow. That's about the only real planned activity, but there will be lots of impromptu visiting going on. On the Fourth Mom has everyone over for a cookout, and then we play horseshoes or croquet and shoot off fireworks in the field after dark. Tuesday we can head back whenever we want. Now, as for the cast, there'll be my brother, John, and his family. They live in town. And my brother, Dennis, who lives in Memphis, will be up for the weekend and staying at the house. Aunt Gladys and Uncle George have five kids, most of whom are married, and a lot of them will come back for the Fourth.'' She paused and took a deep breath after her rapid-fire briefing. ''Those are the main players, but you'll find that a lot of other relatives show up, too,'' she added.

''Sounds like quite a gathering. What about your dad, Laura? You didn't mention him.''

Some of the brightness faded from her face and she turned to look out the window. ''He died eleven years ago,'' she said quietly.

''I'm sorry. You two were close, I take it.''

''Yes, very. I was the only girl in the family, and Dad spoiled me, I guess. He was a real special man, you know? Sometimes even now it's hard to believe he's gone. He died right after Fourth of July—one of the few I didn't spend with the family,'' she said, her voice edged with sadness and regret.

''How come you weren't here? I got the impression this was a sacred ritual.''

''It is now. But I missed a few years when I was married.''

''Why?''

Laura shrugged, and Nick could feel her closing down. ''Oh, you know how it is. Other things interfere.''

Like what? he wondered. But he knew better than to pursue a line of questioning that would alienate her and erase the lighthearted mood they'd established. So he changed the subject.

"You'll need to guide me from here," he said as he turned off the highway.

By the time he turned into the driveway leading to the modest white frame house on the outskirts of town, Laura's earlier mood was restored and her eyes were shining in anticipation. The crunching gravel announced their arrival, and before he even set the brake the front screen door opened and an older, slightly stout woman in a faded apron appeared.

She turned and called something over her shoulder before hurrying down the steps and throwing her arms around Laura.

"Oh, honey, it's so good to see you," she said.

"It's good to be home, Mom," Laura answered, and Nick heard the catch in her voice. He gave them a minute to themselves before climbing out of the car.

Laura's mother appeared instantly contrite. "Oh, goodness, I completely forgot about your young man." She stepped back and smoothed her hair.

"Mom, he's not my young man," Laura corrected her, flushing. "I told you about Nick last night on the phone."

"Of course you did. I hope you'll forgive me," Laura's mother said to Nick.

"I didn't mind in the least," he assured her.

Laura's mother looked pleased. "Well, good. Now, I assume you're Nick Sinclair," she said, holding out her hand. "Welcome to Jersey. I'm Laura's mother, Evelyn Anderson."

Nick returned her firm handshake with a smile, doing a rapid assessment. The years had clearly taken their toll on Laura's mother. Her face spoke of hard work, and the once-brown hair was now mostly gray. But her eyes sparkled and her smile was cheerful and warm. While life may have presented her with difficulties, Laura's mother seemed to have met them squarely and then moved on. Much like Laura herself, Nick thought.

"It's a pleasure to meet you, Mrs. Anderson. And thank you for inviting me. It was very generous of you."

"Not at all. We're glad to have you," she said. "Now let's go in and get you both settled and then you can have some dinner. Laura, I've put Nick in John's old room, if you'll take him up. I've got a pie in the oven that's just about done."

"Okay."

"Take your time unpacking. I didn't know when everyone would be arriving so I just put on a big pot of chili. It'll keep," she told them.

Laura followed Nick around to the back of the car and reached for her bag when he raised the lid of the trunk.

"I'll take care of it," he said, moving more quickly than she and effortlessly hoisting the strap of the small overnight case to his shoulder.

"You don't have to carry my luggage," she protested.

"Neither of us packed very heavily," he said with a crooked grin, holding up his duffel bag. "I think I can manage. You just lead the way and clear the path."

"Okay," she relented, walking ahead and opening the screen door. "Up the stairs, first door on your right," she instructed.

Nick made his way to the second floor and pushed the indicated door open with his shoulder. The room was simply furnished, with a navy blue bedspread on the full-size bed, an easy chair and an oak chest and desk. Rag rugs covered the polished plank floors, and woven curtains hung at the window. As Nick set his bag on the floor, Laura spoke at his elbow.

"I hope this will be okay," she said worriedly. She'd never really noticed before how plain the house was. It had always just been home to her—warm and inviting and welcoming. But to a stranger, it might appear old and worn. Not to mention hot. She noticed the beads of perspiration already forming on Nick's forehead. "Mom doesn't have air-conditioning," she said apologetically. "All the upstairs rooms have ceiling fans, though, so it stays pretty cool at night. During the day we don't spend a lot of time up here, anyway." She paused. "I guess I should have warned you."

"It wouldn't have made me change my mind about coming," he said with a smile.

"Are you sure the heat won't bother you?" she asked skeptically. "I'm used to it—this is how I grew up, and even now, I don't use my air all that much. But most people live in air-conditioning today. Especially in Missouri in July."

"Laura." He placed his hands on her shoulders. "I told you. This is fine. It's a small price to pay for a long weekend with you. Now, where do you want this?" he asked, nodding toward her overnight case.

"I'm right next door." She bent down to retrieve the bag, but he beat her to it. "Nick, it's just down the hall," she protested.

"Good. Then I won't have far to walk."

Laura shook her head. "You sure can be stubborn, do you know that?"

"Yep."

"Okay. I give up. Besides, it's too hot to argue."

Nick followed her down the hall. He could have let her take her own bag. It wasn't that heavy, and he'd seen evidence that she was stronger than she looked. No, his reasons were more selfish than chivalrous. He was curious about the room where Laura had spent her girlhood, and this might be his only chance to see it.

"You can just put it on the chair," Laura said, entering the room before him.

Nick took his time, glancing around as he strolled over to the white wicker chair with a floral cushion, which sat in one corner. The room was painted pale blue, with a delicate floral wallpaper border, and decorated with white wicker furniture and crisp organdy curtains. The floral spread on the twin bed matched the chair cushion, and a large print by one of the French Impressionists hung on one wall.

"Very nice," he said approvingly. "I particularly like this Matisse. Is it yours?"

"Yes."

"I'm surprised you didn't take it with you. It's a very fine print."

"Thanks. It was a high school graduation gift from Mom and Dad."

"And you left it?"

Laura turned away. "My husband wasn't a fan of impressionistic painting," she said with a shrug. "Besides, it would have left a blank spot on the wall here. I figured I could enjoy it whenever we came to visit."

"Which apparently wasn't often."

"Nick." Her eyes flew to his, and there was a note of warning in her voice. "Leave it alone."

He held up his hands. "Sorry."

She looked at him steadily for a moment, and then turned away. "I'm going to change into some shorts and freshen up. I'll meet you downstairs in about fifteen minutes for dinner, okay?"

"Sure."

Nick returned to his room and strolled restlessly over

to the window, jamming his hands in his pockets, a frown marring his brow as he stared out over the distant fields. There was so much about Laura that he wanted to know. Needed to know. But she just wouldn't open up. What could possibly have happened to make her so gun-shy? He had no answers, but he did have three days ahead with Laura, in an environment where she seemed to feel safe. Maybe she would share some memories with him here. At least he could hope.

It didn't take Laura long to change. She was used to having too much to do in too little time, and she'd learned not to waste a moment. She slipped a pair of comfortable khaki shorts over her slim hips, tucking in a teal blue, short-sleeved cotton blouse and cinching the waist with a hemp belt. As she sat down on the bed to tie her canvas shoes, her eye fell on the Matisse, and she paused to look at it. The painting had always soothed her, and right now her nerves needed all the soothing they could get. Slowly she looked around the room that had been home for eighteen years, letting her gaze linger here and there. Everything was the same. The same blue walls. The same crystal dish on the dresser. The same worn spot on the rug. Everything was the same. Everything except her. So much had happened in the years since she had left this house as a bride. There had been so many hopes, heartaches and regrets....

Suddenly Laura's eyes grew misty. She wasn't prone to self-pity, so the tears took her off guard. It wasn't as if she had anything to complain about, she told herself. Yes, her life had turned out differently than she'd expected as a young bride. And some bad things had happened along the way. But the Lord had stood by her through the tough times, and her life now was very blessed. She had a successful business, a loving family, good friends and good health. The Lord always provided for her, even supplying a chauffeur for this weekend, she reminded herself.

Laura abruptly stood, brushing her tears aside. She wasn't going to give in to melancholy. Looking back did no good. She'd learned a long time ago that living in the past was a waste of time and an emotional drain. Live today, plan for tomorrow and trust in the Lord—that was her motto now.

Laura let herself out of her room, closing the door quietly behind her, and walked down the hall, her rubber-soled shoes noiseless on the hardwood floor. Nick's door was still closed, and her step faltered. Should she knock and let him know she was heading down? No, she could use a few minutes alone with the family.

Laura ran lightly down the steps and headed for the kitchen, sniffing appreciatively as she entered the bright, sunny room. John was sitting at the polished oak table unsuccessfully trying to convince eight-month-old Daniel to eat a spoon of strained peas, while Dana helped clear the remainder of three-year-old Susan's dinner off the table.

"Aunt Laura!" Susan squealed, catapulting herself toward Laura, who bent and swept her up.

"My goodness, what a big girl you are now!" Laura exclaimed, hugging the little body close to her. Susan tolerated the embrace for a few seconds, and then squirmed to be set loose.

John gave her a harried smile. "Hi, Sis. We'll clear out of here in just a minute so you can enjoy your dinner in peace."

"Don't rush on my account," Laura said, sitting down at the table and cupping her chin in her palm. Daniel chose that moment to spit out a particularly unappealing bite, and Laura laughed. "I'm enjoying this."

"You wouldn't want to take over, would you?" John asked hopefully.

"Oh, no, you're doing a masterful job. Hi, Dana. How'd you manage to get John to do the feeding chores?" she asked, turning toward her sister-in-law.

"Hi, Laura." Dana was a natural white blonde, and she wore her hair short and curled softly around her attractive, animated face. "We made a deal before we had the second one that feeding, diapering and bathing chores would be divided. And I must say, John's lived up to his side of the bargain really well."

"Did I have a choice?" he asked good-naturedly.

"No."

He shrugged and grinned. "Boy, has she gotten aggressive," he said to Laura.

"No, dear brother, the word is assertive. And good for you, Dana," Laura said with a smile.

"I should have figured you women would stick together," he lamented.

"Oh, get out the violins," Laura said, rolling her eyes.

John's grin softened to a smile. "It's good to see you, Laura."

"It's good to be home," she replied quietly, reaching over briefly to touch his shoulder. "Is Dennis here yet?"

The screen door banged. "Anybody home?" a male voice bellowed.

John looked at Laura and grinned. "Speak of the devil. We're in the kitchen," he called.

Dennis clomped down the hall and stood on the threshold, his hands on his hips. "Who owns the sporty red number out front? Man, what a set of wheels!"

"Hello to you, too, brother," Laura said wryly.

"Oh. Sorry," he said sheepishly, engulfing her in a bear hug that left her breathless. "Good to see you, Laura. So who owns the car?"

"The guy she brought down for the weekend," John said.

"Laura brought a guy down? No kidding! Where is he?"

"Look, you've all got it backward," Laura said, exasperation starting to wear down her patience. "*He* brought *me*. My car gave out, and he very graciously offered to drive me down. He was just being nice, so don't try to read any more into it."

"Just being nice? Give me a break! No guy with a car like that drives three hours to stay in an unairconditioned house in a town small enough to spit across just because he's nice," Dennis said.

Laura felt the color begin to rise in her face. "I knew this was a mistake," she muttered. "I just should have stayed home."

"Come on, you two. Leave your sister alone," Dana said sympathetically. "If she says this man is just a friend, then that's all he is."

"Oh, Laura! I didn't hear you come down," Mrs. Anderson said, bustling into the kitchen. "Are you and your young man ready for some chili?"

Laura looked at the grinning faces of her two brothers and dropped her head onto the table, burying her face in her crossed arms. "I give up," she said, her voice muffled.

Everyone started asking questions at once, and Laura ignored them all—until a sudden hush told her that Nick must have appeared in the doorway. She raised her eyes and his met hers quizzically. He didn't seem uncomfortable by the attention focused on him, just curious. Laura stood, glaring a warning over her shoulder and walked over to Nick.

"Nick, this is the family. My brothers John and Dennis, and John's wife, Dana. And of course we can't forget Susan and Daniel. Daniel's the one with the green slime running down his chin and dripping onto John's shirt."

"Oh, great!" John muttered. He reached for a cloth and ineffectually wiped at the stain.

"Serves you right," Laura said sweetly, and John glared at her.

"Nice to meet you," Dennis said, sticking his hand out. "Great car."

"Thanks."

"I'd shake hands, but I think it might be better if we just said hello," John said, still struggling with the peas.

"You look like you have your hands full," Nick commented with a chuckle.

"Yeah, you might say that," John replied, juggling Daniel on one knee while the suddenly shy Susan, a finger stuck in her mouth, watched the proceedings while clinging to his leg.

"Well, let's leave these two in peace to enjoy their food," Dana said as she came to John's rescue and hoisted Daniel onto her hip. "Nick, it's nice to meet you. I'm sure we'll see a lot of you this weekend."

"We'll be back later, Mom," John said, bending over to give her a peck on the cheek.

"Good. Drive safe, now. Dennis, you're just in time for some chili," she said, turning her attention to her younger son.

"Now that's what I call perfect timing," he said with a grin, turning a chair backward to the table and stradling it.

''Nick, go ahead and find a seat,'' Mrs. Anderson said as she set the table with quick efficiency.

Laura was glad Dennis had shown up in time for dinner. His boisterous chatter kept Nick occupied, giving Laura a chance to think. She should have expected her family's reaction, she supposed. She'd never brought a man home since…since Joe's death. In fact, she'd never brought anyone home except Joe. It was bound to cause a stir. She'd simply have to keep Nick at arm's length and convince everyone that he was just a friend. Except he wasn't helping.

She frowned at the dilemma and looked up, only to discover Nick's eyes on her. Dennis was at the sink refilling his water glass, and Nick's lazy smile and slow wink sent a sudden, sharp flash of heat jolting through her.

''Aren't you hungry?'' he asked, his innocent words at odds with the inviting look in his eyes.

''Wh-what?'' she stammered.

He nodded to her almost untouched chili, and she glanced down.

''Oh. Yes, I am. I guess I've been daydreaming. You look like you're doing okay, though,'' she said, trying to divert his attention.

''It's great.'' He turned to Laura's mother. ''This is wonderful chili, Mrs. Anderson. Does Laura have this recipe?''

''Oh, my yes. She's quite a good cook when she has the time.''

''I know,'' he said. His tone implied that he knew a lot more, and he turned to smile at Laura with that easy, heart-melting look of his.

Laura swallowed her mouthful of chili with difficulty and tried to think of some response, but she could barely remember her name, let alone formulate a snappy retort, when Nick looked at her like that. In desperation, she glanced toward her mother for assistance, but the older woman was watching them with an interested gleam in her eye. No ally there, she thought in disgust.

Dennis had returned and once again monopolized the conversation, so Laura focused on her chili, her mind racing. Her family was jumping to way too many conclusions, she thought. And Nick wasn't helping. If he kept looking at her in that intimate way, it wasn't going to be easy to convince everyone that friendship was all he had on his mind. Especially when she knew better. Or worse—depending on your point of view, she thought wryly.

Chapter Eight

Laura was managing very nicely to keep Nick at bay, she thought late on Sunday, after everyone had overindulged on Aunt Gladys's fried chicken. Nearly thirty people had shown up for the gathering, including the entire Anderson clan and assorted aunts, uncles, cousins, nieces and nephews. The lively exchanges during the meal had now given way to quiet satisfaction as everyone found a comfortable spot in the shade to relax. Except for a spirited game of horseshoes undertaken by the more energetic among the group, everyone else seemed content to do nothing more strenuous than chase away an occasional fly.

From his shady spot under a tree, Nick watched Laura help her mother and aunt clear away the remains of the meal. His offer of assistance had been promptly refused, so he had sought relief from the heat under the spreading branches of this oak, which also provided him with a good vantage point from which to observe Laura. She appeared more relaxed than he'd ever seen her, he noted through half-closed eyelids, his back propped against the trunk of the tree. With her hair pulled back into a ponytail, the trimness of her figure accentuated with shorts and a T-shirt and a good night's sleep behind her, she could pass for a teenager, at least from this distance. Even up close she seemed younger, almost carefree, the lines of tension around her mouth and eyes erased. She smiled more, and Nick began to glimpse the woman she had once been, before some demon from her past had stolen the laughter from her life.

He also knew that she was doing her best to make sure the two of them weren't alone. And he was just as sure that he had to get her alone. Here, in this relaxed, safe setting, she might open up a little, give him some insight to the fears she kept bottled inside. This was his best chance to discover more about Laura Taylor, and he wasn't about to let it pass. Because until he knew the secrets she kept hidden, the source of her fears, he would be at a distinct disadvantage. The only problem was figuring out a way to spirit her away from the group.

In the end, Laura's Aunt Gladys emerged as his unexpected ally. "Land, it's a hot one," she said, fanning herself with part of a newspaper as the women came over to join him. Laura's aunt and mother opened up lawn chairs, and Laura dropped to the ground next to Nick. "Does anyone want some iced tea or lemonade? Nick?"

"No, thank you. I'm still too full from dinner to even think about putting anything else in my stomach," he said with a lazy grin. "That was one of the best meals I've had in a long time."

"Well, I'm glad you liked it," Aunt Gladys said with a pleased grin. She glanced at Laura's mother before continuing, and Nick noted the conspiratorial look that passed between them. "Laura, why don't you show Nick the spring?" she suggested casually. "It's a whole lot cooler down there."

Laura had been halfheartedly watching the game of horseshoes, listening to the conversation only on a peripheral level, but now she gave it her full attention, turning startled eyes to Nick. He saw the panic in them, opened his mouth to politely decline, but caught himself in time. Instead, he idly reached for a blade of grass and twirled it silently between his fingers.

"Oh, Aunt Gladys, it's a pretty long walk. I'm sure Nick's too full to go hiking in this weather," she said breathlessly.

"It's not that far," Aunt Gladys replied. "If I was as young as you two, I'd be heading there myself. I think Nick would enjoy it."

"It sounds very interesting," he injected smoothly. "And I'm all for finding a cooler spot, even if it does take a little effort to get there." Without waiting for a reply, he stood and extended his hand to Laura. "Come on, Laura. You can be my tour guide," he coaxed, smiling down at her.

Laura stared up at him, her mind racing. How could she refuse without appearing rude? She looked to her aunt and mother for help, but they were smiling at her innocently. It was a conspiracy, she thought, realizing she was doomed. Nick wanted to get her alone, and her mother and aunt were clearly on his side. She might as well give up.

Nick saw the look of capitulation in her eyes and let out his breath slowly. He wouldn't have been surprised if she'd refused to go with him.

Laura put her hand in his, and in one lithe motion he drew her to her feet, tucking her arm in his. She saw the look of satisfaction Aunt Gladys and her mother exchanged and vowed to get even with them later.

"We'll be back soon," she said deliberately.

"Oh, take your time," her mother said. "You won't miss anything here."

Laura gave her a dirty look before turning to Nick. "It's down the road a bit and then through the woods," she said shortly.

"If we're not back by dark, send out a search party," Nick said to the two older women. Then he paused and looked down at Laura. "On second thought, never mind."

Laura's mother laughed. "I'm sure you'll take good care of her," she said. "Have fun, you two."

Laura knew she was blushing furiously, and she turned and began walking rapidly toward the road, practically dragging Nick with her.

"Hey, whoa! What's the rush?" he asked.

"I thought you wanted to see the spring."

"I do. But it's not going anywhere, is it?"

Reluctantly Laura slowed her gait. "No," she said glumly.

"That's what I like in a tour guide. Enthusiasm," Nick said, trying to elicit a smile and dispel some of the tension.

Laura looked up at him guiltily. He'd been a good sport about all the family activities over the past two days, blending right in with his easygoing manner and natural charm, and making no attempt to monopolize her time— until now. She supposed she owed him at least this much.

"Sorry," she apologized. "I just hate being railroaded into anything."

He stopped walking, and she looked up at him in surprise.

"If you'd rather not go, it's okay," he said, knowing he had to give her an out, hoping she wouldn't take it. If she wasn't a willing partner in this outing it was doomed to failure, anyway.

Laura seemed momentarily taken aback by his offer,

and he saw the conflict in her eyes. He'd promised to let her set the pace, she recalled, and Nick had been a man of his word—so far. She knew that he hoped something romantic would develop when they were alone, but if she wasn't willing, she trusted him not to push. Maybe that was a mistake, but it was one she was suddenly willing to risk. "No. Let's go. It is cooler there, and you could probably use a break from all this family togetherness."

Relief flooded through him. "I like your family a lot, Laura. But some quiet time would be nice," he admitted with a smile.

"Well, it's quiet at the spring," she assured him.

They walked along a gravel road for a while, the late-afternoon sun relentless in its heat, and Laura looked up at Nick after a few minutes with a rueful smile. "Are you regretting this outing yet?" she asked.

He took a handkerchief from his pocket and mopped his forehead. "Well…that depends on how much farther it is," he said cautiously, the shadow of a grin making the corners of his mouth quirk up.

Laura pointed to a curve in the road about a hundred yards ahead. "The path is right up there. It cuts through the woods, so at least we'll be in the shade. The spring's about a ten-minute walk from the road."

"I can handle that."

They covered the remaining ground quickly and then paused a moment after turning onto the path, enjoying the welcome relief provided by the leafy canopy of trees.

"Whew! It's a lot hotter than it seemed back at your aunt's," Nick remarked, mopping his brow again.

"Yeah. It's got to be well over ninety."

"Is this a cold spring?"

"Very."

"Good. Lead me to it."

Fifteen minutes later, they sat side by side on a log, their feet immersed in a brook that was fed by the spring bubbling up a few yards away. Laura watched Nick close his eyes and smile. "This is heaven," he pronounced.

"It is nice," Laura agreed. "When we were kids we used to spend a lot of time playing here. It was a great place to grow up—fresh air, open spaces, pastures to run in, trees to climb, apples to pick..." Her voice trailed off.

"Sounds idyllic," Nick commented.

She nodded. "It was in a lot of ways. We didn't have much in the material sense, but we had more than our share of love. You may have noticed that this weekend."

"Mmm-hmm."

"I was very fortunate to have such a wonderful family," she continued softly. "We were sort of like the Waltons, you know? When that program was on TV I used to hear people say that no one really had a family like that. Well, we did. My parents taught us by example how to live our Christian faith and gave us an incredible foundation of love to build on. Those things are a priceless legacy." She drew up her legs and wrapped her arms around them, resting her chin on her knees. "That's one of the reasons I got involved with Christian Youth Outreach. Those poor kids have no idea what it's like to grow up in a warm, caring, supportive atmosphere. Outreach can't make up for that, but it does provide programs that help instill Christian values and give kids a sense of self-worth."

Nick looked over at her, the dappled sunlight playing across her face, and noted the faint shadows under her eyes. She worked too hard, always stretching herself to the limit. Yet she still found time to give to others, living her faith in a concrete way. She never ceased to amaze him.

"You know something, Laura Taylor? You're quite a woman," he said softly.

She looked at him in surprise, a delicate flush staining her cheeks, then turned away. "A lot of people do a lot more than me," she said with a dismissive shrug. She took a deep breath and closed her eyes. "This really is a great spot, isn't it? It brings back so many good memories," Laura said, a tender smile of recollection softening her features. Then it slowly faded. "But things never stay the same, do they?"

"It must have been hard to leave here," Nick ventured, sensing a chance to find out more about her past.

She reached down and trailed her fingers through the cold water. "In some ways, yes. But I was very much in love, and when you're in love nothing else matters," she said quietly. "Besides, I had visions of recreating this lifestyle in the city. I figured there had to be someplace there with a small-town feel, and I found it pretty quickly. Webster Groves. When I was first married I used to love to drive through there and admire those wonderful, old Victorian houses. I always figured some day we'd have one." She paused and cupped her chin in her hand, resting her elbow on her knee, and the wistful smile on her face tightened Nick's throat. "It would have had a big porch on three sides, with lots of gingerbread trim and cupolas, and fireplaces, and an arbor covered with morning glories that led to a rose garden. And children playing on a tire swing…" She stopped abruptly and glanced at Nick self-consciously. "Sorry. Coming home always makes me nostalgic," she apologized, a catch in her voice.

He was tempted to reach over and take her hand. But he held back, afraid that physical contact would break the mood. "I didn't mind. I'm just sorry you never got your house."

She shrugged. "Oh, well. It wasn't in God's plan for me, I guess. At least my office is in Webster. Sometimes, in the fall especially, I walk down Elm Street and let myself daydream even now," she confided.

"There's nothing wrong with dreaming, Laura."

"There is when you have no way of making those dreams come true," she replied. "If I've learned one thing in the past few years, it's to be realistic."

"No more dreams?" he asked gently.

She looked at him squarely. "No. Dreams have a way of turning sour."

"Not all dreams, Laura."

"I know. My business is a good example. But it didn't happen by itself, Nick. It took a lot of hard work. Those kind of dreams, the ones you can control, where if you do certain things there's a predictable outcome, are fine."

"Is that why you shy away from relationships? Because people are unpredictable and don't always do what you expect?" He was afraid she'd tense up, resent his question, but the quiet of the woods, broken only by the call of an occasional bird and the splashing of the brook, seemed to have had a calming effect on her. She sighed.

"I suppose that's a fair question, Nick. You've told me how you feel, and I guess you have a right to know what your chances are with me. You were honest with me, so I'll be honest with you. I like you very much. Probably too much. But the odds aren't good."

"Because you're scared?" he asked quietly.

She hesitated, and then nodded slowly. "Yes."

"But, Laura…don't you ever get lonely?"

Laura swallowed past the lump in her throat and looked away, afraid that the tears welling up in her eyes would spill out. "I have my family."

"That's not what I mean."

She knew exactly what he meant, but chose to ignore it. "I also have my faith, Nick. Believe it or not, that helps a lot to ease any loneliness I might feel. It's a great source of strength."

Nick knew she was telling the truth. He had begun to realize just how important Laura's faith was to her. He'd seen the worn and obviously much-read Bible at her apartment, knew she attended church every Sunday. He'd been struck by the peace in her eyes during the church service he'd attended with the Anderson clan that morning—a look of serenity and fullfilment he envied. Nick hadn't attended church much since he was a teenager, and had almost made an excuse to skip the service that morning. But he had honestly enjoyed sharing the experience with Laura and even thought he might begin attending his own church more often after this weekend. But his comment had nothing to do with faith, and she knew it.

"I do believe you, Laura," he said quietly. "But even a strong faith doesn't make up for the comfort of having a human person to share your life with, a hand to hold, someone to laugh with."

Laura debated her response. She could just ignore his remark, change the subject. But he was right, and she might as well admit it. With a sigh she conceded the point. "Yeah. I know. But I've learned to handle it."

Nick watched her closely. The subtle tilt of her chin told him she was struggling for control, and he wondered what could possibly have made her so fearful, so willing to live a life devoid of human tenderness and love.

"This fear you have of relationships is really strong, isn't it?"

"I guess so."

"I assume there's a very good reason for it."

She looked at him silently for a moment and then began

pulling on her shoes, concentrating on the laces as she spoke. "There is."

He reached for his own shoes more slowly, sensing that the conversation was at an end, but wanting to ask so much more. Yet he knew that she'd said as much as she planned to for the moment. Maybe more.

They tied their shoes in silence, and then Laura stood, jamming her hands into the pockets of her shorts. "We ought to start back," she said, glancing at her watch. "We've been gone almost two hours."

Nick rose reluctantly and leaned against a tree, crossing his arms. "You don't mind if I keep trying, do you?"

She gave him a puzzled look. "What do you mean?"

"To break down that wall you've built."

She flushed and turned away. "You're wasting your time, Nick."

"I'm willing to take my chances."

"Suit yourself," she said, wishing he'd just give up and find someone without emotional roadblocks, leaving her in peace, before his persistence eventually wore down her defenses.

Laura spoke very little as they made their way back through the woods. She let Nick lead, and her eyes were drawn to the broad, powerful muscles of his shoulders, his trim waist, the corded tendons of his legs bare beneath his shorts. There was a magnetism about him that was almost tangible, and she found herself imagining what it would feel like to be enveloped in his strong arms, to feel his heartbeat mingling with hers. Lonely? he'd asked her. Oh, if he only knew! So many nights when she'd longed to be held, yearned for a tender touch, a whispered endearment. But always she went to bed alone. And lonely. Suddenly, watching Nick's strong back only inches from her, close enough to touch, a yearning surged through her so strong that she stumbled.

Nick turned instantly and reached out to steady her. "Are you okay, Laura?" he asked, studying her face with a worried frown. He noted the flush on her cheeks and the film of tears in her eyes, and his hands lingered on her shoulders.

"Yes, I'm fine," she said breathlessly, her heart hammering in her chest. "I just didn't see that rock." Her eyes lifted to his, making Nick's heart suddenly go into a staccato rhythm.

It took every ounce of his willpower not to immediately crush her to his chest, to imprison her in his arms and kiss her in ways that would leave her breathless and asking for more. He swallowed, and he realized that his hands were trembling as he struggled for control, trying to decide what to do next.

Laura stared at him, mesmerized by the play of emotions that crossed his face. With one word, one touch, she knew she could unleash the passion smoldering just beneath the surface. And she needed to be held so badly! Held by someone who cared about her, who would love her with a passion tempered by gentleness, who would soothe her with a touch that spoke of caring and commitment. Nick could give her that. Wanted to give her that. It was hers for the taking. She could see it in his eyes.

Without consciously making a decision, Laura slowly reached out a tentative hand. Nick grasped it, his eyes burning into hers, questioning, hoping, and when he pressed her palm to his lips, Laura closed her eyes and moaned softly, surrendering to the tide of emotion sweeping over her. She moved forward, inviting herself into his arms, waiting for the touch of his lips—

A sudden crashing of brush made her gasp, and, startled, she spun around as his arms protectively encircled her. A doe and fawn were hovering uncertainly only a few yards away, standing perfectly still, only their ears twitching. They remained motionless for a long moment, and then with one last, nervous look at the intruders, they bolted into the thicket.

Laura let her breath out slowly. She was shaking badly, not just because of the unexpected interruption, but because of what she'd almost done. She now knew why she'd been so reluctant to spend time alone with Nick. Just being in his presence awakened long-dormant impulses in her, impulses best left untouched. Another few minutes and she… She closed her eyes, refusing to allow her imagination any further rein. She didn't believe in casual intimacy. Never had. It went against every principle she held. But she'd never been so tempted in her life. She needed to be touched, to be held, to be loved, and the power of those compelling physical needs had stunned her. The Bible was right, she thought ruefully. The flesh really was weak. Maybe the sudden appearance of the deer had been God's way of giving her the time she needed to clear her head and make the right decision, difficult as it was.

Taking a deep breath she stepped away, and Nick's hands dropped from her shoulders. Immediately she missed his touch, missed the warmth of his hands that had penetrated her thin cotton blouse. The loss of contact was almost tangibly painful. But it was for the best, she told herself resolutely.

Turning to face him was one of the most difficult things Laura had ever done in her life. He was standing absolutely still, except for the unusually rapid rise and fall of his chest, and he looked shaken and grim. But he composed himself, running a hand through his hair and forcing his lips up into a semblance of a smile.

"Talk about bad timing," he said jokingly, his voice husky and uneven.

Laura brushed back a few tendrils of hair that had escaped from her ponytail. "We'd better get back," she said choppily.

"Laura…"

He reached out a hand, but she ignored the gesture. "Come on," she said simply. She brushed past him, walking with long determined strides toward the road.

Frustration and disappointment washed over him as he watched her retreating back. The moment was gone. But he had some consolation. The longing he'd seen in her eyes left him with hope. It wasn't much, but it was something. With a sigh he watched Laura disappear around a curve, and then forced himself to follow more slowly. At the rate she was going, she'd be back at the house before he even emerged from the woods.

He was surprised to find her waiting for him when he reached the road. "I can find my way back if you'd rather go on ahead," he said quietly.

"No. I'm sorry, Nick. That was rude of me. I'll walk with you."

She fell into step beside him, an introspective frown on her face, and though Nick tried a couple of times to lighten the mood, Laura was unresponsive and he finally gave up, lapsing into silence.

Once back, Laura's attempts to keep him at arm's length intensified. He wasn't able to say more than a few words to her in private the rest of the evening or the next morning. He realized she was running scared, frightened by what had almost happened in the woods, afraid to let that opportunity arise again. He resigned himself to the fact that the best he could hope for was to sit next to her at dinner.

By the time he filled his plate and made his way toward one of the long tables set up in the yard, however, Laura had already found a seat between her niece and her brother. As Nick surveyed the situation, juggling his plate in one hand and a lemonade in the other, John caught his eye. Nick quirked one eyebrow in Laura's direction, and John nodded imperceptibly.

"Susan, where's your fork?" John asked, leaning around Laura.

"Gone," she said, pointing under the table.

"I'll get her another one," Laura volunteered.

"Thanks, Sis."

As Laura headed for the buffet table, Nick made his move, slipping into Laura's seat. "I owe you one," he said quietly to John.

John grinned. "Laura needs a shove. She's a slow mover," he said.

"So I've noticed."

Laura was so busy talking to her aunt that she didn't realize her seat was occupied until she reached the table, whereupon she stopped short, glaring suspiciously at her brother when he turned.

"Oh, Laura. Nick was looking for a seat. We had plenty of room here." He scooted over, and Nick did likewise, leaving space for Laura to join them.

"I don't want to crowd you," she said crossly, reaching for her plate. "I'll go sit with Mom."

"We don't mind being crowded," Nick said, grasping her hand.

Laura looked around. They were beginning to attract attention, and the amused glances being sent her way made her cheeks flame. With a sigh, she squeezed in beside Nick.

"There. Now isn't this cozy?" John said brightly.

Laura gave him a withering glance. "Just whose side are you on?" she whispered between clenched teeth.

"Yours," he replied in a low voice.

She gave an unladylike snort and picked up her corn. She could feel Nick's eyes on her, but she refused to look at him. She knew she was acting like a coward, running away from a situation she was afraid of instead of facing it. Common sense told her she couldn't put off being alone with him forever. They'd be in the car together tomorrow for three hours, for goodness' sake. But at least while he was driving, his eyes and hands would be otherwise occupied, no matter what his inclinations, she thought dryly, slathering butter on her corn.

Suddenly a large bronzed hand entered her field of vision and removed the corn from her grasp. Startled, Laura turned to look at Nick, who had raised the corn to his lips.

Mesmerized, she watched as his strong white teeth took a bite of corn. Then he licked his lips and smiled with satisfaction.

"Wh-what are you doing?" she asked hoarsely, the sensuous dance of his tongue holding her spellbound.

"Nibbling your ear," he said softly, his words implying one thing, his eyes another. Her mouth suddenly went dry and she reached for her glass of lemonade and took a large swallow. He leaned closer. "This will have to do until the real thing becomes available," he added quietly.

Laura choked on the lemonade, which once more put her in the limelight. Curious gazes were directed her way, and then she felt Nick's arm go around her shoulder solicitously. Her face was flaming, and she dabbed at her mouth with a paper napkin.

"Are you okay, Laura?"

"Yes." She coughed. "I'm fine."

"You don't sound fine."

"I said I'm fine," she repeated grimly, shrugging off his arm.

"Okay. Do you want your corn back?"

"No. You keep it."

"Thanks."

Laura ate as fast as she could, bypassed dessert and left the table to join in a game of croquet. Nick watched her go and then sent John a despairing look.

"I'm beginning to wonder if she likes me," he said.

"Oh, she likes you. You make her as nervous as a cat in its ninth life. If she didn't like you, you wouldn't have any effect on her at all."

"You think so?" Nick asked doubtfully.

"Mmm-hmm. I know my sister."

"Has she always been like this around men?"

"Laura hasn't been around men much, Nick," John said, giving the other man a frank look. "Just Joe. He was her first and only beau, as far as I know."

"So you're attributing her skittishness to inexperience?"

"Partly," John hedged.

"It's the other part I wonder about," Nick said, directing a level gaze at John.

"I don't know much else myself, Nick," John said apologetically. "Laura's always been closemouthed about her private affairs."

"Yeah. So I've discovered." Nick sighed.

"Hang in there," John encouraged him. "You're making progress."

"Yeah?"

"She let you drive her down here, didn't she?"

"She was desperate," Nick said with a shrug.

"That's not the only reason. She wouldn't share her family with someone she didn't care about."

Nick thought about John's words later that night as he prepared for bed. The weekend hadn't gone exactly as he'd planned, but he had learned a lot about Laura's roots and her family. And if John was right, there was still hope for him.

Restlessly he strolled over to the window, trying to catch a breath of air. The second-floor bedroom was especially stuffy tonight, and the ceiling fan didn't seem to be helping at all. Even though it was eleven o'clock, the oppressive heat hadn't relented. He ought to go to bed. The house was quiet, so apparently everyone else had. But he knew sleep would be elusive. Maybe if he got some fresh air, cooled off a little, sleep would come more easily, he thought.

Nick stepped into the hall, quietly closing the door behind him, and made his way down the steps, cringing as the wood creaked. But it didn't seem to disturb anyone, he decided, pausing to listen for stirrings in the house, so he continued down and headed for the back porch, holding the screen door so it wouldn't bang. It *was* cooler out here, he thought, taking a deep breath of the night air.

"Hello, Nick."

Startled, he turned to find Mrs. Anderson gently swaying in the porch swing.

"Did I scare you?" she asked in apology. "I'm sorry."

"That's okay. I thought everyone was in bed," he said, walking closer. He leaned against the porch railing, crossing his ankles and resting his palms on the rail behind him.

"Sometimes on hot nights I like to come down and swing for a while. Walter—Laura's father—and I used to do this, and I can't seem to break the habit. It's a bit lonelier now, though, so I'm glad to have some company,'' she said without a trace of self-pity.

"Laura speaks very warmly of her father.''

"Oh, they had a great relationship, those two. Course, as you may have noticed, we're a real close family. It was hard on all of us when Laura moved to St. Louis. We figured they'd come to visit pretty often, but it didn't work out that way.''

Laura's mother was being so open that Nick had the courage to do a little probing. "Why not, Mrs. Anderson? I can see Laura loves being here with all of you.''

"I don't really know, Nick,'' she said honestly. "Laura never did talk much about her life in St. Louis or about Joe, at least not after the first couple of years.'' She paused a moment, then continued more slowly. "You know, Nick, you're the first man Laura's ever brought home, other than Joe. That's why you've gotten so many curious looks this weekend. I hope we didn't make you uncomfortable.''

"Not at all,'' he said, debating for a moment whether to probe further, quickly deciding he had nothing to lose. "Joe must have been quite a guy, if Laura married him,'' he said, forcing a casual tone into his voice.

Laura's mother didn't respond immediately. "He was nice enough,'' she said slowly, as if choosing her words carefully. "But Walter and I didn't think he was right for Laura,'' she admitted. "He was one of those people who always seems to have their head in the clouds, building castles in the air and never putting the foundation under them. Maybe even getting angry when things don't work out, you know what I mean? Laura's just the opposite. She plans for things and persists until she succeeds.'' She paused for a moment. "Besides, they were so young when they got married. Too young, we thought. But there was no convincing them, so in the end we gave in. Like I said, Laura never did talk much about her life with Joe. Even when they separated, all she said was that they were having a few problems. She didn't offer any more of an explanation, and we didn't pry. Laura's always been a real private person. But she surely had a good reason. Laura isn't one to walk away from obligations or commitments, and she's a great believer in the sanctity of marriage. So for her to leave Joe—well, I can't even imagine what must have happened.''

Nick stared at Laura's mother, grateful for the darkness that hid the dumbfounded look on his face. Laura had left her husband? Why hadn't she told him? And what had broken up her marriage? She'd said earlier this weekend that she'd been in love with Joe, loved him enough to make leaving her hometown and the family she cherished bearable. Knowing she was a widow, he'd more or less begun to attribute her reluctance to get involved with him to fear of once again losing a man she loved. But now that explanation didn't seem as plausible. More likely she was afraid of making another mistake, and for that he couldn't blame her. But her fear and caution went beyond the normal bounds.

Mrs. Anderson held her watch toward the dim light. ''My, it's getting late! Time I went to bed.'' She stood and smiled at Nick. ''Hope you didn't mind me bending your ear.''

''Not at all,'' he replied, struggling for a casual tone.

''Well, I do worry about Laura. And it's nice to have someone who cares about her to share that with. Though I expect everything we talked about tonight is old news to you. You probably know much more about it than we do,'' she said good-naturedly.

Nick watched the screen door close behind her. *No,* he thought, *I know far less. Even less than I thought. But I'm learning.*

Chapter Nine

Laura lay in bed sleepless for a long time Tuesday night, thinking about the past four days. Nick had been unusually quiet on the ride back from Jersey, and it was clear she need not have worried about being alone with him in the car. He was probably regretting that he'd ever made the offer to take her home, she thought miserably, punching her pillow. And if she was honest about it, she couldn't blame him. From his standpoint, the weekend had probably been a disaster. Forced to take part in a family gathering where the only person he knew avoided him like the plague was not conducive to a pleasant experience, she had to admit. He had obviously come to the same conclusion, silently carrying her bag upstairs when they'd arrived at her apartment and leaving her at the door, making his escape as quickly as possible.

Well, she'd wanted to discourage him, she told herself. The success of her plan should make her happy. So then why was she so miserable? And why did the loneliness she'd long ago learned to deal with now suddenly leave her feeling so empty and restless?

Laura tossed back the covers, the hot night air feeling much more oppressive here than it had in Jersey. She briefly considered turning on the air conditioner, but the older window unit was inefficient and one night's indulgence would probably boost her electric bill twenty dollars, she thought glumly. That was more than she was willing to spend. The heat would dissipate eventually, she told herself, and sleep would come.

Sleep did come, but not until nearly three, and when the alarm went off at five-thirty Laura moaned. So much for coming back from the weekend refreshed and rested, she thought dryly as she swung her legs to the floor and yawned.

By the time she was dressed, Ken, her foreman, had arrived per arrangement to take her to the office. He had also agreed to drop her at the garage tonight so she could pick up her car.

"Morning, Ken," she said sleepily, taking a last gulp of coffee from the mug cradled in her hands.

"Hi, Laura." He tilted his head and regarded her quizzically. "You look tired."

"Yeah, well, that's what happens when you only have two and a half hours' sleep," she said wryly.

"Did you get back late?"

"No. Just couldn't sleep." She grabbed her portfolio case and headed for the door. "Let's stop by the job sites first. How did things go yesterday?"

Laura now had two crews working, and Ken filled her in as they drove, dropping her at the office by nine-thirty.

"I'll be back about four to give you a progress report, if that's okay," he said.

"Fine," she assured him. "I have plenty of paperwork to keep me busy. It sure will seem odd to spend a whole day in the office, though," she said.

He grinned. "Yeah, the crews won't know what to think."

"Well, I'll be back on the sites tomorrow," she said with a smile. "So don't let anybody slip up."

"Don't worry. I'll keep an eye on everything."

Laura watched Ken drive away, grateful again that she'd found someone of his caliber to fill the all-important foreman role. She'd done the job herself until the volume of work became too great, but she had to admit it was a relief to let someone else share part of the burden. Ken had only been with her for about six weeks, but he was a quick study and had proven to be reliable and trustworthy. She found herself delegating more and more to him as paperwork and new design projects demanded an increasing amount of her time. The Arts Center job had been the catalyst for growth, as she had hoped it would be, and Nick was also sending other commissions her way. She was beginning to feel that maybe, just maybe, she'd turned the corner. But her cautious nature wouldn't let her go quite that far, at least not yet. Still, business was certainly booming, and for that she was grateful. Soon she might even feel secure enough to allow herself the indulgence of air-conditioning at night, she thought with a grin.

It was nearly four before Laura stopped long enough to call the garage, and as soon as Larry answered she knew there was a problem.

"I was just getting ready to call you," he said. "I'm afraid the part hasn't come in yet. I kept thinking it might still show up this afternoon, but at this point I'm beginning to doubt it."

Laura frowned and rubbed her brow. "Well, it's not your fault, Larry," she said with a sigh. "Do you think it will be here tomorrow?"

"Oh, sure. I don't know what held it up today. It'll probably come first thing in the morning. I'll call you as soon as your car's ready."

"Okay."

"I'm sorry about this," he said apologetically. "I know it's an inconvenience."

"That's okay. I'll manage until tomorrow."

Laura hung up slowly, a resigned look on her face. So much for tonight's plans. The grocery store and laundromat would just have to wait until tomorrow. She rested her chin in her hand and looked over her cluttered desk with a sigh. There was so much to do, and now she had a whole empty evening stretching ahead of her. Too many hours alone to brood about Nick, she realized. She might as well work late tonight and then catch a bus home.

Ken arrived promptly at four, and after he quickly briefed her on the day's progress, Laura told him about the car.

"No problem," he assured her. "I can pick you up again tomorrow. Besides, the guys will have another day's reprieve from the slave driver," he said with a grin.

His good humor was infectious, and Laura smiled. "Oh, yeah? Well, tell them I'll make up for it Friday."

"I'll pass that along," he said, his grin broadening. "Ready to leave?"

"Actually, I think I'll work for a while and catch a bus later."

"Are you sure?"

"Yes. Go on home to that beautiful wife and darling new baby," she said, waving him out the door.

He grinned. "You don't have to convince me. I'll see you tomorrow."

It was hunger that finally made Laura set aside her work, that and aching shoulder muscles. She was used to heavy work, but hunching over a desk and drawing table all day must use entirely different muscles, she thought, gingerly massaging her neck. She glanced at her watch and was surprised to discover that it was already eight o'clock—definitely time to call it a day.

As Laura reached for her purse her gaze fell on the telephone, and she knew that the sudden hollow feeling in the pit of her stomach was symptomatic of more than hunger. She hadn't allowed herself to think of Nick all day, but subconsciously she knew that she had been hoping he would call. Each time the phone had rung her pulse had quickened, but it was never his deep, mellow voice that greeted her. He'd probably written her off for good, she thought, pulling the door shut and turning the key in the lock. And she had no one to blame but herself.

Laura made her way dejectedly to the bus stop, telling herself it had worked out for the best, that it was what she wanted, that her life would be much less complicated without Nick in it. The only problem was that it would also be much lonelier, she admitted.

Laura had to wait longer than she expected at the bus stop, and by the time she finally boarded and was on her way dusk had descended. She hadn't taken the bus in a long time, and apparently they ran much less frequently in the evening than she remembered.

That conclusion was borne out at the next stop, where she waited about twice as long as she expected for her connection. By the time she finally disembarked two blocks from her apartment, it was dark and she felt so bone tired that her walk home seemed to stretch out endlessly ahead of her. The lack of sleep was finally catching up with her, and all she wanted to do at the moment was stand under a warm shower, eat something and go to bed. She watched the bus disappear in a cloud of noxious fumes and, wrinkling her nose in distaste, turned wearily toward home.

Once off the main street, Laura was surprised to discover just how dark the neighborhood was at night. She didn't make a practice of wandering around once the sun set and had never noticed that the streets were so poorly lit. Since the side streets were not heavily traveled, the darkness wasn't even broken by car headlights. Nick had asked her once about the safety of the neighborhood and she had dismissed his concern, but now she looked at it with a fresh eye. It wasn't the best part of town, she'd always known that, but she'd never had any problems. So why was she suddenly nervous?

With an impatient shake of her head, she dismissed her sudden, unaccountable jitters. It was just the power of suggestion, intensified by her weariness, she told herself.

Laura had almost convinced herself that she was being silly when she felt a strange prickling at the back of her neck. It was an odd, unsettling sensation that sent a cold chill coursing through her body. Her step faltered, and she turned to look behind her. Nothing. Just shadows. Nevertheless, she picked up her pace, hugging her shoulder bag more tightly to her side.

Laura gave a sigh of relief when she at last turned the corner to her street and her apartment came into view. Now that home was in sight, her jitters eased. After all, there was only one more patch of darkness before she came to the entrance of her building.

Laura had very little warning before it happened. There was the sudden sound of running feet close behind her, and then she felt her purse being jerked away from her shoulder. Instinctively she tightened her grip. Dear God, she was being mugged! she thought incredulously.

The attacker was momentarily taken aback by Laura's

resistance, and they both froze briefly, stunned. Laura noted that he had a hat pulled low over his eyes, but in the darkness she couldn't tell much else about him except that he was tall and broad shouldered. The freeze-frame lasted only a second, and as he moved back toward her fear coursed through her body. She responded with a well-placed knee, and his grunt told her that she'd hit pay dirt. Without pausing, she snatched the purse strap out of his hands and began to run, hoping her aggressive response would discourage him.

She heard a muttered oath of anger, but instead of abandoning the attack, the man pursued her. She didn't get more than a few steps before a hand closed on her arm. She stumbled, and then was jerked roughly around. She didn't even have time to scream before a powerful fist slammed into her face.

Laura's head snapped backward from the impact of the blow, and she staggered, then fell, the breath knocked completely out of her lungs. Her nose began to bleed profusely, and one eye was watering so badly she couldn't see. She gasped in pain as she once again felt the assailant relentlessly tugging on her purse.

"Let go," he muttered, "or you'll get more of the same."

Laura heard his words, but her fingers didn't relinquish their viselike grip on the purse.

"Okay, you asked for it," he muttered.

Laura looked up, just in time to realize his intention, but too late to do anything to protect herself. A second later the hard toe of his boot viciously connected with the tender skin over her ribs, and she gasped as a searing pain shot through her side. With a moan, she curled into a tight ball in a posture of self-protection and fought the waves of blackness that swept over her.

Hazily she realized that the assailant had once again gripped her purse, grabbing a handful of her blouse at the same time. The buttons gave way in response to his vicious yank, and Laura heard the fabric rip. She moaned softly, each breath now an agony of effort, and once more blackness descended.

Nick pulled to a stop in front of Laura's apartment, hoping for an impromptu trip to Ted Drewes. As he turned off the engine his eyes scanned the deserted neighborhood. It was obviously not a place where couples and families took evening strolls, he thought wryly.

Or was it? he wondered idly a moment later, his eyes caught by a movement in the shadows down the street. He grew instantly alert, however, when he realized that a struggle was taking place. One of the two figures was prone on the sidewalk while the other, clearly male, tried to grab something—a purse, he noted.

Nick sucked in a sharp breath and then reacted instinctively, his heart hammering as adrenaline pumped through his body. He flung open the door and sprinted toward the mugger, shouting furiously.

"Hey! You! Leave her alone!"

The mugger whirled around, saw Nick and, after one last, futile tug on the woman's purse, abandoned the attack and took off running in the opposite direction.

In a split second Nick decided it was more important to go to the woman's aid than chase the mugger. He turned to her, and it took only a second for sudden suspicion to turn into terrible certainty. Panicked, he dropped to his knees beside her, the mugger forgotten. Her blouse had been nearly torn off and blood covered her face. One eye had already swollen shut and she seemed barely conscious, her breathing labored. The color drained from his face and he felt his stomach turn over.

"Laura?" Dazed, he reached out a tentative hand, feeling as if he were in a terrible nightmare. But her soft moan made it clear that the attack had been all too real.

"Laura, can you hear me?" he asked urgently, gripping her shoulders. Her only response was to curl into a tight ball, holding her side. Nick withdrew his handkerchief and held it against her nose, glancing around desperately for help. He couldn't leave her here and he was afraid to pick her up. He had no idea how severely she was injured.

Nick could barely remember the last time he prayed, but he suddenly found himself sending an urgent plea for assistance. *Dear Lord,* he pleaded silently, closing his eyes. *Please help us. Please!*

Suddenly, as if by miracle, Nick heard a siren, and his eyes flew open. A police car, its lights flashing, was turning the corner. His shoulders sagged in relief as he mouthed a silent thank-you, and he stood and waved. The car rolled to a stop and an officer got out.

"What happened?" the policeman asked, kneeling beside Laura.

"She was mugged."

"I'll call an ambulance," he said, rising.

Laura's eyes fluttered open, and though she had trouble focusing, her hearing was fine. An ambulance meant a hospital, and the last time she'd been to a hospital was the night she'd left Joe. She had no wish to return to a place of such unpleasant memories.

"No," she said hoarsely.

Nick took her hand. "Laura, sweetheart, you have to go to the hospital. You could be seriously injured," he said gently.

Laura's eyes turned to his. "Nick?" Her voice quavered, and he felt as if someone had kicked *him* in the gut.

"Yeah, honey, it's me."

"No hospital," she repeated stubbornly.

The police officer hesitated, and Nick looked up at him. "Call an ambulance," he said curtly. Then he turned his attention back to Laura. "Laura, I'll stay with you the whole time, okay? I won't leave you."

Laura looked up at him, and even in the dim light she could make out the lines of worry etched in his face. She tried to reach up and smooth them away, but the attempt brought a searing pain intense enough to make her realize that Nick was right.

"Okay," she said raspily.

"That's my girl," he said, squeezing her hand, making an effort to smile reassuringly.

Laura tried to smile in return, wanting to reassure him that she was okay, but the effort was beyond her. Instead, she closed her eyes, taking comfort in the warm clasp of his hand.

Nick saw her eyes close, wondered if she'd lost consciousness again and began to panic.

"So where's the ambulance?" he snapped when the officer rejoined them.

"It will be here any minute," the officer reassured him. He glanced down at Laura. "She looks pretty banged up," he said.

"Yeah."

"I take it you know her?"

"I was on my way to see her. She lives in an apartment over there," he replied, pointing out Laura's building. "I had just parked when I saw them. I don't know what would have happened if I hadn't…" His voice broke, and the officer reached out a hand to grip his shoulder.

"It was lucky for her," he agreed.

The faint echo of a siren was the most beautiful sound Nick had ever heard, and though he knew it must have taken only minutes to arrive, he felt as if he'd lived a lifetime. Laura's eyes flickered open as the two paramedics bent over her and Nick relinquished her hand.

"Nick?" Her voice was frightened.

"I'm right here, honey," he said.

The paramedics performed a quick examination and then went to retrieve the stretcher. Nick squatted beside Laura again. "I'll ride with you in the ambulance."

She nodded gratefully, her eyes clinging to his with a vulnerability that made his heart contract. He was filled with a sudden rage at the injustice of this, and at that moment he felt capable of murder.

As the paramedics bent to lift her to the stretcher, Laura moaned, and Nick saw the tears running down her cheeks.

"Can't you guys be a little more gentle?" he barked, wishing it was him on that stretcher instead of her.

The paramedics glanced at the policeman, who just inclined his head toward the ambulance. Then he turned his attention back to Nick. "I'll follow you to the hospital. I'll need a statement, since you were a witness, and hopefully the victim will be able to talk to me later."

"Her name is Laura. Laura Taylor," Nick said, his voice tight. Then he strode toward the ambulance and climbed in beside her, noting how icy her hand felt when he took it in his.

"Her hands are cold," he said shortly as the ambulance pulled away from the curb.

"Shock," one of the paramedics replied.

Nick lapsed into silence, and Laura didn't open her eyes again until she was being wheeled into the emergency room. He stayed beside her, determined to honor his promise despite the nurse who was bearing down on him.

"Sir, you can wait over there," she said.

Nick glared at her. "No way. I said I'd stay with her, and I intend to do just that. I'll keep out of your way."

The woman took one look at the stubborn set of his jaw and nodded. "I'll let the doctor know."

"You do that," he said, his eyes never leaving Laura. As they rolled to a stop, he bent over her and stroked her forehead. "Laura," he said gently, taking her hand. Her eyes flickered open. "We're at the hospital. I've got to stand back so the doctor can take a look at you, but I'll only be a few steps away, close enough to talk to, if you want." Her eyes were frightened, but she nodded and he released her hand.

Nick moved to the side of the room while the nurse removed the tattered remnants of her blouse and eased the jeans down her hips. Nick swallowed and looked away, respecting her modesty, knowing she would be embarrassed by being so exposed before him. With an effort, he kept his eyes averted as the doctor did a cursory exam and spoke with the nurse in low tones. Not until she was wheeled to X ray did he leave her side, reassuring her that he'd be waiting.

Wearily he made his way toward the waiting room, where he found the policeman. After one look at Nick's face the officer disappeared into a side room, reappearing a moment later with a cup of coffee.

"You look like you could use this. Actually, you look like you could use something a lot stronger, but the closest thing they have in this place is rubbing alcohol."

Nick accepted it gratefully, noting in surprise that his hands were shaking. He took a long, scalding swallow, then he let his eyelids drop, forcing himself to take several deep breaths. It helped, but he still felt unsteady. When he opened his eyes, he met the policeman's sympathetic gaze.

"If I sounded a bit short-tempered before, I'm sorry," Nick said hoarsely. "I know you all were doing everything you could. And you sure showed up at the right time."

"A neighbor called and reported a disturbance," he explained. "And there's no need to apologize. I understand the strain you were under. Is she okay?"

Nick sighed and sank down into a plastic chair, the kind he always found so uncomfortable. Only tonight he didn't notice. "I don't know. She's in X ray."

"Can you tell me what happened?"

"Only what I saw. I think I must have come along toward the end," Nick explained.

The officer took notes as Nick spoke, looking up when he paused. "Could you give me a description of the assailant?"

Ruefully, Nick shook his head. "It was too dark. The guy took off before I got close enough to see anything, and he had a hat pulled low over his eyes. All I know for sure is that he was big—football-player type."

The policeman nodded. "Maybe Ms. Taylor will be able to add something to this," he said.

"I'm not sure she'll be up to talking to you tonight," Nick cautioned.

"If she's not, we'll do it another time," he said easily.

Nick's attention was suddenly distracted as he saw Laura being wheeled back into the examining room, and he was on his feet instantly. She had been left alone for the moment, and he moved close, alarmed by her pallor. Her face looked as white as the sheet drawn up barely high enough to cover her breasts. His eyes flickered across the expanse of skin, noting the long, angry bruise that marred the creamy flesh at her shoulder, apparently inflicted by the strap of her bag. He also noted something else—a three-inch-long scar of older vintage near the top of her right breast. He frowned, wondering about its origin. But before he could speculate, Laura called his name softly and his eyes flew to hers. Her hand reached for his through the bars of the gurney, and he gripped it tightly, reassuringly. His other hand smoothed the hair back from her face. The blood had been cleaned away, but her nose was puffy and one eye was purple and swollen nearly shut. His throat tightened painfully and he found it difficult to swallow.

"I guess I don't look so hot, huh?" she said, trying to smile.

"You look beautiful to me," he said hoarsely. Her eyes filled with tears, and he leaned closer, his breath warm on her cheek. "It's okay, sweetheart. It's okay to cry."

"I ne-never cry," she said, her words choppy as she fought for control.

"Well, maybe you should make an exception this once," he said softly.

The door swung open and, after one more worried look at Laura, Nick straightened up. The doctor glanced at him before his gaze came to rest on Laura. "Would you like him to stay while we discuss your condition?"

"Yes."

"All right." The doctor moved beside her. "You're a very lucky woman, Ms. Taylor. No broken bones, no internal injuries as far as we can determine. You've got quite a shiner, though, so I'd suggest an ice pack when you get home. The nose will be tender for a few days, but it will heal without any help. The ribs are another story. None are broken, but they're badly bruised. You'll need to take it easy for at least a week or so to give them a chance to start healing."

"A week?" she asked in alarm.

"At least," he confirmed.

"But, Doctor, I—"

"I'll see that she takes care of herself, Doctor," Nick interrupted, ignoring her protest.

Laura turned her head on the pillow and stared at him, but she remained silent.

The doctor looked from one to the other and gave a satisfied nod. "Good." Then he turned his attention to Laura. "There's a police officer here who would like to talk to you if you feel up to it."

Laura's hand reached for Nick's again. "I suppose I might as well get it over with."

"I'll send him in," the doctor said. "Then the nurse will help you dress and we'll give you something to relieve the pain so you can rest." He moved to the door and motioned to the officer.

Laura's details of the attack were even more vague than Nick's, and she looked at the policeman apologetically. "It happened so fast, and it was so dark… All I know is that he was big. And strong."

"Age? Race?" he prompted.

She shook her head slowly. "I'm sorry."

"Do you usually walk at that time of night?"

She shook her head. "No. I had taken the bus home, and—"

"Wait a minute," Nick interrupted. "What happened to your car? I thought you were picking it up tonight."

"It wasn't ready."

"Then why didn't you call me for a ride?" he demanded angrily.

"Mr. Sinclair." There was a warning note in the officer's voice.

Nick sighed and raked a hand through his hair. "Sorry."

"Go on, Ms. Taylor."

Laura finished her story and then looked at him resignedly. "I suppose there's not much chance of catching him, is there?"

"Honestly? None," he admitted frankly, closing his notebook. "He didn't get your purse, did he?"

"No. I had a pretty good grip on it."

"Let me leave you with one piece of advice, Ms. Taylor," the policeman said in a matter-of-fact tone. "I hope this never happens to you again. But if it should, forget your purse. Let it go. Your life is worth a lot more. That man could have had a gun or a knife. And I can guarantee you that if he had, you wouldn't be here right now. You'd be in the morgue," he said bluntly. Laura stared at him, tears welling up in her eyes. When he spoke again his voice was gentler. "I'll wait outside and give you folks a ride home whenever you're ready."

Nick could feel Laura trembling, and he stroked her head. "He's right, you know."

"But that guy was trying to take my purse," she said stubbornly.

"So let him have it! Good grief, Laura, was it worth this?"

"It's mine," she said, squeezing her eyelids shut. "I won't let anyone take what's mine. I won't be a victim again," she said fiercely, the tears spilling onto her cheeks. She opened her eyes and looked up at Nick. "Take me home, please," she pleaded.

He hesitated for a fraction of a second, still trying to figure out her last remark, and then reached down and smoothed the hair back from her face. "I'll get the nurse."

He waited outside while the woman helped Laura dress, and the doctor came over to speak to him. "I've given her a pretty strong sedative. She's had a bad shock, and the pain from her injuries will get worse before it gets better. This will knock her out for about twelve hours. By then her eye and nose should feel a little better. But those ribs are going to be sore, so she'll probably need this by tomorrow," he said, handing Nick a prescription. He paused for a moment before continuing. "She really shouldn't be left alone tonight."

"She won't be."

The doctor nodded. "That's what I thought."

The nurse appeared at the door, supporting Laura, who was walking hunched over, one hand pressed to her side. Her blouse, damaged beyond repair, had been replaced by an oversize surgical shirt that made her appear small and defenseless. Her face was gray with pain, and Nick moved to her side. "Maybe you should stay tonight," he said worriedly.

"No! I want to go home, Nick." Her eyes pleaded with him and, though it was against his better judgment, he relented.

"Okay. But not to your place. I'm not leaving you alone tonight. I want you close where I can keep an eye on you. You'll stay with me."

Laura looked up at him and opened her mouth to protest, but after one glance at his stony face she shut it. It was obvious that arguing would get her nowhere, and she wasn't up to it, anyway. She'd be perfectly all right alone, of course. But she had to admit that his concern had done more to relieve her pain than any drug the doctor could have offered.

Chapter Ten

By the time they got back to Laura's apartment, the sedative she'd been given was making her feel strangely light-headed. She was grateful for Nick's steady arms as he eased her into the front seat of his sports car, then squatted down beside her.

"Laura, is there anything you absolutely have to have from your apartment tonight?" he asked slowly, enunciating each word.

She frowned, trying to concentrate, but her mind felt fuzzy. "No, I don't think so."

"Okay. Then we'll head over to my place. It won't take long," he said, giving her hand an encouraging squeeze before gently closing the door.

Laura dozed as they drove, rousing only when he stopped at a drugstore.

"I'll only be a minute, and I'll lock the doors," he said, turning to her. "Will you be all right?"

"Yes."

He studied her carefully, a frown on his face. "I know

you're hurting, sweetheart. But hang in there. We're almost home.''

Oddly enough, she wasn't hurting. In fact, every bone in her body had gone limp and she felt as if she were floating. It was a pleasant sensation, and she let herself drift off again, hardly conscious of Nick's return and completely unaware of the worried frown he cast her way.

But reality came back with a vengeance when they arrived at Nick's condo and she tried to get out of the car. Even though he was helping her, a sharp, piercing pain shot through her rib cage, rudely assaulting her senses and leaving her gasping for breath.

Nick leaned in when she hesitated, took one look at her face and, without a word, put one arm under her knees and another around her shoulders, lifting her effortlessly out of the car. Even that hurt, though he'd been as gentle as possible, and tears stung her eyes. She bit her lip to keep from crying out, burying her face in his chest and clutching the soft cotton of his shirt as he cradled her in his arms.

Nick looked down at her bowed head, felt the tremor that ran through her body and wished he had some magical way of transporting her upstairs. But this was the best he could do. And the fact that she hadn't protested being carried told him more eloquently than words just how badly she was hurting.

Taking care to jostle her as little as possible, he pushed the door shut with his foot and strode to his condo, his step faltering only when he reached the door. He paused uncertainly and then leaned close to her ear, his breath comfortingly warm against her cheek as he spoke. ''Laura, honey, I've got to put you down while I open the door. Can you stand on your own for a minute?''

Laura wasn't sure she could sit, let alone stand, but there was obviously no choice, so she nodded.

Carefully Nick lowered her legs to the ground, keeping one arm around her shoulders as he reached for the key. "Okay?" he asked gently.

She gave a barely perceptible nod, trying desperately to keep her knees from buckling.

From the way she clung to him, Nick knew that she was on shaky ground. The moment he had the door open he once again lifted her gently into his arms, and she nestled against him in a trusting way that made his throat constrict with the realization that, for the first time in this relationship, he felt truly needed. And surprisingly, for a man who'd studiously avoided the demands of a serious relationship, he found that it felt good. Amazingly good.

Laura shifted slightly in his arms, which effectively forced him to refocus his thoughts. Without bothering to turn on the lights downstairs, he quickly made his way through the dark living room and up the stairs to his bedroom, flicking on the light with his elbow as he entered. Laura felt herself being lowered to the bed, and when his arms released her she opened her eyes, took a deep breath and smiled at him shakily.

"I'm impressed," she said.

Nick was relieved that she was able to smile at all after what she'd been through, and he squatted down beside her. "What do you mean?"

"You must lift weights or something to be able to lug me all the way from the parking lot to the condo and then up those stairs."

"Well, I didn't want to tell you, but Superman was my cousin. Muscles run in our family," he teased gently. "When you feel better, I'll show you my cape." He was rewarded by another smile. "I'm going to fix an ice pack for that eye,'' Nick said, straightening up. ''Just lay there and rest until I get back.''

''Gladly.''

By the time he returned, Laura was dozing, and he paused in the doorway for a moment, his throat tightening as he studied her bruised face, his simmering rage once again threatening to erupt. If only he'd gotten to her a few moments sooner. She, who had always been so independent and strong, now seemed so fragile and vulnerable. He was surprised by the protective instinct she'd brought out in him, finding it a heady, but not unwelcome, feeling.

He moved beside her then, and her eyes fluttered open as he reached down and stroked her cheek. ''Laura, I've got the ice pack. But first you need to change into something more comfortable. Jeans are great—but not for sleeping.''

''I don't have anything,'' she said, her words slightly slurred.

''Well, I have a pajama top that might work.'' He moved to his dresser and rummaged in a drawer, looking for the rarely-used piece of clothing. The pajamas had been a gift from his mother, and he'd never worn them. In quick decision, he removed the bottoms as well as the top from the drawer before returning to her side.

''Laura, can you manage this?'' he asked.

''I think so,'' she replied, looking at the pajama top he was holding.

''Okay. I'll wait outside. Let me know when you're ready.''

Nick closed the door and leaned a shoulder against the wall, folding his arms against his chest. He took a deep, harsh breath and then expelled it slowly as a sudden, numbing weariness swept over him, the traumatic events of the past few hours finally extracting their toll. The sound of running water in the bathroom told him that at least Laura was able to move around a little, although what it cost her he couldn't imagine. Then he heard the water go off, and Nick waited expectantly for her to call to him. After several minutes, he frowned and knocked on the door. "Laura? Can I come in?"

There was a brief pause before she responded. "Yes."

He opened the door and found her still dressed, standing, one hand gripping the bedpost.

"Laura, honey, what's wrong?"

She looked at him, tears of pain and frustration in her eyes. "I can't get undressed," she said, her voice quavering. "It hurts too much."

"Then let me help you," he said without hesitation, quickly moving beside her. Noting the uncertainty in her eyes, he placed his hands on her shoulders and forced himself to smile. "Now, don't tell me you're worried about my intentions. I promise you I've never seduced a woman with a black eye."

Laura's lower lip trembled. She hated being so helpless, so dependent. But like it or not, she needed assistance tonight. Nick was available and willing, and if she had to rely on a man, there was no one else she would have chosen. "I guess I don't have a choice," she said with a sigh.

"Not tonight, I'm afraid. Now what exactly is the problem?"

"It hurts when I try to pull this thing over my head," she said, gesturing to the surgical top.

"Does it hurt when you lift your arms?"

"A little. But I can manage it."

"Okay, then just sit here," he said, easing her down on the side of the bed, "and lift your arms while I do the pulling. I'll stand behind you," he said easily. "It's okay if I look at your back, isn't it?" he asked with a grin.

She smiled shakily. "Yeah. I guess so."

He moved around to the other side of the bed, and she felt the mattress shift under his weight as he came up behind her. "Okay, sweetheart, let's give it a try."

Obediently she raised her arms, and Nick gently lifted the surgical top over her head. As it skimmed her sides he glanced down, his eyes arrested momentarily by the huge blackish-purple bruise stretching across her rib cage. He paused, a muscle tightening in his jaw, his stomach churning with anger and sympathy. She must be hurting— badly—yet she hadn't complained once.

"Nick?" Laura's voice was muffled, but he could hear the puzzled tone.

"We're doing great," he assured her, smoothly completing the maneuver. Then he turned to lay the garment aside, giving her a moment to slip her arms into the pajama top. By the time he came around to the other side of the bed, she was huddled miserably, her face once again pale and drawn. He dropped to one knee and took her hands between his, caressing the backs gently with his thumbs.

"I'm so sorry, Laura," he said, his voice laced with anguish. "I wish there was something I could do to help."

"You've done more than enough already. I'm sorry to have caused you all this trouble."

"It's no trouble. Believe me."

Laura looked into his eyes and believed. Unquestionably. Not knowing how to respond, unable in her present state to deal with complicated emotions, her gaze skittered away.

Sensing her discomfort, Nick rose and placed his hands on his hips. "What about the jeans?"

"I can get them down to my knees. I have trouble after that."

"Okay." He nodded, turning around. "Get them that far and I'll take care of the rest." He heard her stand, heard the zipper, heard the friction of the coarse denim fabric against her skin.

"All right, Nick."

When he turned back she was lying on the bed, the pajama top pulled down as far as possible but still revealing a long expanse of thigh and leg. He took a deep breath, forcing himself to focus on her pain. Any other thoughts were totally inappropriate at the moment, he told himself sternly. With an effort he drew his eyes away from the hem of the pajama top, and noted that the jeans were bunched around her knees. Silently he reached over and quickly eased them down her legs.

"Shoes," she said.

"What?" he asked distractedly.

"Shoes," she repeated, pointing to the athletic shoes and socks she still wore. "I don't think the jeans will go over them. And besides, I don't usually wear shoes to bed."

Nick flashed her a grin and bent to remove them, quickly stripping off her socks, as well. "Well, what's this?" he asked in surprise, cradling her foot in his hand.

"What's what?" she asked, puzzled. When he tapped one of her rosily polished toenails, she blushed. "Oh. You've discovered my one concession to vanity," she admitted sheepishly. "I've always envied women with beautiful nails, but unfortunately in my line of work that's not very practical. This is the next best thing. It's good for my ego, if nothing else."

Nick smiled at this unexpected facet of her character. He would never have believed it if he hadn't seen it for

himself. With her sensible nature, Laura just didn't seem
the type who would indulge in something like polished
toenails. But apparently even she had a frivolous side.
Which was fine as far as he was concerned. He had begun
to think she never did anything for herself. Painted toenails weren't much, admittedly, but they were a start.

"You think it's silly, don't you?" she said, her cheeks
still flushed.

"On the contrary. I think it's charming."

She smiled shyly and closed her eyes as everything
began to grow hazy again. "I think I'll rest for a bit,"
she mumbled sleepily.

"Good idea. I'll hold this ice bag on your eye for a
while, okay?" She nodded, wincing when he first placed
it against her skin, but then gradually drifting into welcome oblivion.

Nick stayed with her for another half hour, and when
he was satisfied that her deep, even breathing indicated
sleep, he pulled the sheet up and tenderly brushed his lips
across her forehead before turning the light off.

Once in the hall, he wearily rubbed the back of his
neck. Laura was docile tonight because she was hurting.
But he knew when she woke up tomorrow she'd be hyper
about her business, so diversionary tactics were needed.
He frowned, trying to remember the name of her new
foreman. Ken something. Nichols…Nolan…Nelson, that
was it. With any luck, he'd be in the phone book.

Ten minutes later, after a satisfactory conversation with
Ken, he headed back upstairs to the loft sitting area that
overlooked the living room and opened up the sofa bed,
glad now that he'd had the foresight to buy it. Although
he'd never imagined that he'd be the first to use it, he
thought ruefully.

By the time he took a quick shower downstairs and

made up the bed, it was nearly two in the morning. But though he was bone tired, he still felt too keyed up emotionally to sleep. Rather than even try, he prowled around restlessly, verifying that he had breakfast food in the kitchen, going through his mail, looking over a few plans in the downstairs bedroom that he'd turned into an office, checking on Laura every few minutes. When at last his body revolted, he climbed into the sofa bed, yawned hugely and turned out the light.

Sleep came more quickly than he expected, a deep sleep that dulled his senses. So it took a long time for him to wake up, brought back to consciousness by something he couldn't immediately identify. Groggily he glanced at the illuminated dial of his watch and groaned. Three-thirty. His eyes flickered closed and he was beginning to drift back to sleep when Laura's soft sobs suddenly penetrated his sleep-fogged brain. Instantly alert, he swung his feet to the floor and moved quickly down the hall, pausing briefly on the threshold of her room, which was illuminated only by a dim night-light. In the shadows, he heard Laura thrashing fretfully around on the bed, mumbling incoherently, sobbing quietly. She must be having a nightmare, he thought, moving quietly beside her, and he wasn't surprised, not after what she'd been through. She'd probably be plagued with them for months, only the next time he wouldn't be there to comfort her, he thought, a muscle clenching in his jaw. He bent to gently touch her shoulder when suddenly Laura flung out an arm.

''No, Joe, don't! Please don't hurt me!'' she cried.

Nick yanked his hand back at her impassioned plea, and his heart actually stopped, then lunged on, hammering painfully against his chest. She wasn't having a nightmare about tonight's attacker. She was having a nightmare about her husband! What had that bastard done to her? he wondered in sudden fury.

Laura's thrashing grew more intense, and Nick became alarmed, fearing that she would injure herself even further. He crouched beside the bed, reaching over to gently stroke her hair. "It's okay, sweetheart. It's okay," he murmured soothingly, aware that her whole body was trembling.

Her eyes flickered open, and she stared at his shadowy figure dazedly. "Nick?" Her voice was barely a whisper.

"It's me, honey," he said huskily. "Everything's okay. You just had a bad dream, that's all. Try to relax and go back to sleep."

"Could...could you stay with me for a little while?" she asked in a tremulous, little-girl voice that tore at his heart.

"Sure." He took her hand, and she grasped it with a steel grip that surprised him. "I'll be right here."

He continued to stroke her hair, murmuring soothing words, and slowly she relaxed. Her breathing grew more even and gradually her grip on his hand loosened as she slipped back into sleep.

When she seemed to be resting easily, Nick carefully extricated his hand and gingerly stood up, much to the relief of his protesting calf muscles. He frowned as he stared down at Laura, her face now at peace as she slumbered. He ought to go back to bed, he supposed. But he just couldn't leave her. Not yet, anyway. He wanted to be at her side if she awoke again in the grip of another nightmare.

Wearily he sank down in an overstuffed chair near the bed. It had been a very long day. And it looked like it was going to be a very long night.

Nick let his head drop onto the cushioned back and

stared at the dark ceiling, torn by conflicting emotions that he didn't understand. He cared about Laura. Deeply. But what was he getting himself into? She was obviously troubled, clearly scarred emotionally, and he was no psychologist. He ought to get out of this relationship while he still could.

Only it was already too late, he acknowledged with a resigned sigh. He couldn't walk away, not now. Not after he'd seen the vulnerable look in her eyes tonight. And maybe not ever. But they couldn't go on as they had. He'd heard too much tonight, learned more from those few words spoken in sleep than he'd learned from all of their waking conversations. The time had come to demand some answers, to examine the reasons why she was so afraid of commitment. It wouldn't be easy for her. But psychologist or not, he knew with absolute certainty that until they confronted the demons from her past, they had no future together.

Laura awoke slowly, disoriented and sluggish. It was a struggle just to open her eyes. She raised her arm and stared at her watch, squinting as she tried to make out the time, but for some reason she had trouble focusing.

One thing did come suddenly—and clearly—into focus, however: her attire. She was wearing a man's pajama top! And just where exactly was she anyway? she wondered in sudden panic, her gaze sweeping over the unfamiliar surroundings. It jolted abruptly to a stop on Nick's sleeping figure, slumped uncomfortably in a chair near the bed, his leg slung over one of the arms.

Suddenly memories of the night before came rushing back—the horror, certainly, but even more prominently the care and tenderness of the wonderful man just a touch away. In sleep, his face had an endearing, boyish quality that she'd never seen before. His hair might be tousled, and he might look rumpled and unshaven, but as far as she was concerned he was the handsomest, most appealing man she'd ever seen.

Of course, the bare chest might have something to do with that perception, she admitted, her eyes drawn to the T pattern of dark, curly hair that rose and fell in time with his even breathing. Her own breathing was suddenly none too steady, and she had a sudden, compelling urge to reach over and lay her hand close to his heart, feel the rise and fall of his broad chest beneath her fingers.

At just that moment, as if sensing her gaze, Nick awoke—abruptly, immediately and fully. His gaze locked on hers, his stomach instinctively contracting at the purple, swollen eye and puffy nose, harshly spotlighted in the brightness of day. He rose stiffly from his uncomfortable position and then moved toward the bed in two long strides, squatting down beside her.

"Good morning, sweetheart," he said, his voice still husky from sleep. He reached over and stroked her hair, his eyes never leaving hers. "How do you feel?"

She frowned and gingerly touched her face, then her side, wincing at even the slightest pressure. "I'm a little sore," she said breathlessly, her voice unsteady.

"I have a feeling that's the understatement of the year," he replied with a frown, his lips compressing into a thin line.

"I'll be fine," she assured him. "But…did you sleep in that chair all night?" she asked, her eyes wide.

"What was left of it," he said with a wry grin.

"You must be exhausted! I'm so sorry to cause all this trouble," she apologized, her eyes filling with tears.

Nick reached over as one spilled out to trickle down her cheek, wiping it away with a gentle finger, his throat constricting painfully. "Laura, you were no trouble. Trust me," he said, his own voice uneven. She still looked unconvinced, and his instinct was to kiss away her doubts. But given her physical—and emotional—fragility at the moment, that was probably not wise. Mustering all of his self restraint, he tenderly touched her cheek and then stood up. "I'll run downstairs and get you a pill, okay?"

She nodded silently, still feeling off balance and uncharacteristically weepy.

His concerned eyes searched hers, and then he turned and rummaged in the closet for a shirt and slacks. "Just stay put till I get back," he said over his shoulder, sliding the door shut and making a quick exit.

When he reached the loft, he rapidly pulled on the cotton slacks and thrust his arms into the hastily retrieved shirt, distractedly rolling the sleeves to the elbows. Based on her pallor and lines of strain in her face, Laura needed a painkiller quickly. He took the steps two at a time, and returned in record time with the pill and a glass of water.

Laura was up, gripping her side and leaning against the bedpost for support, when he entered the room. "I thought I told you to stay put," he said with a frown.

"Nick, do you know what time it is?" she asked, panic edging her voice.

He glanced at his watch. "Nine o'clock."

"I should have been at work an hour ago... Ken won't know what happened... He was supposed to pick me up at seven-thirty... My car's ready today," she said disjointedly.

"Relax, honey," he said, depositing the pill and water on the dresser and easing her back down to the bed. "I called Ken last night. Everything's under control. He'll fill in until you feel well enough to go back."

"But I have so much to do. I can't take another day

off. I can at least go to the office. That won't be too taxing, and—''

"Forget it, Laura," he said flatly, cutting her off.

She stared at him. "Excuse me?"

He sighed, regretting the dictatorial approach. Maybe logic would work better. He sat down next to her and gently took her hand. "Look, Laura, you're in no shape to get out of bed, let alone go to the office. Do you honestly feel up to doing anything today?"

She stared at him, savoring the warm clasp of his hand on one level, thinking about his question on another. The truth was, she didn't. But that had never stopped her before. She hadn't been able to let it. It hadn't mattered how she'd felt; the job had to be done. But then again, she'd never felt quite this bad. Her ribs ached, she could barely see out of her left eye and her nose was almost too tender to touch. Besides, every muscle in her body felt as if it had been pulled taut. But there was work to be done. "No, I don't," she admitted. "But I can't afford to lose a day," she said resolutely.

"For the sake of your health, you can't afford not to," he told her bluntly.

She looked at him in exasperation. "Nick, you just don't understand. I'm it. Taylor Landscaping is a one-person show at the management level. You have someone to fall back on. I don't. I can't take a day off."

Laura took a deep breath and stood, gripping the headboard to steady herself. Tears pricked her eyes and she forced them back, but she couldn't do anything about the trembling in her hands. And Nick wasn't blind.

He remained on the bed for a moment, looking up at her back, ramrod straight, and the defiant tilt of her head. She was probably going to hate him after this, he thought ruefully, but there was no way he was letting her set one foot outside this condo today. He wouldn't be surprised if her stubborn determination carried her through a day at the office. Laura wasn't a quitter, that was for sure. But by tonight she'd be a basket case. He steeled himself for her anger and stood, moving to face her, placing his hands on her shoulders.

"Laura, I'm sorry. No way. I've already called Ken, who sounds very competent, and he's handling everything. You're not leaving here until tomorrow."

"Tomorrow?" she stammered.

"Tomorrow," he declared.

"Nick, you can't do this!"

"I can and I am. I'm bigger than you are. And you're in no shape to resist. I'll sit on you if I have to, but I hope it won't come to that."

Nick saw the anger and defiance flash in her eyes and prepared to do battle. But then he watched in amazement as the flame of anger slowly flickered and went out. Her shoulders suddenly sagged and she carefully sat back on the bed, dropping her head to hide the tears that shimmered in her eyes. He squatted in front of her and took her hands in his, taken aback by her unexpected acquiescence. He'd expected a struggle; instead, she'd caved in. Had he pushed too hard, been too heavy-handed? He knew her emotions were tattered. "Laura, I'm sorry for being so obstinate about this," he said gently. "But I'm doing it for you."

"I know," she said softly, struggling to keep the tears from spilling out of her eyes, but the tenderness in his voice just made it more difficult. It had been so long since she'd felt this cared for, this protected, this cherished. Her heart overflowed with gratitude…and something else she refused to acknowledge. Instead, she met his eyes and tried to smile, but didn't quite succeed. "I'm very grate-

ful. It's been a long time since..." Her voice trailed off
and she looked down at the strong, competent hands that
held hers so comfortingly.

Nick didn't move. He just stared at her bowed head,
struggling to regain his own composure. It wasn't easy,
not when his emotions were pulling at him like a riptide,
threatening to sweep him off balance, a protective instinct
emerging on the one hand, a purely sensual one on the
other. The latter instinct urged him to take her in his arms,
to kiss away her tears, to love her as she deserved to be
loved. She seemed so desperately in need of loving.

"Laura," he said at last, the unevenness of his voice
making him stop and clear his throat before continuing.
Her head remained bowed. "Laura," he repeated, squeezing her hands, this time forcing her to meet his eyes,
which held hers with a compelling intensity. "You are
very special to me. Special, and precious. When I think
about what could have happened last night..." He closed
his eyes for a moment and took a steadying breath, struggling for composure before fixing his intense gaze on her
once again. "You're not in great shape," he said, reaching up to her eye with a whisper touch, "but you'll be
okay. You'll be okay," he repeated more forcefully, as
much to convince himself as to reassure her, touching her
as he spoke—her arm, her cheek, her hair. "And I don't
want you to ever be alone and frightened again."

She stared at him, swallowing with difficulty. "Is that
why you slept in the chair last night?"

"Yeah. You had a nightmare," he said quietly. "I
wanted to be close in case it happened again."

She studied his eyes—dark, intense and filled with integrity. He seemed too good to be real, and she reached
over and tentatively touched the angled planes of his face.
A muscle twitched in his jaw, and she watched as the

smoldering sparks of passion in his eyes burst into flame. Alarmed, she tried to draw her hand away, not wanting to create false expectations. But he held her fast, his fingers tightening on her wrist.

"Laura?" his voice was gentle, his eyes probing. "What is it?"

"I—I'd really like it if you would just hold me," she said, so quietly he had to lean close to hear. "But that's not fair to you. I can see that…I mean, you want more and right now…I can't promise that."

He placed his fingers against her lips, and her eyes searched his. "Sweetheart, if being held is what you need now, that's what I'll give. Okay?"

Her head nodded jerkily, and he eased her back on the bed, then stretched out beside her, carefully gathering her soft, bruised body into his arms. It was some minutes before he felt her tension ease, and then he brushed his cheek against her hair. "Better?" he asked.

"Yes. But, Nick…I know this isn't enough for you."

"It's enough," he assured her. But then he added a qualification. "For now."

Chapter Eleven

The persistent ringing of the phone slowly penetrated Laura's consciousness. Tenderly cradled in Nick's arms, feeling utterly safe and content, she had drifted off to sleep. When the ringing of the bedside phone continued, she opened her eyes and glanced up questioningly. "Nick?"

"Mmm-hmm."

"The phone's ringing."

"I know."

"Aren't you going to answer it?"

"I don't think so."

"But it might be something important."

"It's probably just the office."

The ringing stopped, and Laura's eyes grew wide. "The office! What are you doing home? Shouldn't you have been at work hours ago?"

"Normally, yes," he replied mildly.

"So?"

"The past eighteen hours haven't exactly been normal," he reminded her wryly.

"No, I suppose not," she conceded. "But I'll be okay here. You don't have to baby-sit."

"Work can wait," he insisted.

Suddenly the phone rang again, and Nick glanced at it in irritation. But Laura also saw the concern in his eyes, and she nudged him with her shoulder. "Go ahead. This will drive you crazy."

He sighed. "Yeah, I guess so." He reached over to pick up the receiver. "Jack? I told you this morning, we'll have to postpone it. I'm not leaving Laura today." Silence, while he absently continued to stroke her shoulder. "Yeah, yeah, I know, but you don't need me for the presentation." Silence again. "Look, just cover for me. Tell him…I don't know, tell him anything."

Laura frowned. Nick obviously had a commitment, apparently an important one. The thought that he was willing to forgo it on her behalf filled her with a warm glow, but at the same time, she'd struggled long enough herself to know that it was never wise to upset a client.

"Nick," she whispered.

He glanced down. "Jack, hang on a second." Depressing the mute button, he reached down to stroke her cheek, his brusque, businesslike tone of moments before suddenly gentled. "What is it, honey?"

"Go to your meeting. It sounds important."

"You're more important," he insisted.

She smiled her thanks, but shook her head. "I'll feel guilty if you don't go. There's no sense in both of us falling behind, and I'll be fine." She could see the flicker of indecision in his eyes, and with a determined smile she gently eased herself away from the warmth of his body and swung her feet to the floor, trying not to wince at the sudden pain in her side. Carefully she stood, and by the time she turned back to him her features were placid. "Come on, you'll be late," she urged lightly.

Nick hesitated a fraction of a second longer and then released the mute button, glancing at his watch. "Okay, Jack, I'll be there. But not until one-thirty. That will give us time to look over the presentation and make sure we're in sync before Andrews arrives... Yeah, I know."

Nick replaced the receiver and stood, facing Laura across the bed. "I hate to leave you," he said with simple honesty.

"I'll be fine," she assured him again. "And you'll be back."

"You can count on that. And as soon as possible," he said huskily. Laura felt the warmth creep up her cheeks at his tone and glanced down, tugging self-consciously at the brief hem of the pajama top she wore. Nick cleared his throat. "Do you need anything from your apartment? I could stop by on the way back."

"Other than my toothbrush, I think I'm okay for another day. Except...do you have an old shirt or something with buttons I could borrow? I'd rather not put that thing on again," she said, gesturing distastefully toward the discarded surgical top.

"I'm sure I can find something. And I may even have a spare toothbrush." He returned triumphantly a few moments later with the latter item, still cellophane enclosed, and quickly riffled through his closet. "Will this work?" he asked, withdrawing a striped cotton shirt.

"Perfect. I'll just roll up the sleeves and it will be fine."

"Can you get dressed on your own?"

"I think so. But I'd like to take a shower first."

Nick nodded. "I'll put some fresh towels out for you and come back in a few minutes."

It took Laura a lot longer to shower than she expected. First, a glance in the mirror over the sink made her stop in midstride, alarmed at the extent of the damage. She looked terrible. Her nose wasn't too bad—just slightly puffy—but the purple-and-red eye, still half-swollen shut, made up for it. She wished she had some makeup, but she doubted whether anything would be able to disguise the discolored area. She'd barely come to grips with the appearance of her battered face when she'd been shocked by the huge, ugly blue-black swath of skin splayed over her ribs. It had made her momentarily queasy, and she'd forced herself to take a few deep breaths, telling herself that she was okay, that the bruise would eventually fade. But no wonder she hurt so much!

Carefully she stepped into the shower, adjusting the water temperature before turning on the spray. The sudden force of water against her ribs, however, made her gasp in pain, and she quickly angled away from the spray, shielding her side. Nick had been right about her going to work today, she admitted. She was in no shape to sit at a desk, let alone visit the job sites. Just the exertion of taking a shower had drained her. But the warm spray felt good, and she let it massage her body with its soothing caress.

At last, Laura reluctantly turned off the water and toweled herself dry, carefully avoiding the injured areas. She dressed slowly, easing the jeans over her legs, grimacing as she bent to pull them up. The voluminous shirt was easier, and as she slipped her arms into the sleeves she caught the unique scent that she had come to associate with Nick—warm, vibrant, slightly spicy…and very masculine. For a moment she buried her face in its folds, wistfully inhaling the essence. Then with a sigh she slipped it over her head.

Laura pulled a comb from her purse and carefully worked the tangles out of her wet, tousled hair. By the time she finished it was almost dry, hanging loose and long, with a few stray tendrils curling around her face.

"Laura, are you okay?" Nick's soft knock and worried voice came through the door.

"I'm fine. I'll be right out," she called. After neatly folding the wet towels and placing them on the edge of the tub, she picked up her purse and opened the door.

Nick's perceptive eyes swept over her. "How are you feeling?"

"Better. The shower helped."

He grinned and folded his arms, tilting his head as he looked at her. "You know, that shirt looks a whole lot better on you than it ever did on me," he said.

"It's a little big," she said, a smile hovering around the corners of her mouth.

"Big is in. It's a very attractive look."

Laura shrugged. "I don't feel very attractive," she admitted.

If any other woman had said that to him, Nick would have assumed she was angling for a compliment. With Laura, the remark had been artless and without pretense. He moved toward her and placed his hands on her shoulders. "Sweetheart, you are the most irresistible woman I've ever known," he said huskily. And then he lightened his tone. "Even with that shiner."

Laura looked up at him in surprise, suddenly realizing that he'd been using terms of endearment ever since last night. They seemed to come so naturally to him, and had sounded so natural to her, that it had taken all this time for the fact to register. Before she could evaluate its significance, however, he was leading her out the door.

"I'm afraid I'm not much of a cook, but you can't

afford to skip any more meals and I didn't want you to have to fix anything yourself,'' he said over his shoulder. ''I hope this is at least palatable.''

He stepped aside when they reached the loft, where a tray rested on the coffee table in front of the now-made-up sofa sleeper. Laura's eyes grew wide. It wasn't so much the contents—scrambled eggs, toast, an orange that had been carefully peeled and separated into chunks, a steaming cup of coffee—but the thoughtfulness of the gesture that stirred her heart. Her throat constricted with emotion, and when she turned to Nick the warmth in her unguarded eyes made him catch his breath. ''Nick, I... After all you've already done, this makes me feel so...'' She gestured helplessly.

He grinned, inordinately pleased by her response, and took her hand, steering her toward the sofa. ''Don't say anything else until you've tasted it,'' he warned teasingly. He settled her comfortably and then glanced at his watch. ''Do you mind if I get dressed while you eat?''

''No, of course not.''

By the time she'd finished the last bite of what she would always remember as one of the best meals of her life, Nick reappeared, dressed in a lightweight charcoal gray suit, crisp white shirt and paisley tie. He smiled when he saw the empty plate. ''Well, I guess it wasn't too bad. Or else you were starved.'' When she started to speak, he held up his hand. ''No, don't tell me which. I prefer to keep my illusions.''

Laura smiled. ''Thank you,'' she said simply.

His expression grew suddenly serious and he sat down beside her, grasping her hand as he studied her eyes. ''Laura, are you sure you'll be all right? I can still stay if you want me to.''

''I'll be fine,'' she assured him again. ''I took the pill

you left on the tray, and I already feel very relaxed and sleepy. I'm just going to nap this afternoon, and it makes no sense for you to sit around and miss an important appointment while I sleep.''

Nick bowed to the logic of her argument. ''Okay. But I'll be back early—no later than five. Do you like Chinese food?''

''Love it.''

''I'll pick some up on the way home.'' He stood, taking the tray with him.

''Oh, Nick, let me take care of that,'' she protested.

''No way. You're not to lift a finger today. Promise me that, or I'm not leaving.''

She shook her head. ''You really do have a one-track mind.''

''Promise?'' he persisted.

''Promise,'' she agreed.

Laura's day went almost exactly as predicted. She took a few minutes to explore Nick's condo, admiring his spare but tasteful and obviously expensive furnishings. The cathedral-ceilinged living room, overlooked by the loft, featured a two-story wall of glass that offered a restful view of the wooded common ground. She peeked into his office, impressed by its neatness, and through the window she glimpsed what looked like a clubhouse and swimming pool. Compared to this, her apartment really was the pits, she thought. No wonder he had remarked on the neighborhood a few weeks ago. And rightly so, she thought wryly, wincing at the twinge in her side as she turned.

After a quick call to Sam, who was shocked by the mugging but clearly pleased by Nick's attentiveness and concern, Laura took another pill and lay down. Within minutes she was asleep.

The sound of Nick's voice calling from downstairs

awakened her later in the afternoon, and by the time she had oriented herself and was struggling to sit up, he appeared in the doorway, his jacket already discarded, his face a mask of concern. He moved beside her immediately, his intense, dark eyes critically examining her. For a moment he hesitated, and then he reached over and touched his lips to her forehead. "I'd like to give you a better hello, but that's about the only spot I know of that isn't bruised," he said huskily, brushing her hair back from her face as he spoke.

Laura smiled hesitantly. "My lips are okay," she said softly.

Nick's momentary surprise was quickly followed by a pleased chuckle, and the deep, throaty sound of it sent a hot wave of desire crashing over her. "Are you saying you'd like to be kissed?" he asked with a smile.

She swallowed. "Only if it's what you want."

"Oh, I want," he said huskily, and the ardent light in his eyes left little doubt about his wants. "I just don't want to hurt you."

Laura's mouth went dry. Already her lips were throbbing in anticipation of his touch. "We'll be careful," she whispered.

Nick gave up the fight. He'd told himself she was in no shape, physically or emotionally, for intimacy right now. He'd told himself that he would keep his hands off until she was stronger. He'd told himself that she wasn't herself, that the trauma of the previous night could make her needy in ways she would later regret. But he was only human, after all. And the tender, welcoming look in her eyes was too much for him. With a soft groan he lowered his lips to hers, gently nipping at their pliant fullness, until her mouth stirred sweetly beneath his. He felt her shudder as he tasted the warm sweetness of her mouth, and her response nearly undid him. Gently he lowered her to the bed and stretched out beside her, cradling her head in his hands, his fingers lost in the thick fullness of her hair. How he'd waited for this moment, to have her close to him. His lips left hers, moving down to her neck, and she arched her throat for his touch, breathing heavily. Her arms clung to him, urging him closer. Nick let one hand travel downward until it rested lightly at her waist. Laura was so lost in the magic of his touch that it took her a moment to realize that his hand was gently but firmly tugging her shirt free.

Laura knew where this was leading, knew she was breaking every rule she'd ever made about allowing any man to get close to her again, knew that it went against everything she believed about casual intimacy. And yet she seemed powerless to stop what was happening. When Nick had appeared in the doorway tonight she'd had no plan to initiate this embrace. But he'd looked so wonderful standing there, so dear and so handsome and so very special. And she was very grateful for all he'd done for her. Yet she was honest enough to admit that gratitude wasn't the only explanation for her behavior. Last night had been like déjà vu, a bad dream come again to life, awakening old memories and old pain. Today she felt vulnerable, needy, scared—aching physically and emotionally. Nick, with his gentle touch and caring concern, could make her fears and pain disappear, at least for a little while. Her Christian faith put strict limits on intimacy outside of marriage, and she knew she was pushing those limits. Tomorrow she'd probably be sorry. But for now, she needed to be held, to be cared for and protected, to bask in the warmth of his caresses.

Laura felt her shirt being pulled free, felt his hand hesitate briefly at her waist before sliding slowly up her back.

The warmth of his fingers against her bare skin made her sigh. "Oh, Nick," she breathed, her own fingers kneading his hard, muscled shoulders. He urged her closer, his lips once more capturing hers with an urgency that stole her breath away.

It was her sudden, sharp intake of breath that stilled his hands and made him draw back. Her face had gone white and tears glimmered in her eyes. "Nick…I'm sorry," she said breathlessly. "My side… I forgot…"

Her voice trailed off at the stricken look on Nick's face. "Oh, sweetheart," he whispered, cradling her face in his hands, stroking her cheeks with his thumbs. "I'm so sorry! Did I hurt you?"

"It's okay. It just…surprised me. It doesn't hurt now." She wanted to smooth out the deep creases that had appeared on his brow, ease the sudden tension in his jaw, erase the self-recrimination in his eyes.

"I told myself not to touch you. I knew better," he said angrily.

"Nick, it's my fault. I—I more or less asked you to."

"Yeah, well, you're not thinking straight. You're probably half out of your mind in pain and you're doped up on those high-powered pills. Laura, let me take a look, okay? I promise not to hurt you. I just want to make sure I didn't do any more damage."

Laura knew he needed to reassure himself, so she nodded silently. With utmost care he pulled up her shirttail, sucking in his breath at the bruise that extended from her breastbone to the bottom of her rib cage. "Dear God, it looks worse than yesterday," he declared in dismay.

"Bruises usually do," she said lightly, easing the shirt back down. "But it will fade, Nick."

"No thanks to me."

"Nick, I'm okay. And hungry. Where's that Chinese

food you promised me?'' she asked, trying to divert his attention.

For the rest of the evening he treated her like spun glass, helping her up and down the steps, getting a cushion for the back of her chair while they ate, wrapping an afghan around her before they settled in to watch an old movie on video that he'd brought home.

When he tucked her in for the night, gently pressing a chaste kiss on her forehead, Laura smiled. ''You'd make a good mother,'' she joked gently.

''Laura, believe me, my feelings for you are anything but motherly,'' he said with an intensity that left no doubt about exactly what his feelings were. ''My restraint is the result of sheer terror. I never want to hurt you, sweetheart, and if touching you hurts at the moment, I won't touch. The important thing right now is for you to heal.''

Later, as Laura began to drift to sleep, she thought about Nick's parting words. She would heal—physically. It would just take time. It was the emotional healing that still troubled her. Today they'd been closer physically than ever before. Not because he'd pushed, as she'd feared all along, but because she'd pressed him. He'd responded readily, and she couldn't blame him; he'd long ago made his intentions clear. But they'd been heading for a level of intimacy that she believed should be reserved for a committed relationship. And even if he had suggested that, Laura knew she wasn't yet ready—just needy. And that wasn't enough. For either of them.

Nick didn't sleep well. His body was still vibrating with unrelieved tension, and his conscience was battering him for letting his emotions and physical needs cloud his sensitivity and judgment. It was the early hours of the morning before he finally fell into a restless sleep, and even then he only slept lightly, half expecting to again hear Laura's anguished cries, as he had the night before. But all was quiet.

It seemed he had just drifted off when he felt someone prodding his shoulder. "Come on, sleepyhead, wake up," an amused voice said.

Nick opened one eye and stared up at Laura, fully dressed, standing with her hands on her hips next to his bed. "What time is it?" he asked groggily.

"Seven-thirty."

He groaned and buried his head in his pillow.

"Nick Sinclair, even if you have time to loaf, I don't. I need to get to the office."

Nick sighed. It had been hard enough to hold Laura down for one day. He'd pretty much figured two days were out of the question. "Did anyone ever tell you that you're a hard taskmaster?" he growled.

She prodded him again. "Come on, Nick. Here, try this. Maybe it will help." She waved a fragrant-smelling cup of coffee under his nose.

He sniffed appreciatively and grasped the mug in both hands, taking a long swallow before he even opened his eyes. And this time he took a good look at her. Her nose seemed back to normal, her eye was slightly less swollen—though no less purple—and he could only speculate about her ribs. But her face had more color than yesterday, and she seemed to be in good spirits.

"How do you feel?" he asked, watching her over the rim of his cup as he took another swallow.

She shrugged. "Compared to what? Better than yesterday, worse than last weekend. It's all in your point of view. But I'll live."

She was her spunky self again, which meant that she really must be feeling better. Nick was glad, of course, but he felt a sudden, odd sense of loss. For the past thirty-six hours she'd needed him—really needed him—and though the circumstances had been less than ideal, the feeling had been good. Now, suddenly, he felt less needed, less important in her life. He took another sip of the coffee and, trying to throw off his melancholy mood, he glanced at his watch. "Okay, give me fifteen minutes and we can roll."

At her request, Nick dropped her off at the garage to pick up her car, coming around to open the door for her when they arrived. "Do you think you're up to driving?" he asked worriedly.

"Of course," she said with more confidence than she felt.

He sighed and raked his fingers through his hair. "Laura, will you promise me something? If you get tired, go home and rest. Don't force yourself to put in a full day."

"I'll be fine, Nick. Okay, okay." She held up her hands when he opened his mouth to protest. "I'll try not to push myself."

"Promise?"

"Promise."

"Okay. Now, what would you like for dinner tonight?"

"Tonight?" she asked, startled.

"Mmm-hmm. Does pizza sound okay?"

"Well, sure. But, Nick, you don't have to feel obligated. I can manage."

"Yeah, I know. I just hoped you might like to have dinner with me. Besides, you may feel perky now, but I have a feeling that you're going to fade by this afternoon, and I doubt whether you'll be in the mood to cook." More likely she'd just fall into bed without eating, he thought, and skipping meals was not something she could afford to do.

"Well…thank you. That would be great."

"I'll see you about six," he said, walking around to the driver's side of his car and opening the door. "And, Laura…?"

"Yes?"

"Will you take it easy today?"

"I'll try," she hedged.

Nick rolled his eyes and shook his head. "You're stubborn, do you know that?"

She grinned. "Yeah. But it takes one to know one." Then she grew more serious. "Nick…I want to thank you for…well, for everything. You've been really great. I don't know how I would have managed without you. Knowing you were there—just having you with me—made all the difference."

He looked at her for a long moment before speaking. "Hold that thought," he said at last. Then he slipped into the low-slung car and was gone.

Chapter Twelve

Nick called Laura several times during the day. Though she kept her voice determinedly cheerful, he could hear the underlying weariness that intensified with each call. She stuck it out most of the day, despite his urging to go home and take a nap, and by the time he arrived at her apartment with the pizza he wasn't sure what shape she'd be in.

Not good, he thought the moment she opened the door. Her face was as pale as it had been at the hospital two nights before, making the dark, ugly colors of her bruised eye stand out in stark relief.

Nick opened his mouth to tell her she had pushed too hard, took another look at her weary face and changed his mind. She'd clearly already had all she could take today. What she needed now was support, not criticism.

"Rough day," he said quietly. It was a statement, not a question.

"Is it that obvious?" she asked ruefully, shutting the door behind him.

"Mmm-hmm," he replied, aware that she was moving stiffly and slowly—and trying to hide it.

"You look tired," she said, studying his face.

He hadn't really thought it, but she was right. The strain and worry had taken their toll on him, too. "Yeah. I am."

"Why don't you sit down and I'll get you something to drink. I'm sorry about the heat. I turned on all the fans, but I know you're used to air-conditioning. At least you changed into something cooler before you came. Would you like some iced tea, or—"

"Laura." His quiet voice stilled her.

"Yes?"

"Would you please sit down before you fall down? You look half-dead. I did not come over here tonight to be waited on." He took her arm and guided her to the couch, and she went unprotestingly, the stream of adrenaline that had kept her on her feet all day suddenly running dry. All at once she was overcome with a numbing lethargy, and she sank down gratefully onto the soft, chintz-covered cushions of her couch.

"Would you like a cold drink?"

She gazed up at him, her eyes slightly dazed with fatigue. "Yes, I think I would. There's some soda in the fridge."

She heard the clatter of ice and then he was back beside her, a glass in each hand. "I put the pizza in the oven to warm for a few minutes."

She nodded, silently sipping the sweet liquid, fighting a losing battle to keep her eyelids open. When her head began to nod, Nick reached over and gently took the glass from her fingers, then he pulled her against him, carefully avoiding contact with her bruised ribs. She nestled into the crook of his arm, her cheek resting against the hard contours of his chest, and sighed.

"I'm not much company, am I?" she said apologetically.

"Don't worry about it. I didn't expect you to play hostess."

"I'm just so tired."

"I know." What Laura needed tonight was food and sleep, in that order and preferably as quickly as possible, he concluded. What he needed was beside the point, he thought longingly as her firm, supple body molded to his caused stirrings of emotion best held in check. This was not the time. "How about some pizza?" he asked, his chin resting on her hair.

Laura wasn't hungry. Just tired. But she knew she needed to eat, and Nick had gone to the trouble of bringing food, so she nodded.

She perked up a little as she munched on the spicy, rich pizza, enough to remember that she wanted to invite Nick to dinner the next night. He protested at first, suggesting instead that they go out so she wouldn't have to cook, but she insisted.

"I really want to, Nick. It's Saturday, so I can rest all day. And I like to cook. It's not exactly strenuous, and I find it relaxing. Besides, I want to thank you for everything you've done these past couple of days."

"You don't need to do that, Laura."

"I want to. Unless…that is…well, I understand if you have other plans," she said, her voice suddenly sounding uncertain.

He reached across the table and took her hand, forcing her to meet his eyes. "I don't have any other plans," he said firmly. "I'll be here." He gave her fingers a gentle squeeze and then released them, standing to clear away the remnants of their meal. When she started to help, he placed a hand firmly on her shoulder. "Just sit," he commanded.

"Can I at least move to the living room?" she asked with a tired smile.

"Sure. I'll be right in."

By the time he rejoined her, she was sitting in a corner of the couch, her legs tucked under her, her head resting against the back, her eyes closed. He thought she might have dozed off again, but when he quietly sat down next to her, her eyelids flickered open.

"Dinner was great. You're going to spoil me," she said with a smile.

"You could do with some spoiling."

"Well, I'm not used to it, that's for sure."

Nick reached over and took her hand, gently stroking the back with his thumb. "Laura?"

"Mmm-hmm?"

"Will you be okay here tonight by yourself?"

"Of course," she lied. In reality, she was as nervous as the deer they'd spotted in the woods, but she wasn't about to admit that to Nick. He'd insist on spending the night on her couch and he looked wiped out. After the past couple of days, he deserved a decent night's sleep in his own bed.

"I could stay," he offered.

"No. You need to get some rest. I'll be fine."

"But what if you have another nightmare?"

"I won't. I was fine last night, wasn't I?"

"Yeah, but subconsciously you knew I was close by."

She couldn't argue with that. The simple fact was she *would* sleep better with Nick here. She was still spooked from the attack, and she knew that when quiet descended on the apartment after he left, every sound would seem magnified—and menacing. But she couldn't live the rest of her life afraid. "Nick, please…I've got to stay by my-self eventually. It would just be postponing the inevitable," she said resolutely. "The memory of the attack will fade in time."

"That's true. But at the moment I'm more concerned about other memories."

She frowned. "What do you mean?"

"I mean the nightmare you had the other night wasn't about the attack," he said quietly.

"How do you know?"

"Because I heard what you said. Laura…it was about Joe."

A stricken look crossed her face, and she bit her lip. "Oh," she said in a small voice, turning away.

He reached over and stroked her arm, and then his hand strayed to the top of her right breast, his fingers resting lightly on the spot where he'd seen the scar two nights before. "Did he do this to you?" he asked, a sudden edge to his voice.

He felt her stiffen even before she pulled away. "What?"

"The scar. I saw it at the hospital."

She drew a deep, shaky breath. "Nick, what happened between Joe and me is in the past. Let's leave it there."

"I'd like to, because I know it's painful for you. But I can't. Because whatever happened between the two of you is coming between us, whether you want to face that or not. We've got to talk about it, Laura."

She wrapped her arms around her body and shook her head. "No."

With a muttered oath he stood abruptly and walked away from her, the rigid lines of his back speaking more eloquently than words of the strain of the past two days and his longer-term frustration. He was clearly a man on the edge, pushed to the limit of his patience, struggling to maintain control. Laura had never seen him this upset, and it frightened her. Not in terms of physical danger, the way such anger once might have frightened her, but in the knowledge that Nick could very well walk away—and with very good reason. He deserved to know more than she was willing—or able—to tell. She just didn't have the courage to dredge up her painful past for anyone—not even Nick.

It seemed as if an eternity passed before he at last turned and looked at her. When he spoke, she could hear the anger—and the underlying hurt—in his voice. "How long is it going to take for you to realize that you can trust me, Laura? Can't you see how much I care about you? Why won't you share your past with me?"

Laura huddled miserably on the couch, the sting of tears hot behind her eyes. "Nick, please. What happened with Joe is over."

"No, it isn't! If he wasn't already dead I could kill him with my bare hands for what he's done to you! For what he's still doing to you," he said savagely.

She stared up at him, her face devoid of color. "It wasn't like that," she whispered.

"No? Then explain to me why you're so terrified of commitment, so afraid to trust. Explain that," he said, pointing to the scar.

Laura blinked back tears. She felt hollow inside, and a deep emptiness echoed within the walls of her heart. "If you need answers, Nick, I can't give them to you," she said wearily. "I told you at the beginning it was a long shot with me." Her voice broke and she swallowed, struggling for control. "Maybe you better just give it up."

Nick looked at her for a long moment, and then he took a deep breath. "Maybe I better," he said tiredly, his anger suddenly spent. "Because I sure can't continue like this. When I saw what that mugger did to you, I felt like somebody had kicked me in the gut. It's tearing me up inside right now, wanting to share this with you, wanting to share everything with you, and watching you retreat behind your wall, knowing that the door is locked and I don't have a clue where to find the key."

"I—I'm sorry, Nick."

He sighed heavily. "Yeah. Me, too." He jammed his hands into his pockets and walked over to the window, staring out into the darkness. The ticking of her clock echoed loudly in the oppressive stillness that had descended on the room. "What do you say we call it a night?" he said at last. "You need to get some rest."

"I am tired."

He nodded. "Lock the door behind me, okay?" She rose shakily and followed him to the door. He turned and looked at her for a long moment, one hand resting on the frame. "You've got to get out of this place, Laura. It's not safe."

She nodded. "I know. I was planning to move anyway when my lease is up."

"How long is left?"

"Seven months."

"Seven months! That's too long. You need to move now."

"I can't break the lease, Nick."

He sighed, recognizing the stubborn tilt of her chin. He hesitated, as if he wanted to say more, but in the end he didn't. "Good night, Laura."

"Good night," she whispered.

Then he turned and was gone.

Nick ran his finger down the phone listing. Ralph Reynolds. Robert Reynolds. Rudolph Reynolds. Samantha

Reynolds. That was it. He quickly punched in the numbers, praying she'd be home. He'd had all night to think about his evening with Laura, and he knew he should never have started that discussion with her. The timing was lousy. If he hadn't been so tired, so stressed out, he would have realized that. She had been in no shape for a confrontation, for a true confessions session, and he had been wrong to press her. But he had to have some answers, and Sam was his only hope.

Nick recognized the voice that greeted him and slowly let out his breath, relief washing over him. "Sam? This is Nick Sinclair."

"Nick?" The surprise in her voice quickly changed to alarm. "Is Laura okay?"

"Yes, she's fine," he assured her. "Or as fine as can be expected after what happened. Would you by any chance have time to meet me for lunch?"

There was a fractional hesitation, a question hovering palpably in the air, and Nick was grateful when Sam left it unasked. "Sure. I have to show houses at ten and two, so how about around eleven-thirty?"

"Fine. Just name the place."

Nick arrived early at the designated restaurant and was waiting in a quiet, secluded booth when Sam appeared in the doorway, her striking red hair announcing her arrival even before he caught a glimpse of her face. When she turned to scan the room he motioned to her, rising as she joined him.

"Nick, it's good to see you."

"Thanks for coming."

"It sounded important," she said as she slid into the booth.

"It is." A waiter appeared, and Nick glanced at Sam questioningly.

"Iced tea, please," she said.

"The same for me," Nick told the waiter, then turned his attention back to Sam. "I'm sure you're wondering why I asked you to meet me," he began.

"You might say that," she replied mildly.

He sighed. "The trouble is, I'm not sure myself. It's just that I don't know where else to turn." He paused as the waiter deposited their drinks and they gave their orders. Then he took a long swallow of his iced tea.

"You really do have a problem, don't you?" Sam said.

"Yeah. Laura."

"I figured as much."

He twirled the ice in his glass and stared broodingly into it. "Sam, I care about Laura. But she's running scared. It's like she puts up a No Trespassing sign on certain areas of her life."

Sam nodded. "I know. She's a very private person."

"I realize that. I also realize she's been burned. Badly. From what I can gather, her husband was not only a first-class jerk, but abusive."

"Did she tell you that?"

"No. I just put two and two together. Her mother casually mentioned the separation when we were there for the Fourth. Then I saw the scar above Laura's right breast at the hospital. And the night of the mugging, she had a nightmare. Not about the attack. About Joe. She was pleading for him not to hurt her." A muscle in his jaw twitched convulsively, and his lips compressed into a thin, white line.

"I knew it was bad, but it must have been even worse than I thought," Sam said in a subdued voice. "He really did a number on her, didn't he?"

"It sure looks that way." There was a moment of silence, and then Nick leaned forward intently. "Look, Sam. I don't want you to betray any confidences. But is there anything—anything at all—you can tell me about what happened to Laura in that relationship? I want to help, but my hands are tied. I don't know enough."

Sam toyed with her glass. "Don't you think this should come from Laura?"

He sighed and raked his fingers through his hair. "Yes. And I've tried to get her to open up. I pushed pretty hard last night, in fact. Probably too hard. All I succeeded in doing was upsetting her. I came to you because you're her best friend, and I thought…" He shook his head. "I don't know what I thought. I'm desperate. Because the truth is, I'm falling in love with her."

Sam quirked an eyebrow. "Have you told her that?"

"Are you kidding? She's frightened enough as it is, and love can be a very scary word."

Sam eyed him speculatively. "I see what you mean."

Their food arrived, and Sam stared down at her plate for a long moment, her brow furrowed. Nick waited, praying she'd trust him enough to tell him something. Anything. Finally she looked up. "Okay, Nick," she said in sudden decision, and he slowly expelled the breath he'd been holding. "It took me a long time to win Laura's trust, and I'm not about to jeopardize our friendship. But she does have blinders on when it comes to men, and I like you. I think the two of you could have something really special if she'd only give it a chance. So I'll tell you how we met, and I'll tell you what I know about the night she left Joe, because I was involved. But that's it. And to be honest, I don't know much more, anyway. Laura has never talked much about her marriage, and even with my big mouth, I sometimes know when to keep it shut.''

She speared a forkful of tuna salad and chewed thoughtfully. ''Laura and I met when we were both in night school. In the ladies' room, of all places. Not exactly an auspicious beginning,'' she said dryly. ''Anyway, I remember thinking that she looked like she could use a friend. We ran into each other a few more times, and something just clicked. I can't explain it, because we're obviously Mutt and Jeff. She's a lady through and through, discreet, polite, considerate. All that good stuff. I'm more the irreverent loudmouth, the class clown, the kid who was always getting in trouble. But despite our differences, we became friends.

''It hasn't been easy for Laura, that much I know,'' she said pensively. ''Not that she's ever complained. That's not her style. You've seen her apartment? Well, that's a palace compared to where she and Joe lived. It was a dump,'' she said bluntly. ''But it was all they could afford, and she refused to ask her family for help. To be honest, I doubt whether she's ever told them the real reason she left Joe. Anyway, she's had to fight every step of the way to get where she is, and she did it with sheer guts and determination.''

''Tell me about when she left Joe,'' Nick prompted, when Sam paused.

She laid her fork down carefully. ''That was a bad night,'' she said with a frown. ''Laura called me from a pay phone at the corner of her street, hysterical and almost incoherent. When I got there, she was still in the phone booth, shaking like a leaf, not so much hysterical anymore as in shock. She was wearing a jacket, even though it was warm that night, which I thought was odd. After I got her into the car, I asked her what happened, and she said that

Joe had gotten drunk again and that he'd hurt her. Then she opened the jacket and I saw the blood all over her blouse.''

Nick clenched his napkin into a tight ball, closed his eyes and swallowed convulsively.

''Nick?'' Sam paused, and with a worried frown reached over and touched his hand. ''Are you okay?''

He opened his eyes and expelled a long breath, then reached for his drink. ''Yeah. Go on.''

She hesitated briefly, then continued. ''Well, at first she wouldn't let me look, but I insisted. And I can be pretty pushy. It's a good thing I *was* pushy that night, because when I saw that cut I took off for the emergency room like a bat out of…well, you get the picture. The hospital took one look at her physical and emotional state, came to the obvious conclusion and called the cops. Laura wouldn't press charges, no matter how hard we tried to convince her to, but she did decide to leave Joe. That night. She insisted on going home to collect her things, so I drove her back to their apartment and waited at the door. Joe was sleeping it off by then, so there was no problem. I guess she left him a note. I never asked. Then I took her back to my place.''

There was a momentary pause as Nick stared into his glass, then he looked up at Sam. ''Did Joe try to get her to come back?''

''I think so. I know he called a lot. Fortunately I answered one of the first calls and told him to keep his distance or I'd bring in the cops. I guess I was pretty convincing, because as far as I know he never actually came over.''

''And Laura never went back?''

''No. But it was really hard on her, Nick. I'm sure you've discovered by now how strong her faith is. She really believes in the sanctity of marriage and she took those 'for better or worse' vows seriously. In case you haven't figured it out, she lives by the book—the good book, that is. She doesn't just talk about her Christian principles—she practices them. Anyway, I know she felt guilty about leaving Joe, despite what he did to her. She never once mentioned the word divorce and always acted as if their separation was only a temporary thing. I know she tried to get Joe into counseling for his problem. But he wouldn't go. She did tell me that she talked to her minister, who advised her to put her personal safety first, and I put my two cents in. But I think she might actually have gone back to him one day, if Joe hadn't been killed.''

"What happened to him?"

"He was in a car accident two weeks after Laura left him.''

There was silence for a long moment, and then Nick spoke quietly, the anger in his voice barely held in check. "How many times did he hurt her before the night she called you?"

"I have no idea."

He rested his elbows on the table and interlocked his fingers, his untouched lunch forgotten. "I guess I suspected all this. But I was hoping I was wrong. No wonder she's so petrified of intimacy!"

Sam nodded. "I've been talking to her like a Dutch uncle, but I'm afraid I haven't made much of a dent. Maybe you'll finally break through."

"I don't know, Sam. That's a pretty impenetrable fortress she's built around her heart."

"Hang in there, Nick," she said, touching his hand. Then she glanced at her watch. "Good grief! I've got to run," she said, gathering up her purse and jacket. "I'll tell you something, Nick,'' she said as she slid to the edge of the booth. ''She's a fool if she lets someone like you get away. You don't happen to have any brothers, do you?''

He quirked his lips up into the semblance of a smile. ''Afraid not.''

Sam lifted one shoulder in resignation. ''It figures.''

She stood, and he rose and took her hand in a warm clasp. ''Thank you.''

She shrugged. ''I didn't tell you much more than you'd already figured out. I know this isn't easy on you, but Laura's worth waiting for.''

But for how long? he asked himself in despair as he watched Sam disappear in the crowd. And with what results?

Chapter Thirteen

Laura had no idea if Nick intended to keep their dinner date, but she went ahead with preparations anyway, guilt pricking at her conscience as she worked, telling her that she wasn't treating Nick fairly. She took and took, but gave nothing back. Not even trust. And he deserved that at least.

Distractedly she rolled the chicken cordon bleu in bread crumbs, placed them in a pan and put them in the oven. Why was she so afraid to share her past? Was it pride? Embarrassment that she'd let herself be treated so badly? Concern that her bottled up anger and resentment would be destructive once released? Fear that the information would be used against her? Or the guilt she had never been able to fully put to rest?

Probably all of the above, she thought with a sigh as she laid a linen cloth on the table and set out crisply starched napkins and sparkling wineglasses, placing two long tapers in candlesticks.

Laura didn't know why she was so afraid. All she knew was that the fear was real. Why was Nick even bothering with her? she wondered in dismay as she riffled through her closet. There were probably thousands of women out there who would spill their guts to him and welcome him into their arms—and their hearts.

Laura's hand paused on her one good summer dress as she recalled the strength and comfort she had found in his embrace. And she'd found something more as well, she acknowledged. A tide of yearning, so strong it left her flushed and breathless, swept over her. No one had ever made her feel like this, not even...not even Joe, she forced herself to admit. With Nick it was different. Was it because she'd been so long without male companionship? Or was it more than that?

She slipped the teal green silk shirtwaist over her head, cinching the belt and leaving the bottom button open to reveal an enticing glimpse of leg. Then she turned her attention to her face, noting resignedly that the black eye hadn't faded one iota. No cosmetic magic was going to camouflage this shiner. She had to content herself with mascara on her good eye, lipstick and blush. Finally she brushed out her hair, leaving it loose and full. Usually it was too hot in the apartment to wear it down, but tonight she'd splurged and turned on the air-conditioning.

Should she tell Nick about her marriage? she wondered again as she distractedly fiddled with the buttons on her dress. Or maybe the more pressing question was whether she wanted to continue this relationship. Because if she did, this was the moment of truth. Nick had made that clear last night.

Restlessly she moved around her bedroom, tugging at the uneven hem of the comforter, straightening a picture, adjusting the blinds. The room was neat as a pin already, though, leaving her little to do. Her eyes did one more inspection, coming to rest on the nightstand where she'd left her Bible. Slowly she walked over and picked it up, paging through to the familiar twenty-third psalm as she sank down on the side of the bed. The Lord is my shepherd, there is nothing I shall want, she read silently, slowly working her way through the verse. As always, the lyrical beauty as well as the content refreshed her soul and brought her a sense of peace. Now if only she could decide whether to share her past with Nick!

Laura returned to the living room and inspected the small, carefully set dinette table, caught a glimpse of her meticulous appearance in the hall mirror as she passed, and smelled the aroma of the special, time-consuming dish she rarely prepared. And she realized with surprise that she'd already made her decision. She'd orchestrated the setting and ambience to show Nick she cared; now all she had to do was follow through with words. She closed her eyes. *Dear Lord, please stay beside me tonight,* she prayed silently. *Let me feel your presence and your strength. I don't know if Nick will even come, but if he does I owe him the truth. Give me the courage to share it with him.*

The sudden buzz of the doorbell startled her, and her eyes flew open, her heart soaring. He was here! He'd come, after all! With shaking fingers she slid back the locks and pulled open the door.

At first all she could see was a huge bouquet of long-stemmed red roses and baby's breath. Then Nick's face appeared around the greenery, an uncertain smile hovering at the corners of his mouth. "Hi."

"Hi."

"I wasn't sure I'd be welcome."

"I wasn't sure you'd come."

"Laura, I'm sorry about last night. I was completely out of line. You were in no shape for a heavy discussion."

"Well, I feel better tonight," she said, stepping aside for him to enter. Then she reached over and touched one of the velvet-soft petals of a rose. "These are beautiful," she breathed softly.

"Not very original, though. I don't suppose flowers are anything special for someone in your business."

"These are," she said simply. "Thank you, Nick."

"It was my pleasure." As she took the vase from his hands, he sniffed appreciatively. "Hey, something smells great!"

"Dinner. It's ready, if you're hungry."

"I'm starved. I haven't eaten much today."

She placed the roses on the coffee table, and when she turned back she found Nick studying her. His eyes caught and held hers, and there was a warm light in their depths that made a bolt of heat shoot through her. "That's a lovely dress. And you look wonderful in it," he said quietly.

Laura felt a flush of pleasure creep onto her cheeks at the compliment. "Even with a black eye?" she teased.

"Mmm-hmm."

"I think you need to have your vision checked."

"My taste buds are working," he said hopefully.

She laughed and shook her head. "Go ahead and sit down. I'll have dinner on the table in a minute."

She turned away, but he caught her hand and she looked back in surprise.

"How are you feeling?" he asked, scrutinizing her face.

She smiled. "I'll live." She tried to turn away again, but he didn't release her hand.

"Let me help."

She shook her head firmly. "Not tonight."

His eyes traced her face once more, and finally, with

obvious reluctance, he let her go. He strolled over to the table, noting the linen, the crystal and the candles, and he glanced questioningly at Laura, who was hovering in the doorway. "You went to a lot of trouble."

"Not nearly as much as you went to for me," she said quietly.

Although Laura kept the conversation light as they ate the gourmet fare she'd prepared, he sensed an undercurrent of tension. By the time they settled on the couch after dessert, he knew something was up. She seemed distracted and preoccupied, and when he reached over and gently touched her arm, she jumped.

"Oh!" Her hand went to her throat and her startled eyes flew to his. "Sorry," she said with a shaky laugh.

"Laura, what's wrong?"

She stood and restlessly moved around the room, touching the flowers, straightening a picture on the side table, adjusting a lampshade. Finally she sank down into a chair across the coffee table from Nick. He remained silent, guarded, a slight frown on his face and an unsettled feeling in the pit of his stomach.

"Nick...about what you said last night," she began hesitantly.

"I said a lot of things last night. Most of which I regret."

She shook her head. "No. You were right. You've been incredibly patient as it is. Why you're interested in someone with as many hang-ups as me..." She shook her head uncomprehendingly. "But the fact is you seem to be. You've never shown me anything but kindness and understanding, and you've shared your past with me. So I— I want to do the same with you."

Nick drew in his breath, not sure whether to believe his

ears. It seemed too much to hope for, and he watched her silently.

When he didn't respond, she twisted her hands in her lap and looked down. "That is, if you still want to hear it," she said hesitantly. "It's a rather sordid tale." She tried to smile to lighten the mood, but didn't quite pull it off.

"I'd like to hear it. But I need to tell you something first." He took a deep breath, knowing that honesty was the only course. "I had lunch with Sam today."

Laura's head flew up in surprise. "Sam?"

He nodded and leaned forward earnestly, his forearms resting on his thighs, his hands clasped in front of him. "I didn't know where else to turn. I care about you, Laura, but you wouldn't let me get close. I thought maybe if I understood what happened to make you so afraid, I'd know how to address it."

"What did Sam tell you?"

"Not much. She made it clear that she wasn't about to betray any confidences, and I didn't expect her to. She just told me how you two met, and about her role the night you left Joe."

"She told you I left Joe?" Nick could see the hurt in her eyes, the look of betrayal.

"No," he corrected her quickly. "Actually, your mother told me."

"My mother?" she asked incredulously.

"In a roundabout way. The last night we were there I went out for some air and found her on the porch. In the course of conversation, she mentioned your separation. She assumed I knew."

"Oh."

"That's the extent of my knowledge, Laura. No one violated your confidence."

She nodded, still assimilating what he'd just told her. "You know a lot. More than I expected. Which may make this easier." She drew a shaky breath and stared off into a blank corner, carefully keeping her face expressionless and her tone factual. "Joe and I were what romantics call childhood sweethearts," she began. "I never went out with anyone else. We were always a pair, from the time we were children. When I was eighteen and he was twenty, we decided to get married. My parents never did think we were right for each other, but when they realized we were determined, they supported our decision."

She leaned her head back against the chair and transferred her gaze to the ceiling. "Joe had an associate's degree in data processing, which made him well educated for Jersey, and he had great dreams. So we moved to St. Louis, with not much more than hope to sustain us. As it turned out, the competition here was a lot more fierce than Joe expected, and he just couldn't compete with four-year degrees and MBAs. He finally got a low-paying job, as a data entry clerk, and I worked in a department store to help make ends meet.

"As time went on, Joe began to lose heart. It was clear that his only hope of advancing was to get more education, but he had no interest in going back to school. I finally realized that if we were ever going to have a better life, it was up to me. So I went instead. I'd worked every summer in a greenhouse at home, so I got a job at a nursery and began to take classes in landscape design. I discovered I had a knack for it, and decided to go on for my degree."

Her voice grew quieter. "I don't exactly remember when it started to get really bad. It happened so gradually. I think Joe resented my ambition, for one thing. And I know he was frustrated. Anyway, he started to drink—

heavily—and a side of him emerged that I'd never seen before. He'd get belligerent when he was drunk, and push me around physically. And he would belittle my efforts to get an education. Then he started making fun of the way I looked, especially my weight, which was dropping steadily. He…he even laughed at my faith. He began to lose jobs, one after another, and finally he just quit working. Our life grew more and more isolated, and I felt so cut off and alone. If I hadn't had school, and Sam, and my church, I doubt I would have made it. Those were the only normal things in my life—those, and my family,'' she said with a catch in her voice. She paused and took a deep breath.

"I told myself that he was sick, that what was happening wasn't my fault,'' she continued. "But the guilt was there, anyway. I tried to convince him to get help, but whenever I brought it up he got angry. The last time I suggested it was the night I left. Believe it or not, it was our fourth anniversary.''

Nick didn't know when the tears had started. He just knew that suddenly they were there, twin rivers of grief running silently down her cheeks. The unnatural lack of sound unnerved him, and he sat there helplessly, silently cursing the man who had done this to Laura. He longed to reach for her, to hold her, to tell her that he'd never let anyone hurt her again. But he held back, knowing there was more, knowing that she needed to finish what she'd started. "What did he do to you that night, Laura?'' he asked gently.

Her head swung around, and her startled eyes met his. It was almost as if she'd forgotten he was there. She swallowed with difficulty, and her eyes flitted away again. When she spoke, her words were choppy. "It was late. I was asleep. A crash from the living room woke me up, and I ran in to see what had happened. There was a broken whiskey bottle on the floor, and I went over to help Joe clean it up. But he…he slapped me, and he started saying…terrible things.'' Her voice quavered, and she paused, struggling for control. ''I got scared and I backed away, pleading with him to get help, but he was yelling… I started to turn away, so I didn't even see it coming until it was too late.''

''See what, Laura?'' Nick prodded gently.

''The bottle. He threw the broken bottle at me. I had on a nightgown…my shoulders were bare… It hit me here.'' Her voice caught and she gestured toward her right breast.

Laura was close to losing it, she knew. Only superhuman control and the Lord's help had let her get this far without breaking down. That was why she'd physically removed herself from Nick. One touch from him, and she knew her fragile control would shatter.

Nick watched the struggle taking place on Laura's face. There was no way he could make this any easier for her. All he could do was let her finish and then be there to hold her, to stroke her, to love her.

''I guess I finally admitted then that things were probably over between us,'' she said unevenly. ''So I left. Sam took me in, bless her heart. Joe kept calling, begging me to come back. Sam told me I'd be a fool to give him another chance. So did my minister, in a more diplomatic way. But I still felt an obligation to try everything I could to straighten out our marriage. I was raised to believe that it was a sacred trust and something to be preserved at all costs. Except maybe physical danger,'' she admitted. ''I finally realized that the next time Joe got drunk I might not get off with only a three-inch scar. My safety was literally at stake. Besides, the love I'd once felt for Joe had just about died. All that was left was fear. So I finally made the decision that I wasn't going back unless he got some real help and we went into counseling together. I told him he had to truly change before I'd come back. He was so angry and upset the night I called to tell him..." Her voice trailed off for a moment, and he saw her swallow convulsively. "A few days later, he was killed in a drunk-driving accident." She paused and blinked rapidly. "You want to hear something funny?" she said, choking out a mirthless laugh. "He wasn't the one who was drunk. All those nights I'd lain awake, terrified that he'd run down some innocent person..." She fell silent, her mind clearly far away, but after a few seconds she resumed her story.

"After I pulled myself together, I got an apartment, applied for a grant, went to school full-time and worked a forty-hour week. Eighteen-hour days were the norm. Money was tight, and I lived on peanut-butter sandwiches and macaroni-and-cheese for years. But I made it. I finished school and I got a job with a landscaper. I had Joe's insurance money, which I'd saved, and that gave me the seed money to open my own place after I'd accumulated a little experience. That was six years ago, and I've poured every cent back into the business since then. Now, thanks to the Arts Center job, I think we've finally turned the corner." She paused and expelled a long breath, then turned to face Nick. "So there you have my life story," she said, trying for a light tone and failing miserably, fighting to hold in the sobs that begged for release.

Nick moved for the first time since she'd started speaking. He stood and walked swiftly over to her, reaching down to draw her to her feet. Then he wrapped his arms around her and buried his face in her soft hair, holding her as tightly as he dared. Her whole body was trembling, and she was breathing erratically. Without releasing her, he reversed their positions and sat down, pulling her into his lap and cradling her in his arms.

"It's okay to cry, Laura," he said softly, stroking her hair.

She had struggled valiantly for control, but she finally surrendered, giving in to the deep, gut-wrenching sobs she'd held inside for so long. Her ribs ached, but once released, the tide of tears could not be stopped. She cried for so many things—for the lost illusions of youth; for the guilt she still carried over Joe's deterioration and death; for the lonely years with no hand to hold and no one with whom to share her life; and for her empty heart, and the fear that prevented her from giving love another chance.

Nick just held her, because there was nothing else he could do. His heart ached for the woman in his arms, and he was filled with a deep, seething anger at the injustice of the world.

When at last her sobs subsided, she spoke against his shirt. "How could I have been so wrong about someone I'd known all my life?" she asked in a small, sad voice.

"Not everyone reacts well to adversity and disappointment, Laura. You had no way of knowing what would happen when Joe was put to the test."

"All these years I've felt guilty," she admitted. "I keep wondering if there wasn't something I could have done or said that would have made a difference. Maybe he'd still be alive if I'd stayed."

"And maybe you'd be dead," Nick said bluntly. Then his tone softened. "What happened wasn't your fault, Laura. You stuck it out a lot longer than most people would have. Probably too long."

She shifted in his arms and looked up at him. "Nick?"

"Mmm-hmm."

"After everything I've told you, do you still…I mean, I'd understand if you wanted to cut your losses and get as far away from me as you can."

"Do you want me out of your life?"

"No," she said softly. "But I'm still scared."

Nick let his breath out slowly. Fear he could handle. Withdrawal was something else. But they'd just bridged that hurdle. "I know, sweetheart," he said gently, running a finger down her tearstained cheek. "But we'll work on it together, okay?"

Laura searched his eyes—tender, caring, filled with warmth and concern—and nodded, her throat constricting. "Okay," she whispered. "But I still need to move slowly."

"Slow is fine," he said. "Just as long as we're moving."

Gradually, Laura began to forget what her life had been like before Nick. He became such an integral part of her existence that just as she once could not imagine life *with* him, now she could not imagine it *without* him. He became her wake-up call, making her smile as she sleepily reached for the phone each morning. His was her last call of the day, the deep timbre of his voice lingering in her mind long after the connection had been severed. And in between, he was there—pulling her away for impromptu picnics, dropping by at night to take her to Ted Drewes, clipping funny articles he thought she'd enjoy. She grew to love his dependability, his gentleness, his enthusiasm, his ability to make her laugh, and slowly the lines of tension in her face eased and the shadows under her eyes disappeared. She gained a little weight, and the angular

contours of her face softened and took on a new beauty.
As her bruises healed, so, too, did her heart.

Nick watched the transformation with gratitude and
pleasure. As her skittishness eased, he began to weave
small, undemanding physical intimacies into their relationship. A welcoming kiss whenever they met; an arm
casually draped around her shoulders at the movie theater;
his hand holding hers when they walked. If she grew accustomed to the small intimacies, he reasoned, the bigger
ones would come naturally in their own time. And he
could wait. He'd promised to let her set the pace, and he
intended to honor that vow. But he planned to set the
direction.

Though it was slow going, Nick was not unhappy with
the progress of their relationship. Laura was more relaxed
than he'd ever seen her, laughing more readily, touching
more naturally and easily. Her touches—initially tentative,
as if she was afraid that they would be rejected—gradually
grew bolder under his welcoming encouragement. She
was learning to love all over again, cautiously, but with
a restrained eagerness that delighted him and did more for
his libido than any of the amorous ploys of the more sophisticated women of his acquaintance. As her confidence
grew and she became more secure in their relationship,
gradually she began to initiate physical contact on her
own.

Nick had known from the beginning that physical closeness frightened her. She hadn't spoken about her intimate
relationship with Joe, and Nick hadn't asked, but he imagined that making love had probably become a nightmare
for Laura as the relationship deteriorated and the love had
disappeared. And, given her background and her strong
faith and Christian values, he also knew that she didn't
take physical intimacy lightly. She was the kind of woman

who equated making love with commitment, and she'd been avoiding that like the plague for years. He couldn't expect her to change overnight.

But slowly he guided her toward change, finding ways to touch her that were not threatening but that brought a flash of desire to her eyes. In time she grew to not only allow these touches, but to welcome them. He'd learned to keep his desires on a tight leash, though, and at her slightest hesitation he pulled back. He had come to realize that Laura's values were deeply entrenched and that she simply didn't believe in intimacy outside of marriage. He admired her for her beliefs and intended to respect them. But keeping his desires under control was hard, and getting harder every day.

Laura locked the office and glanced at her watch. She was due to meet Nick at one-thirty, and it was already one-twenty. Fortunately, the client's house was only a short distance from her office, she noted, consulting the address Nick had provided.

Laura rolled down the window as she drove, breathing deeply of the crisp October air. She loved fall, especially here in Webster, when the old, established maples put on their most colorful frocks. Her route took her through the heart of the small community, and she glanced admiringly at the wonderful turn-of-the-century houses.

When Laura reached her destination, she sat for a long moment in the car without moving, letting her eyes roam lovingly over the old frame Victorian. It was set far back from the street, on about an acre of ground, and was everything a Victorian should be. Painted a pale peach, it was embellished with white gingerbread accents, making it appear to be trimmed with lace. A wraparound porch hugged the house invitingly, and tall, stately maples stood on the front lawn. She saw Nick waiting for her on the front porch and waved as she climbed out of the car.

He watched her approach, his body stirring as it always did in her presence. She was dressed as she had been the day they'd met—jeans, work boots, a worn blue work shirt and sunglasses—and her hair was pulled back into a ponytail. But her greeting was certainly different. She ran lightly up the steps and reached on tiptoe, raising her face expectantly. Nick smiled and leaned down, grasping her shoulders and pulling her toward him hungrily for a lingering kiss.

"Mmm," she said dreamily, closing her eyes.

He chuckled, and the deep, seductive sound of it made her feel warm despite the slight chill in the air. "Well, what do you think?" he asked, gesturing toward the house.

"It's wonderful!" she said.

"I thought you'd like it."

"I take it the new owner wants to make some changes?" she said, nodding toward the For Sale sign on the lawn.

"A few. I've already been over the inside, so we can skip that and just go around back. Unless, of course, you'd like to take a look?" He grinned and dangled the key enticingly in front of her.

"Are you kidding!" she exclaimed, her eyes shining. "I've been dying to get inside one of these houses ever since I moved to St. Louis."

Nick fitted the key in the lock and then stepped aside. "After you."

Laura stepped over the threshold—and into the house of her dreams. It was everything she had always imagined—tall ceilings, gleaming hardwood floors, private nooks and crannies and alcoves, fireplaces, a wonderful

L-shaped stairway in the foyer that hugged the wall, a gorgeous art glass window and plenty of light and space. She examined it all rapturously, reverently running her hand over the fine wood moldings and marble mantels. When she'd explored every inch, she turned to Nick. "I don't know what the new owners have in mind, but I wouldn't change a thing. It's perfect."

"If all my clients were that satisfied with the status quo, I'd be out of business," he said with a grin.

"You aren't going to do anything to change the character, are you?" she asked worriedly.

"Nope. Just some minor updating. Ready to take a look at the grounds?"

"I suppose so," she said reluctantly, casting one more lingering, longing look at the foyer before stepping outside. "Can't you just imagine this house at Christmastime, Nick?" she said softly. "Snow on the ground, golden light shining from the windows, smoke curling above the chimneys, a wreath on the door... It's a perfect old-fashioned Christmas house. So warm and welcoming." She sighed. "What a wonderful place to call home."

"You make it sound very appealing," Nick said, locking the door and taking her arm as they strolled around the back.

"I don't have to try very hard. It's a very romantic house."

Laura pulled up short when they reached the backyard. It was heavily shrubbed on the edges, affording complete privacy, and several big trees were spaced over the lawn. Little had been done in the way of landscaping, but Laura could visualize the potential.

"Are your clients open to suggestions?" she asked.

"Yes."

"Well, my first thought is a gazebo—white lattice, of

course. And a formal rose garden is a must. Somewhere there should be a trellis, overflowing with morning glories, that leads to a private area with a bench and a birdbath. And there's plenty of room for an English woodland country garden, sort of wild, yet controlled, you know? That's what gives them their charm. But we have to leave lots of open space for a croquet court. This is a perfect yard for that.'' She paused, and Nick heard her soft sigh. ''It could be so lovely here. I hope the client will let me do this right.''

There was a wistful note in her voice, and Nick squeezed her hand, then tugged her gently toward the back of the house. ''Let's sit for a minute, Laura.''

She followed, still scanning the grounds, visualizing the perfect backdrop for this house. It was the kind of home she'd always hoped to have, and even if that was never to be, perhaps she could create her dream for someone else to enjoy.

Nick pulled her down beside him on a small stone bench set under a tree near the house, and stroked the back of her hand with his thumb. ''Laura?''

''Hmm?'' With an effort she pulled her eyes away from the yard and forced her attention back to Nick.

''Laura, I...'' He stopped, as if he didn't know what to say next, and drew in a deep breath. He seemed at a loss for words, which was completely unlike him, and Laura stared at him curiously. ''About the client for this house...''

''Yes?'' she prompted, when his voice trailed off.

''Well...it's me.''

Her eyes widened in shock. ''What?''

''I've put an option on this house.''

"You? But, Nick—it's a wonderful house, don't get me wrong—it's just so big for just one person."

"I know. I was hoping that you might share it with me."

Chapter Fourteen

Laura stared at him, her eyes wide with shock. "Nick...are you...are you asking me to marry you?" she stammered.

"I guess I'm not doing a very good job at it, am I?" He tried to grin, and then drew a deep breath, letting it out slowly. "Laura, the simple truth is I'm not getting any younger. The years have gone by a lot faster than I expected. I want a home, and a family, and a house with a white picket fence and a tree swing—the whole nine yards. And I want it before I'm too old to enjoy it." He stroked the back of her hand absently with his thumb, his eyes locked on hers. "I've been involved with my share of women over the years," he said honestly, struggling to find the right words because it was vitally important that she understand exactly how he felt. "But I've never really been 'involved,' not in the true sense of the word. In fact, I went to great lengths to *avoid* involvement, because I didn't want the complications and responsibilities that go with it. And then you came along, and suddenly everything was different. I *wanted* to share your life—and your responsibilities.'' He paused and searched her eyes. "I guess that's what happens when you fall in love," he said quietly.

Laura tried to swallow past the lump in her throat. For the past few months she'd gone blithely along, relishing her developing relationship with Nick, refusing to think about the inevitable day of reckoning. Now it had come, and she wasn't ready. All the old fears, which had gradually subsided under Nick's gentle nurturing, resurfaced with alarming intensity. He was talking love and commitment and vows, and it scared her to death. There was no question that she loved Nick. But she'd loved Joe, too, and that had been a mistake, one that was still exacting a price.

Nick's eyes were locked on hers, trying to gauge her reaction to his proposal, watching the play of emotions cross her face. He'd known it was a risk to ask her to marry him, but it had been a calculated one. He knew Laura well enough to know that she was completely without guile or pretense. The affection she so willingly returned could be taken at face value as a true measure of her feelings. He'd hoped those feelings would be strong enough to overcome her fears, but now, searching her troubled eyes, he wasn't so sure.

"Nick, I—I don't know what to say."

"'Yes' would be nice." When she didn't respond, he took a deep breath. "Things have gone well between us, haven't they?" he asked gently.

"Yes. But why can't we just leave them as they are?" she pleaded.

"For how long?" His voice was sober, direct.

"I—I don't know," she replied helplessly. "It's such a big step. And I made a mistake once before."

"That was a long time ago, Laura. You were only eigh-

teen years old—just a kid. And you had no way of knowing what would happen to Joe.''

''But…but I'm so afraid it could happen again,'' she
whispered.

Nick didn't say a word. He tried to understand, tried to
remind himself that Laura's traumatic past was clouding
her judgment, but he was still deeply hurt by her lack of
trust. He'd done everything he could to prove that he was
different than Joe, that he was trustworthy and dependable
and even-tempered, that he cared about her and loved her
unconditionally. And he had failed. Instead of the joy he
had hoped to see in her eyes, there was only doubt and
uncertainty. He glanced away, feeling as if his heart was
being held in a vise, the life slowly being squeezed out
of it. He gazed at the house he'd allowed himself to dream
of sharing with the woman beside him, and felt something
inside him begin to die. Finally he looked back at her.

''I don't know what else to do, Laura,'' he said wearily.
''I'd hoped the fear had dimmed by now. But I'm beginning to think it never will.''

Her eyes filled with tears, and she blinked them back.
She wanted to tell him she loved him, but the words
wouldn't come. Just saying them seemed too much of a
risk. But she didn't want to lose him. Without Nick, her
life would be empty, emptier even than before. She
touched his arm and looked up at him desperately.
''Nick…maybe we could just… Lots of people live together nowadays,'' she said.

He gazed at her in surprise, completely taken aback.
Yes, lots of people did live together. But Laura wasn't
cut out to be one of them. It went against everything she'd
been brought up to believe about love and commitment,
flew in the face of her deeply held Christian principles.
Her willingness to even consider compromising her values

spoke more eloquently than words of the depths of her feelings for him. But it would impose a very heavy burden of guilt on her and, in the end, she would come to not only regret such a choice, but resent him for forcing her to make it. It just wouldn't work.

Nevertheless, Nick was tempted. He was losing her—she was slipping away even as he watched—and now she'd thrown out a lifeline. Maybe this was better than nothing, he thought, trying to convince himself. But how long would the arrangement last, even if she did go through with it, which he doubted? Would she ever feel secure enough to marry him? And if not, then what? What if she walked away, somewhere down the road?

As hard as it would be to let her go now, it would be even harder once they'd lived together intimately.

Slowly he shook his head. "I'm sorry, Laura," he said, his voice filled with regret. "I love you. I want to build a life with you—for always. It's got to be all or nothing."

Laura began to feel physically ill. Her world was crumbling around her, and she felt powerless to stop it. The man she loved was about to walk away, taking all of the sunlight and warmth and tenderness out of her life. The tears that had welled up in her eyes slowly overflowed and trickled down her cheeks.

"Nick, I can't marry you," she said brokenly. "I'm not ready for that step and…and I don't know if I ever will be."

He took her hands, his gut twisting painfully at the shattered look in her eyes. She seemed so vulnerable and defenseless that he almost relented, just to ease her pain. Almost. But in the end, he shook his head.

"Laura, I love you," he repeated, his voice hoarse with emotion. "Part of me always will. I wish we could have made this work.'' Gently he released her hands and slowly stood.

Laura's heart was pounding in her chest, her eyes desperate. ''Nick, I...'' She tried again to say ''I love you,'' but the words stuck in her throat. ''I'll miss you,'' she said instead.

''I'll miss you, too.'' He bent down and placed his lips gently and lingeringly on hers, in a kiss as light as the wayward leaves that drifted down around them.

''Will I see you again?'' she whispered.

''In the spring, I guess, when the landscaping starts for the Arts Center.'' He desperately hoped that by then the pain of this parting would have dulled. ''Goodbye, Laura. And good luck. I hope someday you find someone who can bring you the happiness you deserve.''

As the sun darted behind a cloud, she watched his back, ramrod straight and broad shouldered, disappear around the corner of the house. The air grew chilly, and so did her heart.

With Nick gone, there was an empty place in Laura's life that couldn't be filled. She tried working even longer hours, but that once reliable distraction barely eased the pain. She went back to doing more outdoor labor, but the physical tiredness couldn't mask her emotional fatigue and despair, nor did it help her sleep any better. Night after night she lay awake, thinking about what might have been, wondering if Nick missed her as much as she missed him, aching for the closeness she had grown to cherish. She had never felt more alone in her life.

Even her best friend seemed to desert her. Sam had always been the one she'd turned to for support during the difficult years after Joe died and through all the tough times when she'd been trying to establish her business.

But Sam offered little sympathy. Laura knew her friend thought she was a fool for letting Nick walk away. She'd pretty much said so to her face, in her blunt, outspoken way.

Her family was too far away to be able to provide much consolation, even if she'd told them about her relationship with Nick, which she hadn't. All her mother knew was that they had been seeing each other, never that it had grown serious. As much as she loved her family, it had never been her custom to share the intimate details of her life.

Even in her darkest days she'd always found solace in talking over her problems with the Lord, but even He seemed distant. She just couldn't find the words to pray, beyond a desperate plea for help and guidance. But God worked in His own time, and no direction had yet been provided.

So Laura was left alone with her pain. She tried to tell herself that she'd done the right thing, that entering into a relationship when she wasn't ready would be wrong for everyone involved. At the same time, she couldn't blame Nick for walking out. She'd made it clear that marriage wasn't an option at the moment, maybe never would be. He wanted to share his life with someone on a permanent basis, to raise a family, to create a home, and she couldn't offer him that. Because Joe had left her with a legacy of fear that was debilitating and isolating, had shaken her confidence in her own judgment so badly that even now, ten years later, she was afraid to trust her heart. Nick had tried his best to convince her to risk loving again, and he'd failed. And if Nick—with his integrity and gentleness and love—couldn't succeed, she doubted whether anyone could.

Laura carried that depressing thought with her into De-

cember, through two long, lonely months without the
sound of his voice each morning and night, without his
impromptu visits, without the laughter he'd brought into
her life. Her solitary existence, once carefully nurtured,
now seemed oppressive.

Laura didn't even bother to put up a tree, a custom
she'd never abandoned, even at the worst of times. But
her heart wasn't in it this year. The Christmas decorations
looked garish, the carols sounded flat and the weather was
dismal. Her only concession to the holidays was the small
crèche she always displayed on the mantel. As she placed
the figure of baby Jesus in the manger she reminded herself that the Lord had never promised an easy road in this
world. She accepted that. She always had. But did it *always* have to be so hard? she cried in silent despair.
Weren't there ever happy endings?

And then, with a jolt, she realized that the key to a
potentially happy ending *had* been offered to her. She had
refused—because she was afraid. And the simple fact was
that despite the emptiness of the past two months, she still
carried the same oppressive burden of fear.

Her loneliness only intensified as the holidays grew
closer. Laura's mother had decided to visit her brother's
family in California, and though Laura had been invited
to spend Christmas with John and Dana and the kids, trying to look cheery for several days in front of her family
seemed too much of an effort. Sam had gone to Chicago.
Laura told everyone she was too busy to take time off
anyway, but in reality business was slow. People typically
didn't think about landscaping at Christmastime. They
were too busy planning holiday gatherings and buying
gifts for family and friends.

On Christmas Eve Laura closed the office at three
o'clock, realizing as she slowly walked to her car that she

had nowhere to go until the evening service at seven. Her cozy apartment, once a welcoming haven, now seemed empty and hollow. She tried strolling around a mall, but the laughing crowds, so at odds with her depressed mood, only made her feel worse.

In the end, even though the service wasn't scheduled to start for an hour and half, she just went to church. Maybe here, in the Lord's house, she could find some peace and solace.

Laura sat forlornly in the dim silence feeling more alone and lost than she had in a very long while. *Oh, Lord, show me what to do!* she pleaded. *I love Nick. And yet I let him walk away because I'm afraid. I need to move on with my life, find the courage to trust again. Please help me.* She closed her eyes and opened her heart, and slowly, as she poured out her fears and confusion to the Lord in an almost incoherent stream of consciousness, she began to feel a calmness steal over her.

The church was filling with people when she at last opened her eyes, and by the time the candles were lit and the service started, she had attained some measure of peace, though no insights. But she had faith that the Lord would offer those in His own time. If she was patient, He would show her the way.

As Brad Matthews stepped to the microphone, she forced herself to put her problems aside and focus on the words of her childhood friend. He was a wonderful minister, and he had offered her a sympathetic ear and sound advice during her darkest days. He was also an accomplished speaker, and she always found value in his thoughtfully prepared sermons.

Tonight was no exception. In fact, it almost seemed as if the end of his talk had been prepared especially for her, she thought in growing amazement as she listened to his words.

"And so tomorrow all of us will exchange gifts with the ones we love," he said in his rich, well-modulated voice. "They'll be brightly wrapped, in colorful paper and shiny bows. But let's not forget that those gifts are only meant to represent the true gift of this season—the gift of love. My friends, that is why we are here tonight. Because God so loved the world that he sent his only Son to save us. That gift of love is what makes this day so special. No one who knows the Lord is ever truly alone or unloved, because His love is never ending and He is always with us.

"God gave us the gift of perfect love when he sent us His Son. And that love is manifested here on earth in many ways, most beautifully in the love we have for each other. Love one another as I have loved you. That was His instruction.

"Well, all of us know that, as humans, we can never achieve the perfection of God's love. But it should stand as a shining example of what love is at its very best. It is unselfish. It is trusting. It is enduring. It is forgiving. It is limitless. And it is unconditional.

"On this Christmas Eve, let us all reflect on God's love and the gifts of human love with which we are blessed in this earthly life. And let us remember that God never promised us that love was easy. It isn't even easy to love the Lord. Christianity is a celebration, but it's also a cross. And it certainly isn't always easy to love each other. But love of the Lord, and the reflection of that love in our relationships with the people in our lives, is what sets us apart as Christians.

"So during this Christmas season, give yourself a special gift. It won't be as flashy as a new CD player or a computer, but I promise you it will be longer lasting. Because CD players and computers break. And love can, too. But the difference is that love can not only be mended, but strengthened. Sometimes all it takes is two simple words, spoken from the heart: I'm sorry. The power those two words contain is amazing.

"At this season of God's love, which manifested itself in the humble birth of a baby two thousand years, show the Lord that you've heard His voice. Mend a broken relationship. And I guarantee that the joy of Christmas will stay in your heart long after the gifts under your tree are just a memory.

"Now let us pray..."

As the service continued, Laura reflected on Brad's beautiful words, which deeply touched her heart. He was right. Love was a gift, both the divine and human forms. And both kinds of love required trust and a leap of faith to reach their full potential. Maybe that was what made love so unique and special.

A gentle snow was falling when she emerged from the church after the service, the soft flakes forming a delicate, transparent film of white on the ground. As she climbed into her car, an image of the cozy Victorian house Nick had so lovingly chosen for them suddenly flashed unbidden across her mind.

It was probably filled with laughter and music and love as the new owners enjoyed their first Christmas there, she thought wistfully. Without consciously making a decision, Laura put the car in gear and drove slowly toward the house that had come to represent Nick's love and the life he had offered her. Dusk descended, and the snow continued to fall, lightly dusting her windshield as she drove.

When she reached the street, Laura approached the house slowly, surprised to find the windows dark and the

For Sale sign still on the lawn. Sam was always complaining that the real estate market was soft, but Laura found it surprising that a gem like this would still be unsold.

The street was lined with cars, so she had to drive a few houses away before she found a spot to park. Then, digging her hands into the pockets of her wool coat, she trudged up the sidewalk, stopping in front of the house. Her eyes filled with longing as they lovingly traced the contours of the structure. It was just as beautiful as she'd remembered it, but so empty and alone. Just like me, she thought, allowing herself a moment of self-pity. Both of us could have been filled with the magic of Nick's love, but instead we're cold and dark.

She walked up the pathway to the front door and slowly climbed the steps, running a hand over the banister, touching the brass knocker on the door. Then she sat down on the top step, folded her arms on her knees and rested her forehead on the scratchy wool of her sleeves. An aching sense of regret flooded through her as she faced the fact that something beautiful had been within her grasp and she'd allowed it to slip away. Brad had said that love required trust, and a leap of faith. And there were certainly no guarantees. She knew that. Life—and love—didn't come with warranties. But which was worse—to shun risk and spend her life alone and miserable, or to take a chance on love with the most wonderful man she'd ever met? Put that way, and in the context of the past two lonely months, the answer suddenly seemed obvious.

Brad had said that love could be mended, she reflected. But she had hurt Nick deeply. The look in his eyes when she'd admitted her fear was burnt into her memory forever. Because that fear also implied lack of trust. No wonder he'd walked away that day. Love without trust was just an empty shell, and he deserved better than that. If only she could retract her words!

But that was impossible, and it made no sense to yearn for impossible things, she thought bleakly. She just wished she could find a way to make him understand how deeply she loved him, to ask his forgiveness. All she really wanted, or could hope for, was a second chance.

Though her eyes were clouded with tears, Laura realized with a start that the toes of two boots had appeared in her field of vision. Probably a cop, about to cite her for trespassing, she thought dejectedly, quickly brushing a hand across her eyes before looking up.

"I'm sorry, I didn't mean..." The words died in her throat. Nick stood at the base of the steps, his hands in the pockets of a sheepskin-lined jacket, snow clinging to his dark hair, his eyes shadowed and unfathomable, with a fan spread of fine lines at the corners that hadn't been there two months before.

"Hello, Laura."

"Nick?" She took a great gulp of cold air.

"Fancy meeting you here," he said lightly, though his tone sounded forced.

"I—I thought it would look pretty in the snow," she stammered, still not trusting her eyes.

He nodded. "Yeah. Me, too." He glanced at the shuttered windows and placed one foot on the bottom step. "I remember the day we were here, how you said it would be beautiful at Christmastime, so I thought I'd take a look. I see it's still for sale."

A door opened nearby and the sound of carols and laughter drifted through the silent air.

"Yes, I noticed."

"I'm surprised you didn't go home for Christmas."

She shrugged. "I wasn't in the mood."

They fell silent, and Laura looked down, shuffling the toe of her shoe in the snow that was rapidly accumulating at the edge of the porch, trying to make some sense out of her chaotic thoughts. If Nick didn't still care about her, he wouldn't be here tonight, would he? Maybe, just maybe, it wasn't too late to salvage their relationship. She looked up and found that he was watching her. This was the second chance she'd wished for. *Please, God, don't let me blow it!* she prayed. *Help me find the words to make Nick understand how much I care and how sorry I am for hurting him.*

"Nick...I've missed you," she began tentatively.

"I've missed you, too," he said quietly.

"I've had a lot of time to think these past couple of months, and I was wondering... Is there... Do you still..." Her voice trailed off. She was making a mess of this!

"Do I still what, Laura?" Nick asked, his voice cautious.

She took a deep breath. There was no easy way to say it. "Do you still...do you still want me?" she asked artlessly.

He hesitated. "I've always wanted you," he replied, his voice guarded.

"No...I mean, do you still want to marry me?"

Instead of replying, Nick grabbed her hands and pulled her to her feet. She gasped in surprise as he hauled her up onto the porch and over to a dim light by the door that offered only marginal illumination. Then he turned her to face him, his jaw tense, his hands gripping her shoulders almost painfully, his eyes burning into hers.

"Laura, what are you saying?" he asked tightly.

He wasn't going to make this easy for her, she thought. He wanted her to spell it out, and after her previous ambiguity, she couldn't blame him. She drew a deep breath and looked directly into his eyes, willing him to see the love, the sincerity, the apology, in her own. "Nick, I'm sorry for what I've put you through. I'm especially sorry for being afraid to commit to you, for not trusting you, when I've never met a more trustworthy person. But when I left Joe, I vowed never to get involved with anyone again. And I did pretty well, till you came along."

When she paused, he prodded. "Go on."

"These past two months have been miserable," she said, her voice breaking. "Maybe even harder emotionally than when I left Joe. Because when you left you took the sunshine with you. Oh, Nick," she cried, clinging to him. "I want the same things you want—the rose garden and the picket fence and the family. I realize I'm no bargain, that I still have a lot of problems to work through. But I'd like to work on them with you beside me. I'd still like a lifetime warranty, but I'll settle for an 'I'll do my best to make you happy.' And I'll do the same for you."

He studied her face, wanting to believe, but afraid that this was all an illusion, much as he'd thought *she* was an illusion when he'd first seen her slumped on the steps. Then, too, he realized, she hadn't yet said the three words that really counted.

Laura watched his face, saw a flicker of disappointment in his eyes and her stomach knotted into a tight ball. She panicked. He was going to tell her to forget it, that it was too late.

"I…have the feeling…that the offer is…no longer available," she said choppily. "I…know I hurt you, and I guess I can't blame you if…if you can't forgive me."

"It's not that, Laura." He released her and turned to walk over to the porch railing, leaning on it heavily with both hands, facing away from her. "I *was* hurt. Deeply.

But I never really blamed you. If anyone ever had a reason to be wary, it was you. It was egotistical of me to think I could overcome years of debilitating fear in just a few months. In the end, I was just sad. For both of us. But there was nothing to forgive. You were a victim of your circumstances.''

"Then what's wrong?" she pleaded.

"I still want to marry you, Laura, but..."

"But what?" she asked desperately.

"You say you're lonely, and God knows, I can relate to that," he said with a sigh. "But that's not reason enough to get married."

"But it's not just that. I want to be with you, Nick. For always."

"Why?"

"Why?" she parroted blankly. Then suddenly her taut nerves shattered. "Well, why do you think?" she snapped. "Nick, I love you! What more do you want?"

He was beside her in one quick step, pulling her roughly against him, burying his face in her hair as he let out a long, shuddering sigh. "That will be plenty," he said huskily.

"Then do you mind telling me what this was all about?" she asked, still mildly annoyed, her voice muffled by his jacket.

He took her by the shoulders and backed up far enough to look down into her eyes. "Laura Taylor, do you realize that this is the first time you've ever said, 'I love you'?"

She frowned. "Yes, I guess it is. But I assumed you knew."

"How could I know?"

"Well, by the way I acted. I tried to show you how I felt."

"Showing isn't the same as telling."

She smiled, a sudden, euphoric joy making her heart soar. She sent a silent, fervent prayer of thanks to the Lord for granting her a happy ending after all.

"Are you saying you'd rather have words than actions?" she teased, tilting her head to one side and reaching up to run a finger down his cheek.

She heard his sharply indrawn breath and grinned.

"Well, action is good, too," he conceeded.

"I thought you'd agree." She slipped her hands inside his jacket and gazed up into his face, the ardent light in her eyes playing havoc with his metabolism.

"You can count on it," he said huskily, pulling her roughly against him, his mouth urgent and demanding on hers. Laura responded eagerly, tasting, teasing, touching.

"Excuse me…are you folks lost?"

Startled, they drew apart, their breath creating frosty clouds in the cold night air. An older man stood looking up at them from the sidewalk.

Nick put his arm around Laura and drew her close. "No. Not anymore," he said, smiling down at her. "We just came home." Then he turned back toward the street. "We're going to buy this house," he called, and the jubilant ring in his voice warmed Laura's heart.

The man chuckled softly. "Now that's what I call a Christmas present!"

Epilogue

Nick brought the car to a stop and turned to Laura with an intimate smile that made her tingle all over. "Welcome home, Mrs. Sinclair," he said huskily.

Her throat constricted at the tenderness in his eyes, and she swallowed with difficulty. "I love you, Nick," she said softly, her voice catching as her own eyes suddenly grew misty.

"Believe me, the feeling is mutual," he replied, reaching over with a feather-light touch to leisurely trace a finger down her cheek, then across her lips. He drew an unsteady breath and smiled. "Shall we go in?"

She nodded mutely, not trusting her voice, and tried unsuccessfully to slow her rapid pulse as he came around and opened her door. He took her hand, drawing her to her feet in one smooth motion, then let his arm slip around her waist, pulling her close. She leaned against him with a contented sigh as they stood for a moment in the dark stillness to look at the old Victorian house, its ornate gin-

gerbread trim and huge wraparound porch silhouetted by
the golden light spilling from the windows.

"It's beautiful, isn't it?" she said, her eyes glowing.

"Beautiful is a good word," he agreed.

She turned to find his eyes on *her*, not the house, and
she blushed.

"You're even more beautiful when you do that," he
said with a tender smile, touching her nose with the tip
of his finger before taking her hand. As they climbed the
steps to the porch he turned to her. "Are you sure you
wouldn't have preferred the Ritz tonight?"

"This *is* my Ritz," she said softly, letting her free hand
lovingly glide over the banister as they ascended.

"I agree," he replied with a tender smile. For both of
them, the house had come to symbolize their love and the
promise of a rich, full life together.

When they reached the door, he fitted the key in the
lock, and before she realized his intention he swept her
into his arms and lowered his lips to hers, drawing a sweet
response from deep within her. Only when the kiss length-
ened, then deepened, did Laura reluctantly pull away.

"Nick! The neighbors might see us!" she protested
halfheartedly.

He grinned. "They're all in bed. Speaking of which…"
He stepped across the threshold, pushed the door shut with
his foot, and started up the curved staircase.

Laura didn't say a word as a wave of excitement and
delicious anticipation swept over her. She just nestled
against his chest, enjoying the feel of his strong arms as
she listened to the rapid but steady beat of his heart
against her ear.

When they reached the bedroom, he carefully set her

on her feet and removed the light mohair wrap from around her shoulders. Soft, classical music was playing and the room was bathed in a gentle, subdued light.

"I want to show you something," Nick said, taking her hand and leading her to the antique oval mirror on a stand that stood in one corner of the room. He positioned her in front and then stood behind her, his hands on her shoulders. "What do you see?"

She gazed at their reflections, a tender smile on her face. She saw Nick, tall and incredibly handsome in his tux, the elegant formal attire enhancing his striking good looks and broad shoulders. And she saw herself, dressed in her wedding finery. Her peach-colored tea-length lace gown softly hugged her slender figure, and the sweetheart neckline and short, slightly gathered sleeves added an old-fashioned charm that perfectly complemented her femininity. Her hair hung loose and full, the way Nick liked it, and the soft waves were pulled back on one side with a small cluster of flowers and lacy ribbon, giving her a sweetly youthful appearance. But mostly what she saw was the two of them, together, for life.

"Well?" Nick prompted.

"I see a miracle," she replied softly, her eyes glowing with happiness.

"I'm inclined to agree with you on that," Nick concurred with a smile. Then his voice softened and his tone grew serious. "Do you know what I see? The most beautiful bride that ever lived and the most wonderful, desirable woman I've ever met."

"Oh, Nick," she said, her eyes misting. "I never thought I could be so happy!"

"Well, get used to it, Mrs. Sinclair. Because happiness

is exactly what I have planned for you for the next sixty or seventy years,'' he said, turning her to face him, taking both her hands in his as he bent to trail his lips across her forehead. ''Now don't go away. I'll be right back,'' he said huskily, his breath warm against her face.

She closed her eyes, letting his touch work its magic. ''I'll be here,'' she whispered.

When Nick left, Laura turned slowly and let her gaze roam over the lovingly decorated room they'd created together—their first priority when they bought the house. The English country style suited the house, as did the canopy bed that was draped in a floral print of rose and forest green. The thick carpet was also rose-colored, and two comfortable chairs in complementary striped fabric stood close to the fireplace. Yes, this was far preferable to the Ritz, Laura thought with deep contentment. Tonight marked a new chapter in their relationship, and she wanted it to start here, in their own home.

Nick had clearly gone out of his way to make this night special, she thought with a soft smile, her eyes filled with tenderness at his thoughtfulness. Two champagne glasses rested on a low table, and the subdued lighting and soft music created the perfect ambience for their first night together.

Nick quietly reentered, pausing a moment to let his eyes lovingly trace the contours of Laura's profile, bathed in the warm glow of the golden light. It was hard for him to even remember a time when she hadn't been the center of his world. She brought a joy and completeness to his life far beyond anything he could ever have imagined. Today, as they'd recited their vows, he'd felt as if he'd truly come home. Gazing at her now, he was overwhelmed with joy and gratitude for the gift of her love.

Quietly he came up behind her and nuzzled her neck. "Did you miss me?"

"Mmm. As a matter of fact, I did," she said, leaning back against him.

"I brought some champagne."

"I saw the glasses."

"Will you have some?"

"Mmm-hmm."

He popped the cork, poured the bubbly liquid into the two waiting glasses and bent to strike a match to the logs. They quickly flamed into life, sending shadows dancing on the walls. It was chilly for the first day of spring, and Laura moved closer to the welcome warmth.

"Cold?" Nick asked as he handed her a glass.

"A little," she admitted.

He gave her a lazy smile. "I think we can take care of that," he said, his eyes twinkling.

Laura flushed and looked down, a smile playing at the corners of her own mouth. "I was counting on it," she said softly.

"But first...I'd like to make a toast." Nick raised his glass, and Laura looked up at him, the love shining from her deep green eyes. "To new beginnings—and a love that never ends," he said softly.

Laura raised her glass, and the bell-like tinkle as they clinked resonated in the room.

They both took a sip, and then Nick reached over and gently removed the glass from her trembling fingers. He set the two glasses side by side on the mantel, turned, held out his hand. And as she moved into his arms, Laura had one last coherent thought. The good book was right. To everything there was a season. And this, at last, was her time to love.

*   *   *   *   *

Dear Reader,

Ever since I could put pen to paper, I've enjoyed writing. It's a very special gift for which I am deeply grateful.

Love is a gift, too. A precious and beautiful gift that requires courage and faith and trust—and yes, even risk—to reach its full potential.

It is a great joy for me to write about people like Nick and Laura, who find love and romance without compromising their moral values. And I am delighted to be part of Steeple Hill's Love Inspired line, which recognizes that readers want books that reaffirm the existence of character and honor and principles in today's world, despite media messages to the contrary.

I truly believe that good, old-fashioned romance lives even in this modern age. Virtues and values never go out of style. And heroes like Nick are out there, waiting to be found. I should know. I married one!

Happy endings...that's what romance is all about. May you find your own happy ending—and a lifetime of love!

Irene Hannon

2 Love Inspired novels and 2 mystery gifts... Absolutely FREE!

Visit

www.LoveInspiredBooks.com

for your two FREE books, sent directly to you!

BONUS: Choose between regular print or our NEW larger print format!

There's no catch! You're under no obligation to buy anything. We charge nothing—ZERO—for your first shipment. And you don't have to make any minimum number of purchases.

You'll like the convenience of home delivery at our special discount prices, and you'll love your free subscription to Steeple Hill News, our members-only newsletter.

We hope that after receiving your free books, you'll want to remain a subscriber. But the choice is yours— to continue or cancel, anytime at all! So why not take us up on our invitation, with no risk of any kind!

Love Inspired®